Gardenia DUTY

Gardenia DUTY

KATHLEEN VARN

Columbus, Ohio

This book is a work of fiction. The names, characters and events in this book are the products of the author's imagination or are used fictitiously. Any similarity to real persons living or dead is coincidental and not intended by the author.

Gardenia Duty

Published by Gatekeeper Press
2167 Stringtown Rd, Suite 109
Columbus, OH 43123-2989
www.GatekeeperPress.com

ISBN (paperback): 9781642370485
eISBN: 9781642370492

Printed in the United States of America

Dedication

To the generations of those who reported for duty,
and to the families that served with them.

Prologue

OCTOBER, 1980

She stared at the venetian blinds, blurred by tears, gripping the hospital bed rails. They should have been tears of joy. Her family should have been standing in the sparsely furnished room. Should have, would have, could have.

Suck it up, cupcake, she thought. She knew this day would come. She had to think about what was best for… for *him*. And once she had finally decided, even the excitement of her budding career had been overshadowed. She scanned the room through the blur, now void of the nurse who had taken pity on her solitude. The never-ending loop of self-recrimination flooded her brain yet again.

Funny, she thought she'd be over it by now, that somehow the loop would be flushed—like afterbirth.

How could she have been so careless? Why hadn't she focused on school instead of letting herself be attracted to Larry's blue eyes? With that twinkle and his boyish grin, he had relentlessly worked his way into her heart on a girls' night out. Eventually, walks on the beach, romantic dinners and line dancing at The Lazy B. If she had known his orders were only five months away, would she have continued the romance? She didn't let just anyone in. She was the Master of Unavailable and The Life of the Party. But Larry had pulled her off center and made her laugh. She thought he'd bore her. She thought she'd grow tired of him. But no. *Damn you, Larry.* The aching memories made this day that much more difficult.

There was a knock on the thick blonde door. "Dinner time," the nurse said. She stared at the tray as the nurse gently placed it on the table. She peeked under the lid and was hit with the aroma of chicken and broccoli. Typical hospital menu; something from all the food groups.

"Does the chef suggest a wine pairing?" she smiled weakly. Her nurse smiled back and checked the IV bag. There was iced tea and a little carton of milk on the fiberglass tray, the same type served up in school when her biggest decisions were made on a playground, or when sneaking a cigarette on the senior lawn behind the huge live oak.

"When can I shower?" she asked, poking at the mashed potatoes.

"After this bag runs out I'll take out the IV."

Her nurse's deep blue scrubs were adorned by a shiny chrome stethoscope. "Can I do anything else?" Her eyes betrayed the facade of pity for her situation. This may have been her first rodeo, but the nurse had seen too many of her situations. "No, I'm good. Well, not good. I mean, you've been wonderful," she fumbled.

The nurse walked back to the door, patting her feet with a soft hand on the way. She felt the tears welling again. How she needed her sisters. But, no one could know. She needed to get back on track at work and put this behind her. *How the hell do you put something like this behind you*, she thought to herself. She suspected it would always haunt her. "*Please, God, give me the peace I need. I hope you know I'm not heartless. This is for his future. I'm still a kid.*"

There was another knock on the door. As the couple entered the room, he was carrying a fast-food bag, Taco Bell. She carried flowers. It had to be as awkward for them as it was for her. "You're a lifesaver! I hope there are tacos in that bag," she said, with as much bravado as she could muster. But she knew there was a deeper meaning to the first part of her comment.

"Did y'all finally decide on his name?" she asked.

Chapter 1

CHARLESTON, SOUTH CAROLINA – 2004

"Hey, Daddy," Elizabeth said softly. "You okay?"

He opened his eyes from the back-porch swing and smiled weakly. His binoculars sat in his lap. It was purple martin season. For years, he'd been luring them to a homemade gourd contraption. Every season as the martin population increased, he'd altered and refined it. He'd even used one of his deep-sea fishing reels to raise and lower the houses from the twelve-foot steel pole.

"Good, everything's good," Bobby said. He patted the swing seat, inviting his daughter to join him. "Are you done for the day?"

"Yes, I only had a few clients today," she answered. "I heard Mallory popped in last weekend to help get the garden going. Guess she drove up from Beaufort?"

She picked up the glasses and looked for martins peeping from the gourds. The pole was in the corner of the garden that she and her three sisters had enjoyed since her mom had married her stepfather thirty-four years ago. The soil was a rich organic mixture perfected and renourished each season. The irrigation system delivered deep well water during the hot Charleston summers. Depending on the crop rotation, he would adjust the PVC pipes, joints and sprinkler heads to accommodate the tilled rows.

Every summer, family, friends and neighbors coveted his tomato harvest. Each winter, he scoured the seed catalog for his next crop to be started in his hot house. The greenhouse was another personal project; it resembled a small transparent barn. It stayed littered with open bags of soil, fertilizer, plastic flower buckets, gloves, and little cardboard cartons to start the spring seedlings. Elizabeth was leery to go inside and help start the seedlings because the wasps also felt they were entitled to reside with the gentle farmer. Ever since she'd stepped on a honeybee and had an adverse reaction, she was a reluctant volunteer.

"Yea, we picked out the strongest plants. Mallory tilled and reset the sprinklers," he said. "She's coming back this weekend and we're going to set them in the ground. We ran out of time."

"Mallory said you've been sleeping a lot," Elizabeth said, while she tried to see if his ankles were swollen. She was the only daughter in town to help when her mom called and asked her to check on him, or when any medical intervention was needed. She'd watched his feet harden, turn blue and swell from his heart failure. At least it didn't look like there was a lot of fluid retention today. The last time he struggled with his congestive heart disease, his kidneys failed and allowed his lungs to fill with fluid. The helplessness in the ICU as they almost lost him was over-whelming. His recovery was miraculous, but deceptive.

She knew and always remembered— he still clung to his deeply instilled male pride in protecting the women in his life and resisting any dependency. In spite of their pleas to seek medical attention, he pushed against the inevita-ble. Daily routines and errands were smoke screens to the reality that his heart was failing. He hadn't revealed the conversation at his last doctor's appointment. If it were good news he'd have shared. When he didn't, Elizabeth knew there were no more options.

His home and garden were his final sanctuary. His southern roots were in the dirt. Flush or bust, his life and career taught him resilience. He'd learned his share of mortality lessons throughout his childhood and on into a career in the military.

"I'm just fighting a cold," he said. He put his arm around his daughter and changed the subject. "So, have you heard from any of your other sisters?"

Elizabeth got the message. "Got a beer?" she asked. "I'll fill you in."

He slowly leaned into the cooler next to the swing and handed her a well-chilled beer. As she cracked it open, a soft breeze carried the scent of the nearby gardenia bush. What had been a gangly overlooked mess of a shrub when he'd first started cultivating his backyard was thriving and bloom heavy. Gardenias had always held a special place in his heart. Many a photo had been taken in front of that bush. Petals had been pressed into scrapbooks alongside childhood memories. Fragrant bouquets often found their way to a Mason jar on the kitchen table. The martins twittered as they dove in and out of the gourds. She smiled at him and began with, "Audrey called. I think everyone is planning to head this way for Mother's Day..."

Chapter 2

ASHLAND, ALABAMA – 1957

It was his turn, and young Bobby had tossed and turned all night in anticipation. A clean shirt and pants lay folded on the chair beside his bed, along with a pair of polished Buster Browns. He could still recall when he was just five years old and his oldest brother had returned from boot camp in his uniform, creased and impeccably clean. World War II had no meaning in his young life. Instead, what he saw when Jonathan walked into their house, decked out in white crackerjacks and shiny patent leather shoes, was that there was no dirt or dust clinging to him. Working on the family farm made that a requisite for each family member, but not Jonathan, not then.

That Navy uniform had marked Bobby deep. When he ran to hug his brother, Jonathan kneeled and placed the Navy flat hat on his blonde towhead. The seed of adventures at sea had been sown in his little boy heart. Throughout his childhood, Mama would read the letters from the South Pacific. In spite of his family's country simplicity, Bobby had cut his teeth on tales of islands and ocean, exotic food and foreign people. He wanted to trade plowing with Pop's horse, Old Paint, to race on the deck of a destroyer—the greyhound of the sea.

But now he was eighteen years old. He understood the impact of war on his small southern community. Families had been forced to support their farms with secondary jobs. His big brother had made it back from the war but not everyone's family welcomed a returning warrior. For over a decade, the government had been requiring males to register with Selective Services. Bobby knew he would be on the top of the draft list. He was a high school graduate and belonged to the Alabama National Guard. The idea of being summoned to join the Army moved him to follow in his brothers' footsteps. He'd seen the newsreels at the local theatre and knew he wanted to see the world.

His father never flinched when Bobby had to register, but now Pop was approaching his seventies and the farm was getting harder to maintain and produce a living for his family. There were only two more of his brothers left to tend the fields. The soil was poor and rocky and the idea of his seventy-year-old father behind the plow plagued him. But Bobby never wanted to be a farmer and there weren't many other options. The graphite mine had closed years ago. The cabinet factory would probably hire him. He was a good carpenter thanks to his brother, Glen. Glen couldn't join the military because he'd had polio. Before Glen married, Bobby would follow him around like a puppy.

He heard his mom in the kitchen and ran to beat his brothers to the bathroom. The sunlight peeked through the window mullions. His sister's rooster, Foghorn, announced the arrival of Navy recruitment day. He combed his hair with a little Brylcreem, hoping it would make him look older. Maybe he would impress Clara Hall and she'd write him while he was in boot camp.

"Hey, Bobby. I gotta go," Vernon called from the other side of the bathroom door. Vernon wasn't old enough to go to high school yet, and his walk to school was less pressing than Bobby's need to catch the school bus. "Hold your horses," Bobby said. He tucked in his plaid shirt, took one last look and opened the door. Vernon shoved past him and slammed the door.

Bobby headed to the kitchen to meet the welcoming aroma of biscuits. "Morning, Mama," he said, grinning as his mother stirred the milk gravy. There were always flaky, buttery biscuits for the grab in his mom's kitchen.

She looked over her shoulder at him with a smile but he saw the sadness in her eyes. Bobby was one of the last to leave her nest. He knew he was leaving a home that his parents built through wars, the Great Depression and so many economic challenges. But Bobby kept reminding himself that at least he was leaving the nest and not a victim of one of the childhood diseases the family had battled against. Diphtheria, whooping cough and polio had left their dark marks on his brothers and sisters. Not all of them had survived.

"Good morning, Bobby," his mother said. "You look like a fine young man in his Sunday meeting clothes. Is House going to the recruiter with you today?"

"Supposed to," Bobby answered, sitting at his place at the long, wooden kitchen table. "Last time the recruiter came to the high school, he said the Navy was letting buddies sign up together."

She placed two open-faced biscuits slathered in gravy with sausage in front of him and patted his back. She usually rumpled his hair and he was grateful she didn't today after he'd combed it special.

Vernon and Harvey plopped down at the table. Their striped tee shirts and casual long pants contrasted with Bobby's finer outfit. It also accentuated their age difference. They weren't yet aware of perfume and car fumes. For his younger brothers, childhood was still a pick-up game of baseball and fishing down in Farmer Mackey's pond.

"Hey, you gonna help me with math tonight?" Harvey asked Bobby. "This ciphering is hard. My teacher said you were good at it when she taught you."

"Sure, Harvey," Bobby said, wiping his mouth and scooting his chair back from the table. "But right now I gotta run and catch the bus." He looked at his mom, kissed her on the cheek and said, "Told House I'd meet him on the front steps this morning." He popped back into the bathroom, brushed his teeth and made sure his hair was still in place.

"Don't forget your lunch," his mom called.

Bobby got off the bus and saw his buddy House pulling up on their family's single bicycle, wearing his chick magnet senior letterman's jacket. His real name was Richard, but all his life because of his size, he carried the nickname, as in, big as a House. Bobby also noticed his penny loafers, surely his brother's; the thought confirmed when his friend carefully nudged the bike's kickstand, no doubt afraid of scuff marks. Ever since his brother had signed up, House had literally stepped into his brother's shoes, left behind when he left for the Korean War.

Bobby knew House wasn't as excited about enlisting as him. But House's future was as uncertain as his own, and the draft had clouded his hopes of a football scholarship. They'd turned eighteen a few weeks apart in January. Elvis Presley had been drafted in December and was headed to join the Army. He and Bobby couldn't compete with him in uniform but they were eager to wear their sailor caps.

Serving did have its advantages. "I'm going to throw mine at my girlfriend," House had bragged to Bobby. "Just like in the movies."

Bobby wanted his very own dixie cup just like the sailor on the Crackerjacks box and the recruiting poster at the high school.

House and Bobby had grown up together in Ashland. Before high school, their older brothers took them to the theatre to see *From Here to Eternity*. The ships, high seas, planes and ports stirred a restlessness in them. In spite of the generations of woodworking and farming blood, their eyes had feasted together on the silver screen of unknown lands. They wanted to belong to a fraternity of American boys not afraid of hard work and sweat. Besides that, there was a paycheck, enough to share with their families. The wars, Depression and farming weren't going to provide the bacon.

"Hey, House," Bobby shouted from the steps of the high school. As they headed to their morning hangout, the bell rang and they both jumped just a little. He and House had official business today. Men's business.

Homeroom was in Room 307. Mrs. Campbell taught Senior English and Drama. House had been recruited by the thespians in their annual play. They loved to put the athletes on stage dressed in skirts and cardigans pretending to be cheerleaders or swooning at the feet of a solo-ist. Sometimes he could get out of it because he was too big for the girls' borrowed outfits. But, Bobby grinned to himself, his buddy was a good sport, especially if Pearl Miller was involved. Mrs. Campbell went through roll call and reminders. Something about the PTA meeting and graduation ranks. "…and for those young men that are meeting with the recruiters, they will be at their respective tables in the school cafeteria after 4th period. If you run over the bell, please have them provide an excuse for your next class…."

The bell rang and classmates spilled into the hallway. Chatter and banging lockers reminded Bobby there were only a few more weeks before graduation as he headed to his first class.

Bobby tapped the desk with his pencil eraser. He'd had enough of oral book reports. Mary loved to show off. She read *Gone with the Wind*. Why read it when all you had to do was go to the movies? What was all the fuss over Rhett Butler anyway? Bobby looked over the teacher's head at the clock. Two more minutes and he'd be meeting House in the cafeteria.

"It sounds like you really enjoyed *Gone with the Wind*, Mary." Mr. Duckworth said, wrapping up her spot-light moment. "Tomorrow we'll hear from Pete, Doris and Vivian. That'll wrap up the last of your senior reading list. Please remember to return all borrowed books to the library before graduation."

Bobby had returned his book a week ago. He'd put off reading *Red Badge of Courage* for as long as he could. He'd rather make furniture for his mom. She didn't know he was secretly working on a going away present. He'd been saving the money he'd earned working in the chicken houses for Mr. Horn. It wasn't hard, but boy those chickens sure did stink. Pop helped him find the lumber to make Ma's new porch chair.

The bell rang and Bobby's heart leapt. It was time to meet the recruiter. *I'm going to see the world*, he said to himself. All that was left was to fill out his Application for Enlistment. He hoped he had done his homework. Hopefully he'd be reporting for boot camp before the end of summer.

Chapter 3

APRIL 2004

From beneath her pillow, Elizabeth heard the phone ringing. She peeked at the alarm clock's angry red digital numbers—7:24. Her husband was already up so she ignored the ring and turned over. Last night, she'd promised her mom that she'd go back and check on her stepdad, even if she had to call out of the office. Maybe she could catch a couple more hours before she needed to be at work. The bedroom door opened softly.

"Dear, it's your mother," Dan said, holding the phone over her pillow. She sat up and covered the phone with her hand.

"Does she sound okay?" Elizabeth asked.

"She sounds fine," he answered. He remained beside her as she took a breath.

"Hey, Mom. Everything—"

"HE'S GONE, Elizabeth. HE'S GONE. HE'S DEAD!" her mother screamed. "YOU'VE GOT TO COME OVER. HE'S DEAD."

"Is everything okay?" Dan asked softly. She stared into his eyes and shook her head no.

"Mom, I'll be right over," she said. "I'll be right over."

The phones simultaneously disconnected. A numbing chill shuddered through her. She knew this call would come but she felt stunned. *If I'd only stayed longer last night. He said it was just a cold.*

"Daddy's...dead," she said, staring at Dan. "She sounds lost. I've got to get over there." Her feet slid off the bed like lead with her mother's words swirling in her head. Dan's eyes teared and he hugged her, but she couldn't succumb to his sympathy, not yet. "I've got to get over there," she repeated and pulled away, heading to their closet.

"I'm going to make you a protein shake. You need something in you," Dan said, heading towards the kitchen. "I'll call Frank at the funeral home. You just get to your mom."

Dan knew funeral business well. He'd lost two sisters and a nephew too soon.

Jeans, sweater and boots on, Elizabeth grabbed the shake her husband held out to her and descended the garage stairs. Her body was on autopilot and adrenaline masked the grief that she suspected was going to hit her like a wrecking ball. She'd never lost a parent or sibling. She'd never been around a dead body, especially not one in her parent's home that would look like her dad.

"Be careful, drive safe. I'll be over soon," Dan said, shutting the door.

As she drove up Savannah Highway, the usual five-minute drive felt like a slow motion bad dream. *Did Mom call my sisters? Daddy's family? Daddy didn't belong to a church. Where are we going to hold the funeral? At least he'd purchased the cemetery lot.* She scratched that off the to-do list. The last light was ahead and she took a deep breath as she turned left. *You're good at thinking fast on your feet, Elizabeth. You've pulled lots of things out of the air at work. You can do this. But I'm supposed to be crying and weeping and I feel no tears,* she thought. *No, first stage of grief is denial,* she reminded herself in her psychologist persona. *Call the office and start rescheduling appointments—* check. As she pulled up to the house, she saw the EMS truck parked in front. It had become a common sight the past few years. A police cruiser was parked in front of it. He stopped her before she could get up the driveway.

"I'm their daughter," she said. He waved her on. Mom was waiting on the porch and started blurting random thoughts as she reached out to hug her.

"I kept trying to get him to go to the hospital. He wasn't eating. He was sleeping most of the time. I told him I was going to call you if he didn't go to the hospital," she said. "He still has his flip flops on. I don't know what to do."

"Have you called the others?" Elizabeth asked, trying to focus her mother's attention.

Her mom looked away and folded her arms, shaking her head no.

"Mom, we have to call. They'll want to know sooner than later," she said. She looked towards the open front door at paramedics coming around the corner of her dad's bedroom. She wasn't sure she could, and prayed she didn't have to, see her dad. She'd sat on the back porch with him just last night. He always protected everyone from worry directed his way. He'd have hated this scene. Elizabeth looked away.

"I can't. You need to do it. Please?" her mother said, slowly descending to the green wrought iron porch swing on which they'd all spent many a day watching the street's activities. "His notebook with the numbers is on the dining room table. I…I don't know what to say."

Without a word, Elizabeth walked into the house, blocking her peripheral vision from the master bedroom, focusing on the small grey vinyl binder that housed addresses and phone numbers of family and friends. She knew some of the telephone numbers but her mind was spinning. She decided to contact her sisters in order, oldest (besides herself) to youngest. It was still early so Audrey should still be home getting ready for work. She knew Audrey wasn't going to handle it well. Still numb, she dialed. As the phone rang, she tried to find the words that wouldn't knock the breath out of her sister.

The phone rang three times. "Hello?" Audrey answered.

"Hey, it's me," Elizabeth started. "I'm calling from Mom's." She paused to give her a moment to prepare herself for the next sentence. Since his heart condition, they were used to close calls and full recovery.

"Is everything okay?" Audrey asked with caution in her voice.

"Ummmm, no," she replied and powered her way to the next sentence. "Mom called me and said that Daddy passed overnight."

Elizabeth heard the deep moan and pictured Audrey sinking to the floor with the phone. "Audrey, I'm so sorry. Mom just couldn't make the calls. She seems pretty stunned."

She let her sister sob and gather herself before giving her any more details.

"How do you think it happened?" she asked.

"He'd been telling us that he was fighting a cold. Apparently, his heart just wore out," Elizabeth said. A lump formed in her throat as she said the word *heart*. He had the biggest and most generous heart—it might've wore out physically but not in its giving. She heard her sister trying to get a grip on her tears.

"When?" Audrey asked, avoiding the word funeral.

"Not sure. I still have to call his sister in Atlanta. Dan's getting in touch with the funeral home," Elizabeth said. "Guess maybe this weekend. I'll let ya'll know when we're further along. Do you want to call Mallory or Rebecca?"

"I'll call both of them. You do the others," Audrey said, relieving her. "I need to figure out how to tell Leigh. She isn't going to take this well." Audrey's daughter Leigh and Elizabeth's own daughter Autumn were more like sisters themselves than cousins, and both so close to their grandfather.

"Neither will Autumn," Elizabeth answered. "They were really close with their Pop-Pop. I'll call you when we know something more concrete."

Elizabeth looked across the room at her mom leaning on the arch, staring into his bedroom. It surprised her. She motioned for her to come over there mouthing the word *awwww*. "Hey, I'd better go. Mom needs me."

"Thanks, Elizabeth," Audrey said, her voice quivering. "Give Mom a hug, please... I don't know what else to say..."

"I know," Elizabeth answered. "I'll call back soon." She placed the phone down, and as she walked across the room, she guessed Mom was staring at Daddy's bed.

"Look at him, Elizabeth," Mom said, trying to pull her within view. In the true spirit of oldest daughter, she tried to hide her reluctance, but she didn't have a very good poker face. "Remember that Christmas card that he loved when you were in high school?"

"The one with the papa, mama and baby mouse in bed?" she guessed.

"Your dad loved the papa mouse snoring with his little mouth open in his stocking cap."

Elizabeth remembered the illustration on the Christmas card. "I still have one of the cards. He wanted me to paint it. The unfinished art project is in your attic," she said, smiling at the memory of his amusement with the T'was the Night before Christmas card, three little non-stirring mice in one bed with their stockings hanging in the mouse hole.

"Look at him. He looks like the papa mouse," Mom said. Her face was a mixture of emotion. Or was it absence? Daddy always made sure he'd planned for Mom's future stability after he was gone. The retired Navy Command Master Chief was a master of running the ship abroad and at home. In his modest way, his rate and value to the command wasn't known to any of his women until the last few years of his career. To his family he'd just been a simple man who enjoyed cooking for his girls and piddling in the marvelous garden that friends and family enjoyed every summer.

"Mom, I can't go in there. But I'll peek," she said and looked in the room. Daddy had either tried to get out or back into bed. He was wearing his blue striped pajamas and his flip-flops were on his feet. His head rested on his pillow and just like her mom described, his mouth was open just like the papa mouse, as if he was snoring. Elizabeth smiled at the irony of the scene.

When she heard a car door, she used it as an excuse to look away.

Dan was standing beside the funeral parlor's van as Frank removed a gurney with a folded black body bag. It felt surreal and foreign.

Frank approached the porch. "Thanks, Frank," Elizabeth said. He hugged her. She noted that she was obviously still on autopilot. "My mom's inside. I think she's still taking it all in."

"Sorry for your loss," Frank said, pulling her aside as they hugged. "Listen, it would be best while we're working with your dad if you could distract your mom." She nodded and led him inside. The sound of their footprints reverberated on the worn parquet tile.

"Mom, this is Frank. He's from the funeral home," she said. "He's here for Daddy." She was shocked by her own businesslike demeanor and paused to regroup. "Do you need a few more minutes?" Her mom continued to stare into the bedroom and shook her head no.

"Hey, Mom, let's go sit on the back deck." She turned and Elizabeth led her to the backyard, grabbing a glass of iced tea on the way. As they approached the porch swing, there lay his straw hat with the red bandana band beside his binoculars. *Damn it*, Elizabeth thought, obviously no way to avoid acknowledging them. The martins were busy chortling and clucking their dawn song, as if they were anticipating her dad's morning visit. Even the scent of the gardenia bush was wafting over the deck like a freshly brewed pot of coffee. The garden was thriving in spite of her father's absence. Without any signs of alarm, Elizabeth gently removed the hat from the cushion and walked to the fan. She couldn't conceal the birds or the fragrance.

"Mom, let's go ahead and run the fan. The humidity is starting and you never know about the gnats," Elizabeth said, sliding the hat and binoculars into the garden bin. "Okay?" She looked for a reaction. Her mom set the glass of tea on the side table and looked towards the dining room window.

"How long do you think they'll be?" She asked, turning towards the backyard, her expression blank.

"I wouldn't think long. Dan will pop out, I'm sure," Elizabeth adjusted the fan to mimic a soft morning breeze. What used to be a typical morning routine felt awkward and unfortunately reminded her even more that he was gone. "Mom? You okay out here for a few minutes? I need to make another phone call and left everything inside."

She nodded, her gaze now riveted on the gardenia bush. She blew her nose. "Thanks hon, that damn pollen is driving me crazy, probably from those gardenias." She turned back to Elizabeth, twisting the mangled Kleenex. "Just get me back inside soon."

Elizabeth knew it wasn't the pollen, birds or floral fragrances. It was the essence of what remained of her mother's soulmate, cultivated through a lifetime. The fruits of his labor were laden with memories from the corner of his garden to the porch swing.

"We'll get through this Mom. We always do," Elizabeth said softly, patting her shoulder before she headed back to begin the final phone calls.

Mallory placed the phone on the cradle and slid into the dining room chair. She could see the duffle bag sitting across the room by the front door. It was dropped on the floor in the foyer when she got home from Charleston on Monday, still waiting to return in two days. She'd left the tomato and pepper plants lined up at the garden rows they'd dug so she could return and help her dad plant on her next visit. His heart had weakened to the point he couldn't prepare it like he usually did. She'd been summoned to help after a phone call from Mom. When she was stationed in Key West, she hadn't visited as often as she should. Now she was in Beaufort. It took only an hour to drive. After the serious congestive heart incident earlier in the year, Mallory understood she'd be needed at home more. She headed to their childhood home as often as possible and had done it with a joyful heart.

As a child, she felt different than her three other sisters. She was the middle child, number three. She resisted compliance and often tested their mom's rules—especially if their father, and later stepfather, were at sea. Three girls had been born while the Navy sent her father to Purdue for the degree that allowed him to re-enlist as an officer. Specializing in surface warfare during the Cold War, it was not unusual for him to be gone for extended periods of time. They couldn't dodge relocation so every couple of years Mallory and her siblings learned to give up friends, and to be challenged to make new ones all over. Eventually, their parents' divorce and a remarriage fork in the road to their beloved stepfather Bobby had them back in relocation mode, this time following their stepfather's naval career path.

Mallory felt the brush of her rescue kitty across her ankles briefly distracting her. "I know, I know. Breakfast." Looking down, her dog stared dutifully at her, sensing the change in her mood since the phone call. "Pop-Pop's gone, Sparky," she whispered to her canine companion. His dark eyes looked intently from beneath the black and white bangs.

Mallory looked through the sliding glass doors to the back yard, freckled with sunshine. The azaleas were in full spring bloom but her heart couldn't feel the pleasure they usually gave her. She sighed. "I need to go find something black, Sparky," Mallory said, and she headed to the bedroom. The only dirt she'd wanted to see was in Daddy's backyard. Not a cemetery.

"Hungry, Mommy." Rebecca slammed the mini-van door with her hip. The weight of Molly gave it extra oomph.

"Let's get some Cheerios," Rebecca said, heading up the stairs. She glanced over the rail at the door to the family business office. She and her husband worked together in the mortgage business from their home. His territory was mid-State. The demands would soon be coming from behind the door to help put out fires. The blazes usually broke out because his impatient eye was on the commission, never getting a client to underwriting. She'd find herself sucked into the messes and he'd disappear. He always insisted he had sales calls to make.

She didn't love the work but she loved being a mom. She embraced the quiet time taking her son Levi to and from school. She headed straight to the booster seat and set Molly down. "Breakfast time," she said as the phone rang. "Here we go, Molly," Rebecca said out loud. John's office was on the first floor and rather than walk upstairs, he often telephoned from his cell phone, as if he were ringing up an outer office secretary.

"Hello?" Rebecca said, trying to hide the dread of his first set of orders. She grabbed the Cheerios and headed towards the refrigerator to grab Molly's sippee cup.

"Hey, babe. Can you make me a cup of coffee and bring it down?" John asked.

"Sure," Rebecca said, walking back to the coffee maker. She hated running up and down the stairs too, but saying no required more damage control than she could muster most mornings.

"By the way, your sister Audrey called while you were taking Levi to school," John said. "Said you needed to call her as soon as possible. Be sure you don't make my coffee as sweet as last time." Click.

She dialed Audrey's number as she measured out John's perfect cup of coffee. Molly was busy eating her cereal, looking at the children's book on the dining room table. The phone rang and she heard her sister pick up. "Hey Audrey, did you call?"

There was an unusual pause. Something somersaulted deep inside as she waited for Audrey's response. "Rebecca, I got a call this morning. Daddy passed away sometime last night," Audrey said. Her voice broke and she knew there were tears on the other end.

Unprepared for the news, Rebecca froze and put the coffee pot down. "Was he home?" she asked. "I hope he was home."

"Yeah. Um, Elizabeth said…she would call with details of the funeral when they knew something," Audrey squeaked out. "I'm sure it will be this weekend. She was still making phone calls. I really thought we had more time. We were going up for Mother's Day."

"Us too," Rebecca said robotically. "I better start figuring out how to leave and keep the business running," she added, already in salvage mode. She checked her emotions and put them on the back burner. "Do you know how Mom is doing? Does Mallory know?" She looked over her shoulder, making sure Molly was occupied.

"I called her just before you. I think everyone's stunned," Audrey said. "I'm sure it doesn't feel real yet." There was another awkward pause as she stifled sobs. "I guess we'll all get the marching orders before the end of the day. Love you."

Rebecca heard the call waiting beep. "Love you, too. Let me know," Rebecca said and flashed to the other line.

"Babe, where's my coffee?" John whined.

"Sorry, I was returning Audrey's call. Daddy passed away last night," Rebecca said. "We need to go to Charleston this weekend." And the tap dancing started in her head.

"...three little non-stirring mice in one bed..."

Chapter 4

ASHLAND – JUNE, 1957

Kissing his mom on her cheek, Bobby hoped that this was the end of the wait. He and House had been retrieving birth certificates, discharges from the Alabama National Guard Reserves and presenting their high school diplomas to the recruiter for what seemed like years. They'd been out of high school for fifteen days and today would determine his future.

Glen and Pops had helped him finish the chair for his mom. His art teacher had sketched an anchor pattern he'd whittled into the headrest. Pops assured him that he would have his mom's gift waiting for her on the porch if they shipped him out after his physical today.

They didn't have a phone line – Ashland was last on the list for telephones and electric service– so they'd agreed on a two-day amnesty on the chair revelation. Bobby wanted to surprise Mom and avoid tears if they sent him home after the physical. In the back of his mind, he was haunted by what he knew was a history of family heart issues. He prayed he had skipped that trait. So many had departed too soon. He had to pass the physical. He just had to.

He was leaving the house with the clothes on his back. The inside pocket of his jacket contained a black comb, toothbrush and a pen given to him at graduation. His wallet contained enough money for bus fare and if necessary, a soda.

"Ma, I've taken bus fare for two ways from my savings in the dresser drawer," he informed her, looking down on her graying hair. She looked tired. She'd born nine children, worked at the graphite factory with Pops when that was flush. They also sustained the family with farming, milling corn and raising hogs. Ashland, Alabama had never really recovered from the economic impacts of the wars. "Please use anything I left. The Navy will be sending my clothes back to you and I should have a paycheck in a few weeks."

"You aren't worried about boot camp?" she asked, fighting tears. "What if you don't make it?"

"Ma, I did boot camp with the National Guard reserves a couple years ago," Bobby assured her. "Jonathan came back after his time. I can do this. Look at our family. We're tight and we've been taught many things. I have to fit in somewhere on a ship. Besides, you'll love me in my uniform," he teased and kissed her cheek.

Aunt Bessie came shuffling out. She'd never married and had been a lot of help for his mom when he and his siblings were younger. She'd cooked and kept the household running when Ma had to take a bus to the powder factory during the Great World War. Aunt Bessie and Pops had taken care of their parents before Pops had fallen in love with Bobby's mom.

Pops came through the back door from slopping. Bobby looked at the backbone of his family and knew this was the right choice. It was his time to pay back his family's blood, sweat and tears in the dirt outside his bedroom window. The crowing of his sister's rooster, Foghorn, reminded him of her recent marriage and relocation with her husband's railroad job. The rooster stayed behind. Bobby didn't want to stay behind.

Bobby looked at his father. In spite of his dungarees and rough appearance, he was held in high regard in town as a man of political integrity. He managed the voting polls every election before Bobby was born. Each of his older siblings had gone with him to open and close the polls. In spite of the now worn out overalls and unshaved beard, there stood a prince of a man. Pops kept his ear to the ground and made sure if someone was in need, he rallied his family to contribute to relief. But his knuckles and knees were swollen and worn. He felt his father's arthritic hand on his shoulder.

Bobby looked his father in the eyes. "If I pass the physical, I'll be on the bus to boot camp in the Great Lakes up by Chicago. I'll leave in the morning from Birmingham. I promise I'll write when I get the chance. I've got to head out and meet House. We have to be there by noon. Anniston isn't as straight as the crow flies you know." His mom handed him a small parcel with some biscuits and ham. Bobby smiled and stored the smell of the kitchen in his heart. Warm biscuits and gravy would always bring him home.

"There are a couple extras for House, too," his mom said. Bobby gave her a hug in appreciation. He didn't think he'd get home to his parents for a while. Communism was looming on the horizon. But, he understood the drill. He'd rather be on the water than in the trenches or bailing out of planes. There was nothing left in Ashland, except a surprise chair that he hoped would ease his mother's heart after he'd gone.

The screen door quietly slammed as he waved and headed to the bus stop to meet House.

Bobby was intrigued by a life at sea, but he knew that for his friend, his brother's loafers were his only shoes to fill for his sick father whose lungs were failing fast. His best friend's mom was wearing out and caring for his dad's failing health due to bad breathing. Was it the dust from years of mining? House needed to prove he could be the man of his family, needed to relieve his mom working at the mercantile and having to care for his ill father. Bobby suspected the ocean air was a better future for his buddy than the dark dust of the mines.

Though neither of the boys could be sure what their futures in the Navy held. The government wasn't really saying anything about the post war status. The word communism was floating everywhere. Not only was it on everyone's minds, it was in Hollywood movies and news reels. But that seemed far from their little lives and their small town's declining economics. There were many old ships being released from the "Mothball Fleet" that had been stored at Treasure Island, the naval base in San Francisco. Old and newer greyhounds were being maintained by the newbies--chipping and painting, preparing for when the government called for them. He knew they would be required to chip and paint until they advanced. Bobby prayed his test results in boot camp would put him in a slot that would minimize the chore. Seaman was his title but he hoped for a decent workstation.

Chapter 5

APRIL – 2004

The rest of Elizabeth's day was consumed by phone calls and funeral arrangements. She began to wonder if all the business of arranging services and the minister, caskets and pallbearers, death certificates and other endless details, weren't just to distract closest family members from the inevitable grief. It was working; she was all business. The obituary was drafted and Elizabeth's sisters were each preparing to bring their families to town before Saturday's visitation.

Her husband Dan was a rock. He guided them through each detail that needed attending, including lunch at Ruby Tuesdays to make sure they all ate something. Elizabeth watched her mom at the salad bar going through the motions. She stared at the condensation tears rolling down her draft beer. Elizabeth wished that she could release her own grief but she was still on duty for her mom—just like her dad had prepared her for.

"You okay?" Dan asked. They were tucked away in a corner booth, strategically chosen so her mom wouldn't feel self-conscious if she had a moment.

"It doesn't feel real," Elizabeth said. "I appreciate all your help." She moved the broccoli around in the cheesy soup, distracted as she watched her mom returning to the table. "I think she's ready to go home."

On cue, her mom said, "I may take this salad home and eat it later." She scooted beside Elizabeth.

"This has been a long day," Dan said. "I'll get the check and a to-go box. We'll get you home. Or you can stay with us, if you want."

"I'll be fine," she said, and withdrew again. "Who's coming tomorrow?"

"Mallory," Elizabeth answered. "She was… already planning on coming this weekend to help plant the garden with Daddy." Elizabeth had seen the pots of young starter tomatoes and peppers lined up at the edge of the garden while she made phone calls. The purple martin families had flitted in the early morning light, hunting breakfast as the babies peeked from the gourds. "Everyone else should be in by lunch on Saturday. Dan reserved some rooms at our hotel."

"Thanks," her mom said, playing with her salad. "Yeah, Mallory worked pretty hard getting the garden ready with him last weekend. But he took lots of naps in between tilling. I should have pushed harder for him to go the doctor."

"I think he went the way he wanted to," Elizabeth said softly. "Command Master Chief went in his sleep, at home, in privacy."

Her mom smiled weakly and scraped her salad into the box Dan set down in front of her. "I just want to get home, change into my jammies and watch TV," she said. "I need to be alone before all this starts up. I don't know how to do all this."

Dan took her hand. "You're not alone. We'll get you through it," he said. Elizabeth nodded in agreement, but privately she couldn't wait for the reinforcements to arrive. She still didn't see herself being relieved from duty yet. She couldn't help wishing they were getting ready for Daddy heading out to sea on a Med. The three to six month absences on his ship always required their female household to stand fast, to keep Mom unburdened. As kids, they'd pushed her buttons but it was usually confined to the earlier part of his departure. His imminent return was always filled with reminded threats to *tell your father when he gets home*. This time he wasn't coming home. Elizabeth swallowed hard.

"Mom, I'm taking you shopping for some clothes tomorrow," she said, back to safer details. "We'll do that before everyone starts arriving. We can check out Steinmart."

"I'm tired. Let's don't do it too early," she said. "I need to get his suit together, too." Her face went blank and Elizabeth felt her mom withering emotionally. They took a long sip of their beers.

"We'll get through this," Elizabeth said, sliding out the booth. She took a last look at her own lukewarm beer, envying the tears puddling on the table. It was the darkest day of her life. She felt the weight of his jacket— Bobby's beautiful dress blue jacket with its gold buttons, ribbons and hash marks for good behavior. She couldn't let him down. In a sense, they had all worn that uniform during his thirty-two-year career and each had stood their watches, preserving their small family circle. But this, this was not a drill. Everyone needed to report to their battle stations.

★ ★ ★

Hotel rooms were reserved for Audrey and Rebecca's family. Mallory would stay with their mom. She'd left her cats behind with plenty of food and water, but her dog Sparky rode shotgun with her from Beaufort. Since they had arrived, Sparky sat at her mom's feet as if he knew she needed support.

Mallory had taken on the chore of starting dinner. The sisters were getting together after everyone had chipped in to plant the garden earlier that day. This summer would be the final garden harvest of Burpee seeds raised in the self-designed green house. It was the first of many firsts they'd have to endure the next year. For 365 days, holidays and traditions would leave their father's chair vacant. No more chances to hear Pop-Pop tell stories of his glory days, of boys sailing from their hometowns, sandwiched between the decks of a destroyer and living within her bowels. Trained and drilled as a single unit without hesitation to pursue peace or humanitarian assignments.

She heard the front door, looked over her shoulder and saw Elizabeth heading towards the kitchen. It was where everyone hung out. The smell of the ham in the oven mingled with the pot of green beans on the stove.

"Beer or wine is in the frig," Mallory said. "I'm ahead of you."

"Don't bet on it," Elizabeth said, reaching into the glass cabinet. "How's Mom?"

"She wants to be alone. Sparky keeps her company. I guess we should try and get her to eat something later. I don't think it's hit her yet."

Mallory turned and leaned on the counter, taking a healthy swig of her Corona.

Elizabeth put her glass to the spigot of the box of Chardonnay. Another of those firsts; they'd never again sit with him on the deck watching his garden progress, the swooping of the purple martins or listen to his glory day stories. Sitting on the porch swing, each with a glass of wine—from a box. They'd always teased him about buying the cardboard boxes of wine. The image of Walter Matthau carrying a box of wine in *Grumpy Old Men* to woo Sophia Loren played in her head as she waited for the glass to fill. He always joked if it worked for Walter; he had a shot at getting lucky, too. Before Elizabeth closed the refrigerator, the front door opened. Audrey and Rebecca quietly passed their mom's closed bedroom door.

"Everyone settled in?" Mallory asked.

Mallory could see that her big sis Elizabeth was relieved someone else was leading the agenda for the night. It showed as she sat on the bar stool and stared into her wine glass. Being the oldest of the four girls, Elizabeth had been the one molded to never show weakness.

"I left John feeding and bathing the kids," Rebecca answered. "He wasn't happy about it." She looked thin and tired. But, she had for several years between parenting and helping with the home business. Rebecca rarely visited, and it seemed as if she had placed herself on the bottom of the totem pole of her life.

Audrey went straight to the refrigerator and grabbed a Corona. "I left Leigh. She wanted to watch TV. I wanted to give her a little space before everything ramps up."

No one commented on Audrey's personal loss. There would be plenty of time to find the right words to discuss it. Audrey looked at Elizabeth. "Maybe Autumn can stay at the hotel with her on Sunday night?"

"Of course," Elizabeth said.

Elizabeth was suddenly flooded with memories. Up until Audrey's husband's transfer with the civil service, their girls were like sisters, cousins that were inseparable and the apple of their grandparents' eyes. It wasn't unusual for them to call and ask for overnights with the girls. Early the next morning after a country breakfast, they'd load them into the car and drive to South of the Border. By the end of the day, they returned them with cheesy souvenirs. One time, Pop-Pop took them to the Summerville dirt racetrack, entrusting the forty-pound girls with a dozen big fat yeast rolls in the back seat. He was engaged in a conversation with his buddy as they waited for the rain to determine the calling of the race.

"Hey, hand us a yeast roll," Pop-Pop requested. The girls' heads snapped and they locked eyes with their grandfather looking into the rearview mirror. The box had been abandoned empty on the floor for over thirty minutes. Butter glossed their lips. Twelve big, fat, yeast rolls protruded from their little bellies, six apiece, as their grandfather stifled a laugh.

Elizabeth had heard that story many years after and it had always stirred the same twinkle of amusement in his eyes, as if it was the first time he was telling it.

"Before I leave, I'm going to pop my head in and check on Mom," Audrey said. They all knew she'd always been the favorite but as adults, it was a silent sister code. Everyone knew their place and as trained Navy dependents; each knew who was best at what. They were a well-oiled team, dedicated to the cohesive expectation to be ready to stand their watches.

"Let's get this ham sliced," Mallory said as she grabbed the potholders often worn by their dad. Elizabeth and Rebecca moved towards the cabinet to grab paper plates and silverware. No one was very hungry. It was a grasp to inject a normal routine into a family gathering. Unfortunately, there was an empty chair.

"Hey, do y'all remember when Daddy made the girls a flying ginny?" Elizabeth asked. The mood of the room immediately changed at the memory of his twirling see-saw, built one summer while the girls were still young. It included a visiting raccoon, with panicked munchkin voices trying to summon the adults to escort them out of the backyard. The intimating bandit had been hunting for spare cat food placed for the feral cat that lived in the woodpile. No one sensed the urgency of their cries. They kept smiling and waving from the kitchen window as the food was laid out at the dining room table— just like tonight. The ghost of the flying ginny never failed to tickle them, even now.

"Well, there is a lot to do between now and Sunday," Audrey said. "We have lots of memories growing up with Daddy. Nothing like growing up Navy."

They all looked at each other and nodded in agreement.

"Who remembers Pufnstuf's kittens climbing up Daddy's leg when he was dating Mom? Who knew he was terrified of cats...."

Chapter 6

GREAT LAKES, IL – 1957

Dear Mama,

I can't believe this is the last letter I will be writing from boot camp. It's gotten easier and I'm excited about where they might send me. I have made a couple of new friends. One of them plays the guitar in the weekly variety show. They nicknamed him Hank because he sounds just like Hank Williams. I'm buying the yearbook for my Company 161. I will show you pictures of the Training Center and the things we had to do and learn. The strangest exercise is standing watch over our hanging laundry. But, I do what I'm told and try to stay under the wire. Even if it is watching uniforms and socks dry.

Me and the guys in my company have gotten pretty good with our inspections. They don't give us very much space for our clothes but the way we fold and stack really does work. We won the Star Flag last week. That means we finally got Dirk to get serious about the hygiene and barracks inspections.

I mentioned him in my last letter. I was getting worried that some of the guys were losing patience and grumbling. They say someone in the barracks next door was forcibly scrubbed in the showers. I don't ever see House except the week we worked Mess Hall. The food isn't great but after all the drills, housekeeping and classroom time, I'll eat anything. But, I don't think I will ever get biscuits like yours unless I'm on leave.

Even though my test scores placed me in Damage Control, I had to learn all the other jobs too. I liked hunting with Pop and Glen but after gun turret instruction, I'd rather work putting out fires. Gun turrets are small and hot, and the shells are loud. For fire control, we learned how to use a water pump. We can use it below deck or on deck. They call it Handy Billy. The Navy has some of the funniest terms for stuff we use. The only thing that I worry about is the other guy helping me put the hoses on. I'm pretty fast with it. I can even get the rope on the pulley and start the gasoline engine almost every time on my first pull. On the day we worked with real fire outside, we hosed Company 145 and knocked a few of them off their feet. I know we shouldn't have, but it was hot. They returned the favor. Chief Toliver didn't punish us but he didn't seem amused either. Sometimes we get away with stuff like that.

About the only non-classroom activities are exercise competitions. Some of the Yankees take boxing a little too serious. You can tell where we're from by the groups that are cheering. Mama, there are guys from so many other parts of the country. I was always excited going to Anniston and seeing the electric lights, telephones and even the new bathrooms. But, when the bus pulled into the bus station in Chicago, the lights on the office buildings went up for miles and for as far as you could see. I wish you and Pop could come to graduation. You wouldn't believe it. It is just like some of the moving pictures downtown. I can't wait for liberty so I can take pictures for you. Now I see why Jonathan loved the Navy and I haven't even seen my ship yet.

It's almost time for lights out. Tell everyone I think of them and miss them. I need to review my signals. That's from my semaphore class. I'm not supposed to smile during the flag drills but I can't help but think of House's crush, Pearl Miller, cheering when we are all doing the numbers and alphabet signals. Tomorrow is laundry day and we are getting ready for final parade. We have to march and drill without our company commander. I probably won't write again until later.

Love to all and hope Pops isn't doing too much. Make sure to tell everyone I asked if Vernon and Harvey are studying hard in school and listening to you.

Love,
Bobby

Bobby folded, addressed and put a stamp on his letter home. He'd left out the parts of boot camp that might worry his mom. He left out why the Handy Billy could be used below deck and above. She didn't need to think of mines, torpedoes and missiles slamming into the hull or fantail of a ship. She didn't need to know about him acing his class on A.B.C. Warfare. The instructors often made him wear his gas mask clipped from his belt. They had covered every type of attack and damage control scenario. Holes, flooding, fire, abandoning ship or floatation if washed overboard. And cussing like a sailor was an everyday conversation. No, his mom just needed to hear about food, housekeeping and parades.

"Hey, Howie," Bobby yelled as he tucked his letter away to drop off in the outgoing. He grabbed his signal book. "Want to go over semaphore signals?"

Chapter 7

GREAT LAKES, IL – 1957

S eabags were lined up outside the barracks. Bobby closed his locker for the last time. He'd arrived eight weeks earlier with nothing but the clothes on his back. In processing changed everything on him from head to toe. His clothing had been mailed home in exchange for dungarees, boot leggings and a watch cap. Haircuts, shots, GCTB test and an interview to define his billet had been shoved in between stenciling his name and service number on uniforms.

With one last look around the room, he recalled the words of his recruiter: "***Honor, Courage, Commitment****: Three words that before Boot Camp probably held little meaning.*

There, they'll become words you'll live by. These Navy Core Values will become the ideals you and your fellow shipmates live by."

Indeed, it became the thread for recruit training. He thought he knew the meanings but from lectures and training films to hands-on battle station drills, he was presented with a new reality. As the recruits worked together with fire, chemicals, weapons, and everyday responsibilities on a ship, they'd become a brotherhood. Graduation including the march, the colors, the national anthem and passing in review was all still fresh in his mind.

Let's go, Bobby!" House shouted from the door of the barracks. "The bus is leaving. We have some time in town before we head home. We can dump our bags at the train station."

Bobby felt his cap to be sure it was on straight. His shoes were impeccably shined and his Navy crackerjacks fit like a glove. "I'm ready," he said. Pivoting on his heel, he gave his room one last salute. "Request permission to go ashore, sir."

House bowed and swept his hand to guide him through the doorway. As Bobby passed, they slapped each other on the shoulders and grabbed their seabags.

Two hours later, their bags were stowed in train station lockers. The Grand Hall of Union Station was filled with businessmen and women rushing to gates and dirty platforms with parked, huffing locomotives.

"Let's find a diner and grab a bite before we're stuck on the train. We'll see who gets the most looks in our uniforms," House said, while Bobby took a picture with his new Kodak. He'd promised to show his family the big city. The marble-clad station was a great start.

The sidewalk was busy with more commuters. "All these people remind me of the ant hills at home after you stir them with a stick," Bobby said. Cars and delivery trucks stopped at red lights. "Look at that ride," he pointed at a red sedan. "That's the new Bel Air. I saw those in *Mechanix Illustrated*. You won't see one of those back home." Bobby took advantage of the red light to snap another photo while the car idled.

"I'll bet those white walls can burn some rubber," House said, somewhat distracted as he looked around for a diner. He tipped his cap at a blonde. She sheepishly looked at him and blushed as she passed. "That was worth every push up and battle station drill. She's a barn burner."

"Simmer down, Seaman Smith," Bobby said, punching House's arm. "Why don't we grab a bite at that bar instead?" He pointed at the neon sign flashing. The words "Petey's Bar & Grill" radiated red and yellow. A white arrow pointed downwards at a peeling painted door. Two other sailors were headed inside.

"First beer is on you," House said, jumping into the street. Shiny black shoes hit the asphalt and their neckerchiefs slapped against their starched shirts.

"This is a good idea, Bobby!" As they pulled on the door, cigarette smoke hit them in the face.

"Maybe we should get some smokes for the ride home," Bobby suggested. "Oh, man! Look at the size of that burger." They grabbed two bar stools.

"Two mugs of beer…on my friend," House ordered. Bobby shook his head and punched his buddy in the arm with a crooked smile.

"I know I look sharp even though this uniform is scratchy," House said, tugging at the crotch. "But, hey, it makes my dick look good."

The two sailors broke out in boyish laughter.

Chapter 8

APRIL, 2004

Elizabeth held her coffee, feeling numb. She stared at her husband reading the *Post & Courier*. For her, the elephant in the room was her step-father's obituary on page B-2. "Entered into eternal rest," was etched in her head since they had taken care of funeral plans. There were so many unwritten qualities, memories and untold stories that were missing in the obituary. How could anyone sum up the life of a giant in a measly paragraph?

She didn't realize how late it was when she left her sisters last night. They'd laughed and cried while they caught up on each other's lives. After they shared dinner, Rebecca's husband called the house, whining about caring for the kids and needing a break. As was typical, she made some shallow excuses and ran to rescue him. Mallory promised to check on their mother throughout the night. Audrey returned to the hotel to put on a brave face for her daughter, and Elizabeth was relieved of her watch, temporarily.

"How you holding up, honey?" Dan asked, looking over his glasses from the newspaper. "You were out pretty late last night."

Elizabeth gave him her best brave smile. "It was good to be back together. And funny, listening to how Daddy influenced each of us in his own way. We discussed getting Mom ready for the visitation tonight. We're meeting in a few hours and planting his last garden that Mallory had prepared last week." She knew her answers were all business and realized even as she spoke that Dan would be helping with the garden. She was just going through the motions, executing her plan of the day.

That was the short synopsis of the situation. But she knew it was so much more. Her dad had been the glue for the five women in his life. They had been tucked into his heart whether he was home or at sea. His unconditional love had been as constant as the North Star. Elizabeth stared into the pond outside their breakfast room. There was hardly an element of nature that didn't flood her with memories, each influenced by her parents' career path. He was the professional sailor and her mom held down the home. It wasn't a Doris Day movie by any means, but her childhood was rich in adventure. But, there were also the challenges from having first a dad, and then a stepdad, absent so much. Her mother tried her best to herd four girls, each a year apart in age. *Poor mom. She wrangled us from potty training to puberty, a houseful of developing hormones and personalities, and many, many times without her life's partner to relieve her of her watch.* As Elizabeth twirled these thoughts around her brain, she reflected on raising her own daughter from a young age. How had her mom done it with four, and on a Navy man's salary? Well, there were lots of TV dinners and potted meat.

But, in her mind, growing up with the Navy was still suspended above them like an unwritten book and she felt like this weekend would be a time of sifting and reflection. She knew they would hold up a beautiful jewel and observe how every facet had been cut. Four sisters possessed their own unique perspective, in spite of growing up in the same house. Depending on the times, each of them had tried to find their voices. As the oldest, Elizabeth was pressured to be the dutiful daughter, setting the example from sharing her Little Debbie to being the first to demonstrate how to receive childhood vaccinations. The spiritual and political journeys changed with the social hurricanes in the 1960s and 1970s. She was beginning to understand her next assignment.

Chapter 9

1957 – TREASURE ISLAND, CA

It had been four months since Bobby had visited his family after boot camp. He and House had spent their last night sitting on the porch discussing their next duty station. It was a humid hot night, the airwaves filled with the chorus of cicadas. Without a word, they accepted there would soon be new sounds filling their ears, those of ship bells and bosun pipes. They were headed to the opposite side of the world. House was going to school at Bainbridge before he would be deployed to the Mediterranean. Bobby would travel to Treasure Island outside of San Francisco. Destination unknown.

"What'cha think, Bobby?" House broke the cicadas' concert. Spanish moss hung limp from the live oaks that were fast becoming a silhouette against the sunset.

"Gonna miss home but I can't wait to see a real ship," Bobby drawled. "Not excited about chipping and painting, but I'll get over it. Beats a plow… and I get a pay check. You ready?"

"Yeah. Kind of excited about being a radioman. Keeps me out of that engine room," House said. "Not that what you're doing isn't important, too." He regretted how quickly he had said that.

"We all work together," Bobby responded, swatting a gnat from his eyes. "Won't miss these little beasts. Did you see Pearl?"

"I tried to. She's off at college," House said. "So much for my uniform and tossing a cap to her as I leave for Bainbridge."

"You got bigger things ahead. The pings of subs, whales and sending encrypted messages from admirals," Bobby said. "You go East, I'll go West. We'll compare notes! Your mail is APO and mine will be FPO. Just stay in touch."

Neither looked at each other as House stood and pretended to stretch.

"I gotta ship out tomorrow. Better head home and spend some time with Ma," House said softly. "Dad's not really doing that great." He bent down, spit on his finger and wiped some dust off of his brother's inherited loafers. "Seabag is already packed."

"We should have that down by now. Who'd believe we'd get all that stuff in those little bags and lockers," Bobby responded, stalling their inevitable good-bye. "How many times did you have to keep yourself from asking your mom to *pass the fucking butter?*"

They patted each other on the back and House muttered, "Slipped out four times."

Bobby watched as House walked to his bicycle. "Aunt Bessie scolded me three times," Bobby shouted to diffuse the separation. "Stay in touch."

The flashback ended as Bobby was buzzed by a horse fly while he chipped and painted on the next ship being pulled out of the Mothball Fleet.

"Hey, Higgins… your new orders are waiting with the CO," shouted petty officer. Bobby snapped alert.

"Permission to go ashore, sir?" He was ready to see the world.

Chapter 10

CHARLESTON, 2004

T he car was silent as Dan drove Elizabeth and their daughter to the funeral home. Elizabeth could feel her husband looking at her but she kept her head turned, staring out the window. She pretended not to notice his concern. Her thoughts were deeper than even he could reach. She wanted everyone to think she was handling it well. Throughout their marriage, he'd always told her how he'd been amazed at her ability to detach in emotionally charged situations. Where was that strength now? She wondered. She supposed she appeared detached to the others. But what of it? It was her job to be the strong one, wasn't it?

"What time is it?" Elizabeth asked. Her question was only a distraction, keeping her mind on the task at hand, herding her family through the maze of grieving the loss of a man who had a great presence in so many lives. Husband, father, brother, uncle, proud grandparent and all the other community labels placed on his lapel. His compassion, nurturing, joie de vie, but tempered intolerance of irresponsibility had been forged on the international seas of his beloved US Navy.

Elizabeth let her thoughts wander back ten months earlier to when she and Dan had headed over to Dad's Sunday cookout for Father's Day. The smell of creamed corn and perfectly grilled steak filled the kitchen. She was the only daughter to make an appearance. The rest of the girls had sent cards and small packages. Their daughter Autumn was in the other room watching *America's Funniest Home Videos*.

"Daddy, what did you marinate the steak with?" Elizabeth had asked. Outside of the aroma, the air was tense and strained with no obvious source. She knew he'd had a stress test that week but he had not brought it up. *Nothing new,* she said to herself. He was always man at the helm, even at home.

As her dad whistled and rolled his eyes to the ceiling, she knew he wasn't going to tell her anything about his recipes.

Not knowing she was walking into a damage control arena, she asked the innocent question, "How'd your doctor's appointment go?"

Her father's reaction stunned everyone in the kitchen, rare tears that he couldn't hold back. Even her mom seemed unaware of the answer to the question. He'd been struggling with congestive heart disease, a defibrillator and stern warnings of overworking his weakening heart for the past couple of years. But everyone in the kitchen was unprepared for his vulnerability.

"I've got some decisions to make," he finally said after he controlled his obvious grief. "Did I tell you about the time I had to yell at the captain to hold the gangway when I stole the milk money from the woman I'd gone home with on liberty?" He wrapped his arms around Rose and gave her a reassuring squeeze.

"Daddy, you wouldn't steal a baby's milk money," Elizabeth said, playing along with his awkward change of subject.

Now, as she was headed to her final good-bye in Chapel C, she recalled when she'd finally been told his only lifeline was to be put on the list for a heart transplant. He'd refused. His decision was a double-edged sword. On one hand, Elizabeth didn't want to lose her dad but on the other hand, she knew her dad would never put himself over a younger recipient. Immeasurable grief mixed with immense respect for the man who always put others first.

"We're on time," Dan said, interrupting her grim thoughts. "One hour until the visitation. Y'all will have a complete hour of privacy before you have to greet and meet," Dan said, his funeral experience reassuring. "I've got your back. I'll be watching. Lock eyes or grab my hand if it gets too tough, okay?"

Elizabeth nodded as they turned into the parking lot. They took one of the parking spots allotted to the immediate family. She looked one last time in the sun visor for make-up flaws, even though no mascara had tested the claim of waterproof yet. The tears were still walled behind a dam of grief that hadn't been released. But she could feel the pressure welling and knew it was only a matter of time before the dam broke.

"Looks like the girls are here," Elizabeth said, as she counted the cars, spotting Audrey's rental, Mallory's Jeep and Rebecca's mini-van. "I think Mallory wanted to bring Mom. Can't picture her hair in the Jeep." She let a small grin escape.

"Audrey may have intervened," Dan grinned back, trying to lighten the mood.

"That's true. It has always been a joke that Mom favored "Audrey, Audrey, Audrey." It was one of the sisters' favorite lines from the "Brady Bunch" show. "She's always been the Cinderella favorite." Audrey and Elizabeth had shared a bedroom her entire childhood. It hadn't always been a piece of cake, but it had forged a distinct bond. When Audrey had moved to Connecticut, the result of her late husband's job transfer, it had left a gaping hole in Elizabeth's life. She hadn't realized how big until Audrey was back. She hoped she and her daughter might stay on for a while; two gaping holes would be too much to bear.

Dan placed the car in park. As they opened the doors, the humidity of the Charleston spring hit them in the face, rising up from the asphalt. Elizabeth shuddered as she noticed the grim hearse parked under the carport, blocking the back door.

Dan grabbed Elizabeth's hand as Autumn embraced her elbow on the other side.

Autumn stalled and looked directly at her mom. "Mom. We'll get through this—together. Right, Dad? The way Pop-Pop would want us to?"

Elizabeth glanced at Dan, then Autumn. She squeezed each of their hands, took a deep breath and they stoically marched towards the door.

As they entered the chapel, Elizabeth felt the weight of responsibility press against her again. Audrey had been away and unable to share in the final months of their father's illness. Mallory's recent transfer to Beaufort gave Elizabeth some weekend liberty but the long weeks in between were all on her. And Rebecca was restricted to an occasional phone call from Greenville. Her attention span was consistently cut short because of the dysfunctional family business. Elizabeth now felt guilty, knowing her resentment was beginning to boil. She took a deep breath and forced a smile as she approached her sisters. Dan was shaking hands with others and Autumn hunted for her cousin Leigh.

"Is Mom in the room?" she asked. As if synchronized, all four looked through the door where their mom was standing beside the casket.

"How does he look?" Elizabeth asked.

"Good, but it's obvious he had lost weight," Audrey said.

"He's still handsome in his dress blues," Mallory added.

Rebecca shifted Molly to her other thin hip. Elizabeth saw her looking across the room at her husband talking with Dan. The cousins were sitting in the corner. The makeup wasn't concealing the rings under her eyes from crying. Elizabeth knew Becca was crying for the loss of the only father she knew growing up, but instinctively she knew there was more to her little sister's tears.

"By the way, after the visitation, some ladies from Dan's church are setting up food for us at my house," Elizabeth said. "You don't have to come but anyone is welcome. It's not too far from here."

Audrey shook her head enthusiastically. "Sounds perfect. I don't want to go back to the hotel so early." They watched Rebecca's eyes dart from John back to the circle of sisters.

"Rebecca?" Audrey prodded.

It was becoming obvious that Rebecca had lost her confidence and her baby-of-the-family gusto. Elizabeth thought, *the abuser starts by isolating them.* As a psychologist, she counseled many women in abusive and toxic relationships. The idea of her sister—baby sister at that, being oppressed by her own husband put one more brick on the already stressful situation. But the signs were beginning to surface. Rebecca's body was too thin and if Elizabeth's hunch was right, it mirrored her spirit. Undernourished, starved and neglected, it would become harder and harder for Rebecca to put up a facade. Elizabeth looked across the room at John holding court as if he was at a social event instead of their stepfather's funeral. Dan looked her way and cocked his eyebrow. She forced a tired smile and turned back to her sisters. *See John, that's what you should be doing.*

"Come with us Rebecca. We'll all help with Molly," Elizabeth said, rubbing her sister's back, encouraging her to stick with them.

"Pro-probably, maybe... I'll see how John feels by the end of the visitation," she stuttered and avoided eye contact, adjusting Molly's dress.

"No, it's about YOU!" Mallory's voice insisted. "We hardly see or hear from you. You need to focus on you, on us, on Mom. That's why you're here."

Audrey put her arm around Rebecca. "She's right, sweetie. I've been in Mom's shoes. She needs all of us. *We* need all of us."

Tears welling in her eyes, Rebecca nodded.

It had been forty-five minutes as the family members mingled in and out, stopping to whisper words of farewell over the casket. Dan guarded his mother-in-law, stationed near the guest book.

"Hey guys, let's go give our good-byes to Daddy while Mom is out here," Audrey said. There was a twinkle in her eye and she seemed to be holding onto something in her pocket. "Mallory, go get Rebecca. Make John hold Molly."

As Mallory went to grab Rebecca, Audrey said, "I really hate how much he controls her."

Elizabeth nodded. Within moments, they were together and headed into the room, shutting the door for their private moment.

They stared silently, each in their own thoughts. Mallory broke the ice.

"Daddy, I'm so glad you came into our life. I know I pushed the limits sometimes, but I always looked forward to coming home. Sitting in the kitchen, drinking cold beer as you cooked for me while we exchanged Navy stories. I loved helping you with the garden last week. I promise to look after Mom, and those tomatoes." Mallory gently stroked his five gold hash marks.

Rebecca was trembling as she looked on, partially shielded by Mallory. "I'm so sorry I didn't come home as much as I should have," she said, her voice little more than a whisper. "I know you always loved me as your own. Maybe even more than Audrey, Audrey, Audrey."

They all chuckled and Rebecca tried to wipe her tears with a mangled, overused Kleenex.

Audrey nudged Elizabeth.

"Everything they said," Elizabeth said, passing Rebecca a fresh tissue. "I loved canning tomatoes and green beans with you. Your tomatoes from the garden were worth every canker sore I got eating tomato sandwiches until the plants wore out. The older I've gotten, the more I see, really see, the sacrifices you made to help us become healthy and independent. Thank you for being the best Pop-Pop to my daughter, too. You were always enthusiastic in creating things for them to play with or stealing them for overnights. I love you, Daddy." Her eyes felt moist but still no tears.

There was a polite pause before Audrey pulled out what she had been clutching in her pocket. With a tender smile, she placed her hand over his heart. "Daddy, when you met Mom, I don't think you realized yet that there were four young girls waiting for her at home. She hadn't been divorced that long. I'm sure that our good-looking young mom was just another girl in port. But after your wedding, you slid into your role in our lives seamlessly. You signed up for all the Saturday morning breakfasts, making biscuits and gravy, lumpia by the dozens as we sat waiting for you and Mom to make the next batch. You even made the egg roll wrappers from scratch on the griddle. But most of all, you loved our Mom. And we were always so excited when you came home—always bringing gifts from overseas," Audrey sighed.

She turned her hand over and in her palm was a home-crafted medal. Everyone peered to examine the unofficial service medal. What looked like a heart shaped pet tag had been spray-painted gold engraved with the word *Sea Daddy*. She'd attached it to what appeared to be a bar of cardboard covered in gold lamé. She opened his lapel and slid it in the coat pocket. Everyone smiled at Audrey's forethought. "Thank you for your service, Daddy. You're the best man that ever walked into our lives."

The room grew silent except for Rebecca's soft sniffling. There was a knock on the door and the funeral director poked his head inside. "The guests are arriving. Are you ladies ready?"

Again, synchronized, they nodded their heads and moved as one to support their mom.

Chapter 11

DECEMBER, 1957

Bobby's feet were light as he headed to the Receiving Station to retrieve his orders. Between chipping and painting destroyers in the Mothball Fleet and eight weeks of welding school, he envied House being assigned to a ship in the Mediterranean. Via his regular letters, Bobby knew House had been jumping from Greece to Italy, working in the air-conditioned radio room. Bobby was sweating in Treasure Island above and below the ships retired from the Great World Wars. He was getting restless and was ready to head to sea. He took a breath before he entered the office.

"Seaman Higgins reporting for orders, sir," Bobby said with a little grin.

"Service number?" the unimpressed secretary asked.

"5207514," Bobby answered. That number was as much a part of him now as his name; it rolled off his tongue. She turned to a stack of brown service records.

"Robert?" she asked.

"Yes, ma'am." Bobby's curiosity was growing. He'd been hounding his petty officer to put in a good word for an overseas transfer. He knew it would probably be somewhere in the Pacific.

"You're to report to Pier 3 West, Fort Mason in two days to USNS Barrett. The bus will depart 1130 and embarkation will be at 1300. When you get to Subic Bay, you'll report to the Naval Station. Review the Orders and you'll find your assignment as #64," she finished, and handed him the five pages. He searched the list of men he was travelling with and found his name at number 64. There were 119 going to the Philippines. The only person headed to the same assignment was his friend, Jerry Fox. He'd heard of the transport ship, USNS Barrett. He'd seen Cary Grant movie scenes on ships like that.

"How long will we be at sea?" Bobby asked, trying to conceal his excitement.

"That depends on how many stops your captain makes on the way," she replied. "You'll be on board with dependents, too."

"Thank you, ma'am," Bobby said. As he left the building, he threw his cap into the air.

It had been six weeks underway on his transport ship. Walking down the gangway, there was a clanging of metal out on the piers. The sharp assault brought him back to the reality of his new assignment. The Subic Bay Naval Magazine was full of naval ammunitions, mostly from injured ships. With a sea bag slung over his shoulder, he followed his shipmates headed towards floating barracks. What a strange place to spend his first night in the Philippines. The Barrett had been luxurious and as close to a vacation as he'd had since boot camp. They walked quietly around the new piers in the dark.

"You'll hear the bosun's pipe at 0530 and be ready, including your breakfast, for transportation to your respective assignments by 0700," the chief said before he allowed them to approach the gangway. The air was humid and there was a slight smell of raw sewage. "There will be a Welcome Committee meeting after you board the buses. Get some sleep men."

Bobby looked for a top berth and crashed. He hoped it looked better in the morning.

0700—Standing on the pier after a very brief shower and shave, Bobby hung with his friend, Fox. The veterans of the base were strolling to their duties. Officers wore khaki shorts and short-sleeved shirts. The enlisted men wore dungarees and short-sleeved shirts. Sweat was already beading on brows and under arms.

'Well, this isn't Hawaii," Fox mumbled.

"The old salts back at Treasure Island gave me shit about being sent here. I think it's going to be a great first adventure," Bobby replied. He'd heard stories of the liberties, bars, beer and bands. He'd never write home about that but was excited to sow some oats. San Francisco sounded tame in comparison and the USO wasn't calling his name. He wanted to experience local flare and local girls.

"Just watch out being hustled," Fox said. "I hear the money handlers aren't the best. Even the beer prices go up when the guys fight in the bars."

"Who told you that?"

"A marine coming back for his second tour. He started out getting the base on its feet a couple years ago," Fox said.

Two grey school busses pulled up, driven by a local. Gaping holes stared at the men where there should have been windows, or at least screens on the windows. "Glad we aren't going through the jungles on that. It's like a Navy target for the Huks. They like to practice on Americans with grenades."

"Cut it out, Fox," Bobby said. "Let's give this a chance." Fox seemed to be getting more negative by the minute.

"Playing with ammo, avoiding snipers, pythons, monkeys and hustlers," Fox said glumly. "I wanted to see the world, not a shit hole."

Bobby ignored his mate. The morning sun glistened on the water. White clouds softly blew over the grey ships with the American flag flapping over the fantails. Maybe it was time to find a new sidekick.

A short bus ride and thirty minutes later, Bobby had first sat in the Welcome Center, he'd learned there was a mixed reception to the American presence in the Philippines. The chief went through rules of transportation, off limit areas in the city, the basic layout of the base and its services. Bobby stared at the map mounted at the front of the room. The hospital was on the hill by Cubi Point. His duty station was by the piers to receive and replenish ammunition. Hopefully, he'd never need to make a serious burn visit up the hill. The residential neighborhoods segregated the officers from the enlisted. He needed to explore and make sure he could stand his watch on time.

Bobby stopped his mind wandering and refocused on the chief's warnings. "You will exit and re-enter through the Main Gate during liberty. Do not leave the authorized areas. Your CO, XO or OOD are available for any questions from money handlers to your watch schedules. You will be assigned to another class to orient you on watch responsibilities and to review proper procedures. Be diligent and aware of anyone acting suspiciously, even if they are in Naval uniform."

The chief paused and looked around the room to make sure his crew was all paying attention before he continued in a somber voice. "The jungles are off limits. Keep your eye out for the kids that may disregard this. There are pythons and other wild life that could be deadly," he advised them. "Check the list by the door for your bus assignment. Welcome to Subic Bay! You're dismissed."

There was a "Welcome to Subic Bay!" pamphlet with even more information. Bobby noticed that all US currency had to be turned in and converted to Military Payment Certificates. MPC would be his future pay and pesos had to be used in the local community.

Dear Mama

I hope you got my letter about my new assignment in Subic Bay in the Philippines. Me and 118 guys were sent over on a ship called the Barrett. We shared the ship with military wives and children. I volunteered to help take care of an officer's dog, named Pooh. Who names a dog Pooh? But, it gave me something to do and hopefully some good notes in my record. I asked how far it was from San Francisco and it was about 7,000 miles. Can you believe I'm that far away?

We pulled into Pearl Harbor. I couldn't believe the sadness we all felt when looking at those sunken ships. It really made me proud to be part of the Navy. My friend, Jerry, and I tried some of the local food. You wouldn't like this stuff called poi. Tastes like paste. I'll take grits any day. But the palm trees are just like they look in the movies, and the beaches are, too.

So, I've completed my fireman school training. I'm a watch stander and working on my third class rating. The Filipinos I work with are really nice. (They are short though). We have a bowling alley and a movie theatre on the base. There is a school for the kids here with their families. They like to try and get dimes from us so they can bowl and let a local set up their pins. Watching them hang out and become part of a small town reminds me of home. I miss all of you and hope to get some leave time in a few months. House is having a good time on the opposite side of the world. I get a letter or two from him.

You'll always find monkeys hanging around the banana trees. The first thing they told us was to stay out of the jungles. I had to laugh at a sign on one of the jungle paths: "STRITLY off limits." Not sure who made that sign but they can't spell. The beaches are even more beautiful than in the movies. We go over to Cubi Point or Grande Island. I spotted my first shark while swimming! The officers are usually off water skiing with their families.

So, I hope all is well and Pops is feeling better. Will miss you on Christmas. I'm sending a package but not sure if it will get there in time.

Love,
Bobby

He folded the letter into the envelope, licked the stamp and carefully wrote the family address. His last letter had been three weeks ago. Since then, he'd attended the class for fire control and watch stander duties at the Naval Magazine. His head was packed with circumstantial protocol. Until the fence had been installed, local thieves would take advantage of nightstanders. Fire extinguishers, tools and parts would be stolen from generators, all hidden in the jungles. Bobby appreciated the fence and the new telephone line that had been installed by a senior officer. Evening watch and midwatch were dark and solitary. The jungle's nocturnal noises often had to be deciphered between human or animal rustling. He was armed with a rifle and warned not to leave his post to approach unknown persons. Even a fire outside the magazine could be a diversion tactic.

But, after unloading ammunition from a damaged destroyer, Bobby was getting his first liberty chit. For two weeks, every depth charger and bit of gun ammo had to be removed from the holds and driven to the Naval Magazine so the hull could be repaired. There was no easy way to get this done but passing them off in the heat. It had reminded him of an old Western movie where buckets were passed to put out the burning building. He definitely felt he could justify blowing some pesos off base.

His new sidekick, Bill Smith, was meeting him at the gate at 1800. Bill had earned the nickname "Crunch" for driving a jeep into the water. Bobby hadn't had the chance to ask why yet, but he was hoping to get the story soon. Bill had been on the base for six months and had insisted he'd be Bobby's sea daddy, both on base and off, or "on liberty." Smith had already learned the ropes and Bobby, as a green Subic sailor, knew he'd benefit from being under Bill's wing.

The uniform of the day was his crackerjack whites. Other more experienced sailors warned him about carrying wallets and the pesos he had exchanged on base. For the past two weeks due to the heavy indoctrination classes and the ammunition transfers, Bobby had stayed on base, hanging out at the enlisted men's club. The food was good and the beer was cheap. The local beer, San Miguel, was his new favorite flavor. The local girls were sweet and loved waiting on them. But he wanted to see what was off the base. He'd heard other sailors' stories and they sounded unbelievable. He wasn't sure if he could participate in some of the racy activities. But his boyish curiosity and boredom tipped the scale. He splashed Old Spice on his freshly shaven face. Well, he *hoped* it would really need a razor soon. *Geez, will I ever get used to that sting?*

Bobby put on his white dixie cup and left the Enlisted Quarters, heading to the gate. He patted his pocket to make sure he had remembered his wallet and letter to be dropped into the corner mailbox. He'd need his ID and liberty chit. He felt the same anticipated excitement he'd felt when he and House wandered around Chicago. Instead of a train, he would be taken to the road Magsaysay across the canal. The sewage, diesel and trash dumped from the Olongapo barrio was part of the tales sailors told making the trip to drink, listen to music and play with the bar girls. He suspected he was going to understand why they called it Shit River in a few minutes.

He headed to the security house at Gate 2. Young military dependents were passing him on their way to the Teen Club movie. He noticed officers and their wives headed to the Officers Club. He was starting to feel like he belonged in Subic Bay.

Crunch was leaning against a building, puffing a cigarette near the jeepnies. Two lines of the colorfully painted old WWII jeeps had been left behind. It was obvious that each driver had put a lot of effort to completely cover the jeep with many paint colors and artwork.

"Let's get this party started, fobbitch. Let's pop your cherry," Crunch said, grinning at his pun. He pushed the real meaning of fobbitch; it was reserved for military personnel who had never seen action or left a base. Bobby resembled that remark. He looked over Bobby's uniform to make sure the Marines working the security gate wouldn't find something over which to harass the newbie.

"I'm ready!" Bobby said, pulling out his wallet. The smell of the river was getting stronger. "I guess tonight will be a lot of firsts!"

"You deserve a cold one or two. Unloading that destroyer was a bitch. Too bad she took a hit by that minesweeper. That was a lot of damn ammo," Crunch said. They walked to the gate, presented their IDs and liberty chits. The MP recognized Crunch and looked at Bobby as if he was memorizing the face of a new arrival.

"How long you been here?" the MP barked.

"Three weeks, sir," Bobby said. "This is my first liberty, sir."

"Are you in charge, PO Smith? Keep this green seaman from getting in trouble?"

"Yes, sir. I'm his sea daddy," Crunch said, with a twinkle in his eye.

"This is not an overnight pass, Seaman Higgins. Stay out of the alleys and other restricted areas. Free to pass and expect you to stumble back by 2300."

Crunch slapped Bobby on the back and Bobby resisted grinning. "Yes, sir," he responded. They had barely approached the bridge when the stench christened Bobby.

"This smells like shit," Bobby said. He looked off the side of the bridge and saw young girls dressed in pretty dresses on the local Filipino banca boats. They looked up and begged the sailors for coins. One group of sailors tossed several dimes into the river cheering when the boys on shore jumped into the smelly water. Then, like ducks diving for food, they disappeared to the bottom and reappeared holding a coin. Bobby was appalled but intrigued at the same time. It couldn't be healthy for them. He'd lost a sister to diphtheria.

"The girls are called Shit River Queens," Crunch informed him. "At the end of the day, the boys split the coins with the girls."

"Doesn't seem right," Bobby said.

"This is a very poor barrio and a lot of locals were moved off the land to build more of the base. If they don't work on the base, they have to be very resourceful in getting money off the Americans," Crunch said.

They continued over the bridge and entered a vending area. Women were cooking over grills, while others beckoned them to tables laden with souvenirs, including beautiful leather photo albums. An old woman stood on the corner with a basket of eggs.

"Don't rush and buy souvenirs yet, the same stuff is out here all the time," Crunch said, stepping into his sea daddy mode. "Those eggs? Balut. You have to either want to impress someone by eating it or you're really drunk."

"I like hard-boiled eggs," Bobby said. "What's wrong with those?"

"Nothing wrong, they are a local food. Duck embryos are in there that are partially developed. I have no curiosity to try one myself, but I've watched sailors and marines eat them. By their faces, looks like they must taste disgusting. One of my friends said there's a different texture in every bite. Not sure if this is a joke, but they say if you're really good, you save the beak for a toothpick."

"I guess I'll put that on the bottom of my budget," Bobby said. "I'll buy another beer first."

As they continued walking along Magsaysay Road, the vendors thinned to make way for storefront bars that lined the dirt road. There was music everywhere and girls tried to entice them into each bar. Bobby suspected in a good rain, the bottom of their crackerjacks would be muddy.

"Okay, here's the deal about some of the bars. You heard the chief warn you of pick-pockets but you have to know what bars not to go to," Crunch said.

"Why wouldn't I go to the one I want?"

"Because there are bars that only radiomen go to, marines go to, EOD guys. You get the picture. It is an invitation to brawl, get arrested, put in the local jail and have to get shore patrol to bail your ass out. When they get to it," Crunch added. "If you blow off steam with one of the girls, be sure to wrap it. If you catch something, it goes in your record. Use the off base clinics if you need antibiotics."

Bobby heard country music ahead. "When do we get to have fun, Daddy?" Bobby said sarcastically.

Crunch laughed and slapped him on the back. "What's your flavor? Country, rock-n-roll? I usually go to The Hay Stack." He pointed up the block. With that, there was a pep in Bobby's step and he heard Johnny Cash.

"I saw him sing 'There You Go' last year," Bobby said. "That sounds just like him!"

As they nodded to the doorman, Bobby spied the little Filipino guitar playing man belting out Johnny Cash. The room was full of local women. He saw the hostess sitting on a stool, predominantly watching each sailor who entered. With San Miguel bottles sweating on the tables, sailors were flocked by girls sitting on their laps. The floor was dirty and he spied a hand-scrawled sign posted behind the bartender's counter: "If you urinate anywhere but the toilet, you will be thrown out."

Crunch pointed to two seats in the corner. They settled in and were immediately the target of the girls.

"San Miguel? One hour in your lap?" a young girl advertised. "Love you long time."

Crunch tossed out the pesos and added a little extra. "Extra cold in the back of the icebox? This is my friend's first time." She grinned and gave a nod to another honey-ko. The bar was filled with the smell of tobacco and beer. It was hot. The sound of the jeepnies and scooters played in the background as the Filipino Johnny Cash belted from his little stage.

Bobby thought to himself, *Can't write home to Mom about this.*

In a low voice, Crunch said, "The girls are commonly referred to as entertainers or honey-ko. If you pick one, you'd better like her. No one will touch you after that. Try and have several in other bars, they will label you as a butterfly. They will blacklist you. So what I'm saying is, don't be hasty."

The beers arrived and two girls immediately perched on their laps. The singer started a new song and Bobby was determined to baptize himself into the heart of Olongapo, even if they only wanted his pesos.

"Did I tell you about the bar that has the alligator in the ditch? You can buy a baby duck and feed it before you hang out," Crunch added like a sea daddy infomercial. "But, it's mostly a Marine's bar. I've heard many a drunken jarhead has bitten the baby duck's head off before they toss it. They're animals."

Bobby was appalled but only responded, "Guess that's why they're in charge of the brig. Glad I'm not a duckling."

Bobby's honey-ko wasn't the youngest in the bar. She was petite and had long, straight black hair. Her eyes reminded him of the root beer marbles at home in his dresser. Her dress was short and tight but clean. In spite of the heat, she wore knee high black boots. She smelled like jasmine.

There was a small stage beside the band area with dancers. There was no enthusiasm on their faces as they tried to entice anyone that wanted servicing. Bobby picked up the "other" menu and read various pleasures for pesos. Crunch leaned back on his well-worn wooden chair, one hand around his honey-ko, the other on his beer, a slight smirk as he observed his seaman.

Bobby tried to digest the entertainers' sex offerings as if it was the decision to try baluk. Unfortunately, his long-ingrained family values were still battling against his basic male desires. He felt a little overwhelmed and queasy as the angel and devil on his shoulder played an age-old tug of war. He shifted his focus to the honey-ko on his lap.

"How do I ask her what her name is?" Bobby asked. "I don't know Tagalog."

"Anon pangalan mo?" Crunch said to the girl on Bobby's lap.

"Ang pangalan ko ay *Floribeth*," she replied and smiled at them both.

Crunch already knew who she was but helped Bobby with a general pick-up line.

"Pretty," Bobby said and tried to focus on the band as he allowed Floribeth a little reprieve from all the hungry eyes and free-roaming hands.

Four San Miguels later, Crunch nudged Bobby from his nodding state. "Bobby, wake up, we have to get you back. You have watch tomorrow night."

The girls had abandoned the table. There was no action other than drinking and the ladies left the bar with their arms linked. Bobby had given his honey-ko an extra peso for being so patient and not pushing him.

Bobby's eyes tried to focus and shake off the exhaustion of his past few days on base. "Yeah, sure," he said. Let's go." As he stood up, he stumbled a little to his left. Crunch grabbed his arm and stabilized him.

"Easy, we have to get back through the gate. We'll grab some monkey meat on the way back," Crunch said as he waved at the hostess and tipped his cap.

Bobby felt a dry heave at the words. "Monkey meat?"

"It's just chicken on a skewer. They sell them on the way back to the bridge," Crunch said. "There is some type of meat all over Subic. This one may help if you wake up too late to get a good breakfast and soak up some of that San Magoo."

Ten minutes later, the charcoaled monkey meat digesting in his stomach, Bobby was sturdier, ready to pass through the gate and crawl into his bunk.

The Marine at the checkpoint turned on his flashlight and checked their IDs and chits. "Welcome aboard."

Bobby and Crunch hadn't quite passed the guard shack and Bobby felt a sharp whack on the back of his head. Assuming it was the Marine, his Alabama surfaced. Crunch grabbed him as he spun around to accuse the jarhead.

"Don't go overreacting! That's the local monkey. They call him Henry," Crunch said, trying to diffuse Bobby's temper. "He hides in that tall tree and thinks he is trying out for the Yankees. Loves to hit a sailor cap for shits and giggles."

"Maybe I'll sell him to the old woman and eat some real goddamn monkey meat," Bobby said, rubbing the goose egg on his skull.

Chapter 12

CHARLESTON, 2004

The black dress was hanging in the closet. Mallory had made sure her mom's dress was also ready. The family would sit in the chairs on the front row under the green tent at the cemetery. It was placed in the section reserved for military veterans and their spouses. The funeral director had confirmed it would be a full military burial. Small reward for thirty-two years of service, five gold hash marks on his dress blues and the love and loyalty of his men. He'd get a full gun salute by the younger sailors; one only his family would be able to appreciate. Still, that's probably how he'd have wanted it.

Mallory had argued with herself over wearing her own uniform or the black dress. She decided that in this instance she was his daughter and one of the sisters. The black dress won. She walked to the kitchen with Sparky, made a cup of coffee and headed to the back porch. Sparky trotted off to sniff and relieve himself. Mallory sat on the porch swing and looked at the newly planted garden. Hard to believe that just one week ago she'd sat here with him and prepared the fertile plot. The young tomato plants looked secure and hopeful for their chance to bear fruit in her father's last garden. With no one watching, Mallory's tears streamed as she watched the purple martins twitter over the garden, popping in and out of their gourd houses.

Her heart was breaking but he'd taught them how to endure whenever he was away. Instead of him returning home, she'd ultimately be joining him. Only the wealth of memories that she was sifting through with her sisters could push a smile past the wall of tears.

Breakfast was over and Rebecca placed the kids in front of the television. She jumped into the shower, leaned against the wall and let the water baptize her grief. How had life gotten so complicated? Growing up as the baby of the girls, her mom had always shielded her from the conflicts. When a sister annoyed her, all she had to say was "I'm telling Mom!"

After all, Elizabeth was used to being blamed. Audrey knew she was the favorite, and Mallory was always in trouble. But as the youngest, the only father she'd known was gone. She'd barely known her birth father; her parents had split up when she was still losing baby teeth. She'd remembered sitting in her stepdad's lap as he tied a string to a loose tooth, convincing her to let him yank it.

She came out of the shower and looked at herself in the mirror. Even the steamed glass couldn't hide her protruding hipbones. No longer the protected baby since marrying John, she knew she'd put herself on the bottom of the relationship chain. Kids, business burdens, household worries...zero support from her partner. Rather, all John ever offered her were a lot of excuses for the blunders that she was constantly cleaning up.

"Bec...How long are you going to be in there?" her husband said, banging on the door.

She rolled her eyes and sighed. "Almost done. Give me a little more time, hon." She often regretted that she'd allowed him to move her so far from the rest of her family. Her children hadn't had the time with Daddy that Elizabeth and Audrey had given their own daughters. But it did keep the family's watchful eyes off of her and the dysfunctional relationship she kept feeding. No, she wasn't feeding it; it was starving her.

"Sure, I'm surviving," Rebecca muttered, combing out her damp locks and ignoring the incessant knocking on the door.

The travel fatigue was diminishing. Audrey and Leigh were leaving the ghost in the room alone. They had barely survived the first year of firsts themselves. Audrey had married her high school sweetheart, Jeff. Up until a few years ago, they'd built a perfect life and family in Charleston. The shipyard was closing and he'd taken a job in Groton, Connecticut. He'd blessed her with the ability to be a stay at home mom but even their perfect little family couldn't fill the loneliness of being away from her sisters. Jeff never complained about the long distance phone bills or plane fares to celebrate Hallmark holidays.

She thought about the night before with most of her sisters. Mallory had followed in their fathers' footsteps, joining the military. She'd never married, but she'd never missed remembering a birthday or holiday for her nieces or parents. She seemed content with her pets. Always the epitome of honor and service, but slightly detached, Elizabeth was hiding behind the funeral details. Audrey hadn't seen her shed a tear yet. Not that she doubted that Elizabeth was hurting. Rebecca was quickly revealing her wishbone instead of a backbone. But none of them truly knew the hole that her husband's absence had placed in Audrey's heart. She knew how her mom felt more than any of them.

She continued to curl her ash blonde hair. She was wearing the same black dress from her husband's funeral.

She smiled thinking about the conversations they were having in the great beyond. Nascar, pig roasts and frying turkeys in the backyard every year until they'd moved. The recipe collaborations were shared in private. Whenever she or her sisters asked, her dad whistled and pretended not to hear their questions.

"Leigh, we need to head out in fifteen minutes," Audrey called out. In her mind, she felt her husband's arms surrounding her as she went to celebrate but grieve for the loss of the other man in their bereft lives.

Chapter 13

SUBIC BAY – 1960

Dear Mama,

I've saved over 30 days leave and have been told I can use it. I plan to come home the beginning of February and take a break. The heat here is brutal but I love my job. My CO has split my time between the Ammo Magazine and the Surface Craft repairs. I've been able to really work on expanding my fire damage knowledge to repairing the damaged boats. I even got to hop on a ship and help retrieve a Filipino boat lost in a typhoon. She wasn't very big, but it was great training and on my record. I think I've been recommended for DG third class, which includes a pay increase.

I'm so sorry that I wasn't home when you had your heart attack. I was so happy but torn that Sarah came home before her and Mike's baby was born. I'm sure that was complicated getting there from Atlanta. But, she'd never let anything prevent her from being with you. I'm sure Pops and Aunt Bessie did what they could but I wish I could've helped. I wrote Sarah and thanked her.

I want to put you and Pops on my military allotment as soon as I can. I hope to do what Jonathan did when he was in the Navy. You and Pops really showed me what it was like to be part of our community and to be aware of others in need. I have so many stories from the men and women I've been living with on this very small Naval base. I am really starting to realize what a great family and town I was raised in.

Can't wait to see y'all. Have some souvenirs for everyone. I've been taking Kodaks. Thank you for your letters. Sometimes they arrive in clumps, but it helps me re-connect. I'll admit it can get very lonely. There is nothing like a letter from home.

Have some good local recipes to share with you and Pops. I've been watching and asking the locals how to make egg roll wrappers from scratch. It's kind of like making biscuits but much thinner. I could eat a dozen off the vendors' carts. You know how we like our fried food.

See you soon. It isn't heaven but I do love the Navy brotherhood. The local dependents remind me of Ashland. The teen club is active and I really like to support their bake sales on the ships at dock. Makes me feel like when House and I were working the theater with Pearl Miller.

Love you, Mama. I'll be home soon.

Bobby

MARCH – 1961

Bobby and the friends he made during his three years in Subic Bay were meeting for drinks at The Haystack. He'd received his new orders and was being flown stateside from Clark AFB. He had heard of the 38-mile bus ride through the jungles and to the mountains. The Huks were still a threat to the Navy grey school busses and there was no protection from a well-aimed grenade or bullet.

Bobby dabbed on his aftershave, and then checked to be sure his dragon cuffs were undetectable. He'd saved a week's pay to have them made. The uniform of the day was his blues. Once he got to The Haystack, he looked forward to rolling his cuffs back to show off the embroidered dragons hidden inside. He could have done mermaids or even a Playboy logo but he loved the gold dragons. And so did the girls. He'd been promoted to Petty Officer Third Class and traded his seaman stripes for his first crow. He'd outgrown his old uniforms and used this as an excuse to have his blues custom made with his new rate. Sneaking in the dragon cuffs was an added bonus. They weren't approved by the Navy but the local tailors knew how to hide them so Shore Patrol didn't discover them and revoke his liberty chit.

It seemed like only yesterday when his chief petty officer put him under the wing of Bill. Crunch had since been transferred to the USS Maddox. Bobby had become a sea daddy to several young seamen himself. He grabbed his hat and headed to catch the bus to Gate 2 and take one of his last walks across Shit River.

As he approached the bus shed, sailors were piling inside. He jogged the rest of the way. The Filipino bus driver held the door for him. "Just in time," he grinned.

The excitement and enthusiasm of the bus reminded him of his first time in Olongapo. Now Bobby was an old timer and preparing to face a new frontier at sea. He suspected liberty would not be as frequent while he learned the ways of a destroyer at sea instead of these familiar local ports.

The squeal of the brakes and swish of the bus door delivered the sailors to the gate. He stood in line as the Marines checked IDs and chits. Two tweens came up to Bobby. "Mr. Bobby, can we have a dime for the bowling alley?" The girl's big blue eyes stared up at him. It had become a routine request when she saw Bobby.

"Happy to assist! And, have an ice cream on me as well," Bobby said, pulling out a couple pesos. She hugged his legs and they ran off.

When Bobby approached the guard shack, he was waved on. The River Queens were begging for coins, the boys were diving for them, the same vendors were ready to hawk their souvenirs and the balut were in the baskets of the women on the corner. He doubted he'd ever experience that local food. Duck embryos or ducklings for an alligator were not a memory he wanted to carry out of Subic Bay.

As he entered The Haystack, the hostess smiled from behind the bar. He headed to the table with all the other guys from his division.

"Bobby!" Red shouted. He was already into his San Miguel and a honey-ko sat on his lap. He looked at her and said, "Get my buddy who's shipping out a good cold one." Obediently, she went to the bartender with his pesos.

"Thanks, Red," Bobby said. He looked around to see if Lilibeth was working. He'd grown fond of Lilibeth and been invited to her home on many a weekend. He'd been exposed to good Filipino food. In return, he'd helped the family learn better English. She knew he was leaving and probably wanted him to take her with him. But he was headed to a ship and wasn't ready to put down roots. His first honey-ko, Floraliza, had grown impatient and hooked up with a sailor who had offered her more than pesos, a coveted gold wedding band.

"What's new, Magoo?" Red asked. His girl was back with the cold beer.

"It's a little early to use Magoo," Bobby said grinning. "I'll miss my nights with San Magoo... drink 'til she's pretty!" They clinked their beer bottles.

"I hear it's getting hot in Vietnam," Red said. "Commies have their eyes on South Vietnam. Guess they're growing war balls since they pushed the French out. I hear China and Russia are smuggling in weapons all along the Gulf of Tonkin."

"Guess I'll wind up in Japan next," Bobby said in a dismissive way. The band was playing songs that a new American country music star was writing. "You heard that new guy, Glen Campbell?"

"Nah, I'm not a music guy," Red said, stroking the pretty Filipino sitting on his lap. "I'm a baseball guy. Wanna guess if I hit a home run tonight?"

Bobby took a deep breath and was reminded of the smells of the bar he'd be leaving. Jeepnie and scooter exhaust, stale beer and tobacco smoke. There was still that undercurrent of sewage. He'd always loved sniffing Lilibeth's hair. He'd taken his time to connect with a Filipino girlfriend and enjoyed surprising her with gifts of scented perfumes and soaps. Suddenly, a soft hand touched his shoulder and he felt a warm kiss on his ear.

"Love you long time! Buy me a washing machine?" Lilibeth said, although they had moved beyond that pick up line months ago. She slid onto his lap. Bobby put his arms around her tiny waist and buried his nose in her perfumed hair. His heart knew the night was ending with a parting of ways and the idea of another sailor in her life pulled on his heartstrings.

"Thanks for coming, Lilibeth," Bobby whispered in her ear. She leaned into his chest, pressing into him as deeply as she could muster. Her eyes closed and he saw a tear slip onto her cheek. He felt guilty, a twinge of abandonment plaguing his effort to have a good time on his last liberty in Subic Bay. He would take her aside and give her the bracelet he'd dropped in his pocket to soften the good-bye. But who was he kidding? There was no way to soften the cold hard fact that he was breaking her heart.

The band began playing *Hunka, Hunka Burning Love*. The faces of the sailors broke out into laughter as Smithy taunted the old hostess onto the dance floor. He spun her and thrust his hips like Elvis.

Bobby sat back and watched for the disaster that was looming on the dirt dance floor. As suspected, Smithy fell backwards but continued making gyrations as the hostess straddled over his body. Her skinny weak legs hopped as if she was playing limbo until she got over his face. She wobbled and fell on Smithy's face, giving him a bloody nose with her pelvic bone. It was a great diversion from the break-up to come at the end of the night.

Three hours and many San Miguels later, the sailors paid their tabs and headed back to the gate. Red had jumped into a jeepnie to spend some time with his bar girl. Bobby could've had overnight liberty but didn't want to complicate saying good-bye to Lilibeth. She needed to find a sailor that would want to marry her. She accepted the bracelet with shining eyes and he gave her a last hug, holding on for a long moment to memorize the feel and scent of her. Then he was off, unwilling to look back at her tear-stained face.

As the group approached the bridge, the smell of chicken drew them over to the elderly woman cooking on a charcoal grill.

"Anybody else want some monkey meat?" Bobby pulled out his last peso. The old Filipino woman gave him a toothless smile and handed him the stick of meat. Her battered grill rested on two rocks, the charcoal reduced to waning embers. "Here Smithy, put something in your stomach. You had quite the night."

The small group laughed and slapped Smithy on the back. He staggered alongside them with the remnants of a bloody nose. "You aren't going to tell anyone what happened, are you?" Smithy asked, his voice pleading.

"Hell yes, I am!" Bobby said. "We all have our moment on the bar floor. Too many San Magoos and you thought you were Elvis Presley."

"Was breaking your nose with a pelvic drop on the menu? What did she charge you for that service?" They all broke out in laughter and started their walk across the now silent Shit River. Bobby hid his dragon cuffs from the eyes of shore patrol for the last time.

Chapter 14

CHARLESTON, 2004

Elizabeth sat in her keeping room, staring at the computer. The funeral was only hours away and she had been appointed to be one of the voices of her sisters. She hated the spotlight, but thankfully Mallory agreed to share it with her. Still, the writing was up to her. How to encapsulate a life in so few words? Elizabeth had more one-on-one stories between her and Daddy since the sisters had all moved away. She wanted to use her dad's sense of humor but she wasn't sure she could muster the smiles and stifle the tears, still yet to flow from her eyelids but always threatening.

In spite of her lack of love for coffee, Dan insisted she needed the warm cup of Joe. She forced a tired smile, stared into her fireplace and journeyed back in time, searching for the memories that would become part of the eulogy.

Across town, Audrey cradled her morning cup of coffee and glanced at Leigh sitting in front of the hotel mirror. She was allowing her daughter to play with a little make-up inside while she sat on the balcony with a great view of the Intracoastal waterway. A porpoise arched through the glassy water. A seagull perched on the top of a mast of a sailboat in the City Marina. Life was moving on.

It had been two years since they'd lost Jeff, tragically taken in a car accident by a drunk driver. She remembered the doorbell ringing as if it was yesterday. She'd gotten Leigh to the bus stop and was getting ready to head to the gym. Above the sound of the blow dryer came the fateful bing-bong, an unusual sound at 8:45 a.m. Her husband had left for the shipyard over a couple hours ago. *Probably a neighbor needing to borrow something,* she told herself. She'd gotten used to her neighbor, Sherry, with four kids popping over for something she needed to use.

As she peered through the peephole, she saw a grey uniform. It wasn't military. She peeked out of the sidelight curtains. It was a highway patrolman. Her confusion raised another notch. She opened the deadbolt. "May I help you?" she asked.

"Mrs. Walters?" he asked, as he identified himself with his badge. "I'm Lt. Stanley."

She hoped it was a fundraiser cold call. "Yes, I'm Mrs. Walters."

"Is your husband… Jeff Walters?" he asked with a bit of trepidation in his voice. She noticed a female officer standing respectfully behind him.

"Yes," Audrey said, still hoping this was a casual house call.

"May we come in?" he asked. Audrey motioned them in and led them to the den. She suddenly felt numb. *Lord, please don't tell me something bad about Jeff.*

"Mrs. Walters, we regret to inform you that your husband was involved in an auto accident," he said, looking down at his notebook.

She paused, fumbling for the right question, for any words that would change the inevitable outcome. "Are you…sure?"

"We would like you to come down to the hospital. Do you own a red Ford pick-up?"

Audrey felt like she'd been stabbed by the words *Ford pick-up*. "Yes, but he's only been gone a couple hours."

"There was a fatality and it may be the result of a drunk driver," he said. "But we've yet to confirm that and the Coroner would like you to identify him at the hospital."

Her eyes searched the faces of the two police officers. It sounded business-like but she sensed the conflict in their message. *Don't kill the messenger,* resounded in her head. She felt unprepared to react, to spontaneously drop her morning routine and flee to prove them wrong.

"What hospital?" she asked.

"The William Backus," the female officer answered. Audrey nodded and stared at the wedding picture propped on her fireplace hearth. Her world began to spin—

Audrey's painful flashback was interrupted by her daughter's call. "Mom?" Leigh shouted from inside.

"Yes…honey?" Audrey reeled herself back to the present.

"Does Autumn get to spend the night tonight?"

Life was still so simple for the cousins. They were clueless about the holes left in the souls of her and her sisters. Or were there holes? Maybe her dad had done it right. He'd always be there. All his hugs, laughs and jokes…

"I'm sure Elizabeth will be fine with that," Audrey answered, forcing herself to smooth over the depth of the day's events.

★ ★ ★

Mallory fidgeted. T-minus four hours before the ultimate good-bye in front of too many people. She retreated to her own thoughts of standing and speaking for the family. They knew their mom was withdrawn and saying very little. Mallory looked at the poem that she'd borrowed from Elizabeth. She'd lost a dear friend due to a brain tumor who'd planned her own funeral. The words of the funeral program seemed to fit perfectly.

TOGETHERNESS

Death is nothing at all. I have only slipped away into the next room. I am I, and you are you. Whatever we were to each other that we still are. Call me by old familiar name, speak to me in the easy way you used to.

Put no difference into your tone, wear no forced air of solemnity or sorrow.

Laugh as we always laughed at the little jokes we enjoyed together.

Play, smile, think of me. Pray for me. Let my name be the household name it always was. Let it be spoken without effort. Life means all that it ever meant. It is the same as it ever was.

Why should I be out of your mind because I am out of your sight? I am but waiting for you, for an interval, somewhere very near, just around the corner. All is well, nothing is past, nothing is lost.

One brief moment and all will be as it was before, only better, infinitely happier and forever. We will all be one together with Christ.

Mallory thought back to her conversation the previous evening with Elizabeth, taking a minute to reminisce on the screen porch. "Do you remember the time in Aberdeen after a thunderstorm there was a bumblebee floating in a bucket?" Mallory asked. She could still recall the yellow and black bumblebee trying to find its way out of the beige bucket of rainwater. It had probably been at it for hours. They'd found it the next morning when their mom shooed out of the house to find something to do.

Elizabeth cringed but had to grin. "Yeah, I remember pleading for *you* to rescue it. Something in me said *don't touch*. Do you remember when you started the lawnmower in high school and that poor little toad had taken refuge under it and the blades spit him out?"

Mallory shot Elizabeth a look of pain. "That bee stung the crap out me and still died. I cried over that toad." Elizabeth had grabbed her hand and reassured her it was not a callous comment. Mallory's heart was soft, no matter how hard she tried to guard it. She wondered if Elizabeth was the same, if that's why none of the sisters had seen a single tear from her yet. Would she take up her eldest child mantle and deliver the perfect eulogy?

★ ★ ★

It's funny what you remember when discussing a child-hood memory, Rebecca thought. She had managed to steal some time on the porch with her sisters the night before. Leigh and Autumn had entertained her children while John cornered Dan about a new business idea.

Of all the things they'd discussed was the year their father was sent to Vietnam. One of her memories was leaving Jacksonville Beach, Florida. Their parents decided it would be best to move them closer to Mom's family.

They'd been piled into the car including Pufnstuf, the family tabby. There was brief stop to say good-bye to friends met serving on the USS Yellowstone. Daddy had carried Rebecca to the car and placed her under one of the blankets. Then everyone snuggled into their favorite space in the station wagon for the ten-hour drive.

Forty-five minutes later, Rebecca had woken up and searched for her teddy bear, Freddie. In a panic, she started crying and asking for help to find Freddie. She hadn't let the movers pack him. The idea of her teddy bear in a box and shoved into the Mayflower van was unbearable. Leaving him in the car by himself while her parents said good-bye to their friends was not negotiable. She propped the scruffy brown teddy bear on her hip and took him into the house. His yellow paw pads were dingy from all the washings. She'd given him a nice chair to sit in while she played with the other kids and ate dessert.

At the first chance, Daddy pulled into a gas station and they searched the car. Rebecca was sobbing heavily and it was fast becoming clear that Freddie was back in Florida. Without any complaint, her stepfather made a U-turn and headed back to get the teddy bear. Needless to say, the tattered bear was still sitting in the chair and they didn't arrive at their new home on schedule.

To this day, Freddie still had his own place in Rebecca's closet. Whenever she looked at that old bear she'd smile and think of her step-dad's unconditional love, how, without complaint he'd healed her broken heart.

She looked out the hotel window down at the pool. John had the kids on the small dock throwing the bread from breakfast into the water. Why couldn't he see her loss and soothe it like her dad? The weight of managing it all was still on her thin shoulders. She popped a pill to dull her pain.

Chapter 15

LONG BEACH, CA – AUGUST, 1961

Bobby had gotten through the jungle, the mountains, a short visit with his parents and orders to report to Long Beach. He'd taken advantage of a month's leave to go home and visit his family and friends. His life was polarized but the Navy and Ashland were both his family. He'd been sobered by the aging of his parents. It was the nudge he needed to get a piece of his salary and benefits sent home.

As the bus pulled in, he retrieved his belongings from the bowels of the luggage hold. His sea bag was slung over his shoulder as he walked to report to his transport ship, the USS Phoebe. She was only a few years old and his damage control skills would be broadened to include the engine room. It was headed to Japan where he would be transferred to his final destination, the USS Leonard F. Mason. His next job would be to use the education and training between the Magazine, watch duty and repairing service crafts for the amazing greyhounds of the sea, destroyers. In ninety days, his final destination was Yokosuka, Japan, to join the Westpac 7th Division. Fortunately, it was a peacekeeping tour.

Exhausted but anxious to claim his berth and fold all his belongings into his tiny personal locker, Bobby climbed the gangway. He lowered his sea bag, looked straight ahead and saluted. "Permission to come aboard, sir."

The sentry reached for his papers, ID, and looked over his clipboard. "Permission granted, Petty Officer Higgins. Present yourself in the aft engine room to Chief Richards. He will direct you to your quarters."

He'd familiarized himself with the Bluebird class ship. She was much smaller than a destroyer and looked forward to his new classroom time. Bobby wanted the at sea training before he reported to his destroyer. The heat of the communist/democratic tug of war was starting to leak into the ears of the sailors. Bobby had seen his share of damaged crafts due to accidental collisions, plane accidents or fire damage. He'd been on the piers with an occasional billet to help retrieve a sunken Filipino boat. It was usually a drill for him, but also a chance to help the locals learn to fix their own. He loved to pass on the knowledge that the old salts had taken the time to show him.

Bobby was a good welder and could craft just about anything without a formal blueprint. But he knew that he was now underway to test minesweeping tactics and be the damage control leader in the event things went awry. He passed the ship store and barbershop towards the stairs descending into the bowels of the engine room quarters and workspace. Tossing his sea bag below, his feet ignored the steps as he slid down the handrails. The smell of paint and fuel would become the perfume of his new home.

He wove through the tucked-up berths and felt the temperature increasing. Another snipe looked up, and Bobby asked, "Master Chief Richard's office?"

"Around the corner, off the carpenter's shop," the sailor said, fiddling with his gauges. "Just arriving?"

"Yeah, PO 3rd Class Higgins," Bobby said, offering his hand.

The sweaty engineman gave him a short handshake and returned to his job. "Petty Officer 2nd Class, Bill Jones," he said. "See you in the mess hall."

Bobby continued through the bowels of the minesweeper to seek out his chief, his watch schedule and his new drills. An explosion at this level would certainly put him in a new damage control situation.

Better not tell mom, he told himself. He saw the engraved nameplate on the door: Master Chief Stanley

Richards. He took a breath and knocked. "Enter," commanded the voice on the other side.

"Petty Officer 3rd Class Higgins, reporting for duty, sir," Bobby said.

"Have a seat," Richards answered, and motioned him to sit in the vinyl chair in front of the metal desk. Clipboards hung from the wall behind him, as well as family pictures. "Welcome aboard. I reviewed your record and you seem very interested in learning to cross over many duties."

Bobby was impressed. "Yes, sir. If someone can't stand in their shoes, I'd like to know that I am able, sir."

His chief sat back and showed no reaction. "You have an accent. Where are you from?"

"Born and raised in Alabama, sir," Bobby answered. Master Chief Richards continued to stare blankly.

"Gotta a problem with color? Race?" he asked.

"No, sir. I'm part of the US Navy. I can't speak for others, but I'm a team player, sir," Bobby said confidently and with conviction.

"Good, here is your berth number. Go sling your hammock. Find your way about," he said, searching the pages of Bobby's file. "Watch standing instruction and duties with Petty Officer Jones at 0900 in the aft fire room. Plan of the Day is posted around the ship. Have you participated in an Oscar drill?"

"Briefly, while on a transport ship," Bobby said.

"We have one tomorrow. Get Jones to review the procedure to retrieve our dummy, Oscar. If an officer grabs you to miss muster, obey him. We'll be testing the department heads for honest reporting."

"Yes, sir," Bobby said, looking directly at his Master Chief.

"Dismissed," Chief Richards picked up his coffee mug and leaned back in his chair.

Bobby stood and saluted as he left to seek out his new bed for the next couple of months. He just hoped they had a few liberties as the ship island-hopped her way towards Japan. He knew he would learn a lot during sea trials. There was no Shit River liberty ahead of him and no girls, just girlie magazines.

Yokosuka, Japan – December 1961

As the bosun pipe announced the call to the mess hall, Bobby sighed with relief that his time at sea was nearly over. Four months and he was ready to hit the pier. He'd played poker, watched the same movies over and over and stood many watches as if there was a threat to his engine room. The only threat that he was aware of was the department thieves trying to find spare parts for their own tasks. It reminded him of the Huks back in Subic Bay that tried to trespass into the Powder Magazine and grab military issue for black market sales.

REPLENS beside those huge oilers with cables being heaved into heavy seas were always exciting but on the edge of dangerous. One snap of a fuel cable or rogue wave shoving the hulls together was constantly on the minds of the sailors. As they held the lines taut, the ships had to head into the seas and they were all covered with the white water of the Pacific.

"Remember Rev. Lindon being transferred over the cable to be relieved so he could head home for shore leave?" Bill asked as he scooped his eggs and gravy.

"Yep, I was on that REPLEN," Bobby said. "That was one rough fuel replenish. The waves were really confusing the cable lines between the Cons. Don't think I've ever seen a high line transfer with a cussing chaplain!"

"I'm sure he'd already been baptized," Bill said with a smirk. "Best REPLEN of my life watching him dunk under the waves and come up saying 'God damn it'... three times."

Bobby had to laugh at the replay. "He was soaked by the time he hit the other ship."

As they'd approached the harbor, the ship wasn't granted permission to dock at the pier. They had to tie up on the side of a destroyer and head to shore on the utility boats. He and Bill had become fast friends. Bill was from Illinois. He'd resisted the idea of being drafted into service and decided to get it over with. After high school, there were few job opportunities in his small town. Even the washing machine factory wasn't hiring. Bobby knew the small town economic scenario too well.

"I know you'll be heading to your destroyer in a few days. Want to hang out?" Bill asked.

Bobby wasn't sure. Yokosuka wasn't like Subic Bay. There were only random notes on the bulletin board warning of the off limit spots and the girls to avoid. He didn't want to complicate his new duty assignment just to blow off some sea steam.

"Do the Marines control the gates?" Bobby asked. "They always seemed to police the sailors a bit more returning than leaving."

"Nah, just keep out of the way of shore patrol." Bill gulped his coffee and slid the tray away. "Well, think about it. I thought it would be difficult to engage with the locals, but the Japanese want us here."

This base was huge compared to Subic Bay. The intimacy and community would not be the same. But, here he was being assigned to the 7th Division to try and keep peace with the communists. It was his first WESTPAC. Maybe he did need to have some mindless fun first. The seas had been rough and the winds became colder as the ship got closer to Yokosuka. Pea coats were pulled out for lookout watches. He'd been through too many overboard drills with the famous Oscar dummy. Everyone took it seriously in the event that one day it would be a shipmate's life that depended on a well practiced search and rescue.

"I have liberty tomorrow after 1400," Bobby replied, "Work for you?"

"Meet you at the gate," Bill confirmed. "I have a few dungaree tasks before I try and beat Cookie's ass tonight. Need to get some of my money back I lost to him in poker."

"Swell!" Bobby said absently and headed back towards the engine room hatch. He paused and looked across the gulf and tried to project where he was headed on his new assignment, the USS Leonard F. Mason.

USS LEONARD F. MASON (DD-852) – DECEMBER, 1961

"Petty Officer Higgins, please report to the stern 0700," the scratchy intercom boomed. Bobby had just finished breakfast and was throwing his shaving kit in his sea bag. He double checked for his orders and threw on his pea coat. The vessel from the Yokosuka boat pool would be waiting to take him to the pier and move him to his first destroyer. He slung the bag over his shoulder and made his way to the fantail.

Bobby approached the OOD and placed his bag beside him. Saluting, he said, "I have permission to go ashore."

"Permission granted," he responded. Bobby walked briskly to the utility boat. Protocol dictated he sit forward. The pier was a short ride away and he needed to be present before 0730. He spotted some snow across the base and the icy wind stung his face.

"Morning. I'm Petty Officer Higgins. This sure is a contrast from the tropics," Bobby said to a seaman. He buttoned the top button of his peacoat.

"Seaman Guffin," the man responded. "Where you off to?"

"Finally on my first destroyer. The Leonard F. Mason," Bobby said, pulling his coat collar up.

"Ah, the Leakin' Leonard," Seaman Guffin said. "I think that's Captain Graham's ship. I hear he's one hell of a captain."

"Yeah, I guess captains can make or break a crew," Bobby said. "I've been pretty lucky so far."

His water taxi pulled up to the pier and he watched as they moored. The sternhook threw the fenders and Seaman Guffin quickly hopped to the pier and secured the line to the cleat. In spite of Bobby's excitement, he tempered his pace to avoid several patches of ice.

He turned the corner and there she was… DD 852. The gangway bounced under his weight. He saluted the ensign and approached the JOOD. He saluted and said, "Permission to board, sir?" He handed his ID and orders to the lieutenant.

"Reporting for duty, uh…Petty Officer Higgins?" he said. "Damage Control?"

"Yes, sir," Bobby said, holding his salute.

With a Navy issued ballpoint pen, the lieutenant filled in the date and time of Bobby's arrival. "Permission granted. Report to the ship's office," he said.

Bobby picked up his sea bag, stifled a grin and walked across the quarterdeck. As he stepped through the hatch, the temperature dramatically switched. Before he approached the office, he took off his coat and stepped aside as a chief passed. *Someday that will be me*, he thought. He stood in front of the window of the office and saw a yeoman hunched over the typewriter. Before he could knock, he was motioned to enter.

"Third Class Petty Officer Higgins reporting for duty, sir," Bobby said, placing his documents on the desk.

"Mess Gear. Clear the mess decks," was announced over the intercom. The passageways and ladder wells suddenly became busy with the day crews. 0800 and Bobby had been whisked off by a petty officer to his berth and given a quick orientation of the ship. The denim bell bottoms and chambray shirts blurred through the passageway and down hatches. It was obvious that he had just come aboard. He'd shed the dark crackerjacks and blend in soon.

"Higgins? Did you hear me?" the petty officer asked. "This is your locker. You have the morning to get organized and changed. Report to Chief Connerty in the aft engine room by 1000. Again, welcome aboard. Plan of the Day is posted around the ship."

Bobby dropped the sea bag on his berth and saluted. "Yes, sir. Ten-hundred."

Chapter 16

CHARLESTON – 2004

Elizabeth noticed Dan quietly pass the door to her office. She was still hovered over her keyboard, buried in preparing the eulogy. The cup of coffee on her desk had grown cold. She ignored the ringing phone. She heard Dan pick it up in the kitchen. Then he was at the doorway.

"It's Audrey," he said. Elizabeth rolled her eyes and took a deep breath.

"Hey Audrey," she said, not taking her eyes off the computer monitor. "Is there a problem?"

"Not really. I'm trying to get Mom organized. Are we using the limo from the service to the graveside?" she asked.

"Yes, but Dan and John are taking the kids," Elizabeth said absently. "Let her know someone from the funeral home will meet her before leading her to the first row at graveside. Oh, and tell her, I heard they arranged full military honors."

Audrey was silent.

"Audrey, are you okay?" Elizabeth prodded. She suspected the afternoon events were picking at the scab of Audrey's recent widowhood.

"I'll be fine. See you in a couple hours," her sister answered. Then the phone went dead.

Refocused on the computer screen, Elizabeth's thoughts drifted back to the last Father's Day she'd spent with her stepdad. Before he'd broken the news about his health it had been the perfect Sunday, filled with juicy ribeyes, fresh local corn and boxed wine. Yep, there was always boxed wine.

"Elizabeth? I'm going to start getting ready. You almost done?" Dan said as he opened the office door.

"Uh-huh," she answered and continued to focus on the monitor. "Still going back in time. Think I've narrowed down the right stories."

She grinned then at another memory that came unbidden, at nine-years-old, being shaken awake by her mom in the bunk beds her dad had made for their new home in Jacksonville Beach, FL. It was close to midnight and school was out for Christmas. Their father was off doing something for the Navy. It was happening more and more but she didn't know why. Her mom didn't want to be alone during the holidays and planned to drive home and be with her family. As Elizabeth dragged herself into the living room, she watched her mother click off the rotating light under the silver Christmas tree.

Maryland winters weren't quite the same as Florida but there would be lots of cousins to lend them coats and gloves. After the required bathroom run, four sisters followed their mom to the station wagon, each in their pajamas, each carrying a pillow. The back was stacked with suitcases, forcing two in the front seat and two in the back.

"Audrey and Rebecca, jump in the front. Elizabeth and Mallory share the back," their mom instructed. "We'll be driving all night."

"Mom, will you let us know when the South of the Border billboards are coming?" Audrey asked as she settled in with her pillow.

"Especially the one with the moving sheep and Pedro is counting them?" Elizabeth added.

"I like the monkey," Mallory said, yawning and trying to stretch out on most of the seat. Elizabeth watched the rear view mirror and pushed Mallory's legs back. They gave each other challenging glances but no one dared complain.

"Mommy, will we see snow?" Rebecca said, laying her head into her mother's lap.

The blinker ticked as they left the neighborhood and headed to Highway 301. "You never know about snow but we may get some icicles to break off and enjoy. Just remember we're there for your grandparents and aunts. I don't want any sass or tattle telling. Get me, Mallory?"

The car was quiet and everyone pretended to be falling asleep. They all knew Rebecca would tattle tale even if it wasn't important. The radio snapped on and that song their mom played on the record player blared. Unintentionally, Mom was going to send them off on the ten-hour journey with *Homeward Bound*. There wasn't a day that music didn't exist in the home. The record player was well broken in and she made sure they had their own small record player as well. Soundtracks to Winnie the Pooh and Disney movies were precious, to be played and acted out on a rainy day. If they got to listen to the Wizard of Oz, the girls would scramble through their mom's closet for a pretty pair of heels to skip on the Yellow Brick Road.

For the next four hours, Elizabeth was in a twilight sleep but aware of her mom snapping the buttons on the radio as they rolled in and out of station ranges. She could tell the difference between the snaps when her mother pressed the floorboard high beam button or a radio button. The car charged through the dark two-lane highway. Elizabeth wakened to the glance of a motel neon sign inviting them to stop and sleep in a bed. But, her mom was relentless in tackling the journey. Every so often she announced the next Pedro sign and let them know how many more miles to crossing the Carolina border.

As they drove past the large Mexican statue's bowed legs, Elizabeth gave into sleep. She wished her dad was with them on Christmas, but more than anything, she hoped Santa would know they were in Maryland.

The grown-ups were in the kitchen and the smell of coffee percolating on the stove wafted through the small two bedroom home. The four girls shared the living room floor, now laden with pillows and quilts. A voice from the kitchen invaded their space.

"Please get up and start getting ready. The Three Stooges matinee is at 10:00 a.m.," their mom's voice called. "Take turns in the bathroom. We have breakfast for you. Chop Chop. It's not very cold out."

Audrey popped up and headed to the bathroom. As she crossed the small eat-in kitchen, the smell of Ivory soap kept her on the path. Her grandfather's prosthetic leg was propped behind the bathroom door.

Elizabeth and Mallory went to the suitcase to pick out an outfit. Rebecca stayed stretched out on the couch. They knew their mom wasn't letting her go.

"Your uncle is going with you this morning," her mom announced. Elizabeth wasn't excited since he was only three years older. Sometimes he would bully her and favor Audrey. But the Christmas movie was something to do. They'd already gotten into trouble the night before for making snowflakes out of typing paper and hanging them from the living room ceiling. As "The Twilight Zone" played re-runs, they'd found straight pins, scissors and white paper. As their mom and her family visited in the kitchen, they thought surprising them with paper snow-flakes pinned to the ceiling were a generous offering.

Elizabeth learned how to make beautiful snowflakes out of folded paper in Art Class. But her uncle was the mastermind who insisted on pinning them into the sheet-rock ceiling.

At the end of the last episode, their parents had a very different reaction when they entered the living room to announce bedtime. "Do you know what your grandfa-ther is going to say when he sees all these pin holes?" The matriarchs immediately began damage control.

Not understanding the rejection, the sisters helped put all the snowflakes in a pile under a table until they could be destroyed secretly the next morning. Elizabeth couldn't help but feel sorry as the joy they had experi-enced that night evaporated. In spite of their mistake, they crossed their fingers that they would get to watch Rudolf the Red-Nosed Reindeer on Christmas Eve night.

But the morning after, everyone piled into the station wagon and each were handed a dime. As they pulled onto Main Street, the line for the movie was half a block long.

"I'll be back in two hours," their mom said. "If it ends a little early, meet me on the corner by the bank."

Compliant children left the car and took their places in line. Within five minutes, they were at the ticket booth passing over their dimes and being handed navel oranges and Whitmore Chocolate Samplers. As they entered the dark burgundy furnished lobby, the smell of stale popcorn and melted butter permeated the air. Passing through the velvet tasseled curtains, they forced their eyes to adjust and find four seats.

"Can we please try and not sit in back of anyone tall?" Mallory asked. Elizabeth agreed; they were all vertically challenged. Audrey and young Uncle Scott were laughing and sharing a bag of popcorn he'd bought with his own money.

As they headed to their seats, the pre-movie cartoon ticked from the projection room in the background and hit the screen. The movie theater was filled with the Christmas children of Havre de Grace. The small American Graffiti town preserved a facade of an innocent and safe social moral compass and soon the Three Stooges movie started with typical banter among Moe, Larry and Curly. Curly tried to eat his clam soup and had a private battle with a clam in his bowl. All the kids were laughing out loud. Milk squirting in his eye was priceless.

As Elizabeth wrapped up her eulogy, she smiled at the much-needed comic relief memory. Trips to her grandmother's for Christmas filled with playing board games, watching Christmas television reruns and small town traditions were blessings. Now, as an adult, Elizabeth realized how much her parents insulated them from a complicated world. Little did that younger Elizabeth know her father was off preparing for Vietnam. Or for that matter, what Vietnam was and why he was going there. She realized her parents' marriage must have been challenged by political paranoia, escalating Navy extended deployments for her stepdad and thousands like him, which left her mom as a single mother of four. Elizabeth and her sisters never knew the loneliness they must have each felt, or the conflicts that simmered between them.

The black limousine with black tinted windows carried five women in black dresses behind the black hearse. Elizabeth stared out the window. Audrey broke the silence.

"I think the service went well," she said, patting her mom's hand. "The pastor described our family and our lifetime experiences like he knew us for years. You and Mallory did a great job with your parts."

"Thanks, sis. I hate public speaking but I needed to do something," Elizabeth's voice was muffled and monotone.

The hearse turned into the narrow asphalt path leading to their dad's plot among so many other military veterans. She remembered two years earlier when he met with the cemetery representative to make arrangements. He'd made the appointment after his doctor confirmed the deteriorating condition of his heart. All she knew was what cemetery he had picked...no other details. Here they were, another road trip, the last one.

The procession slowly carried them to the Garden of Honor. It wasn't lost on Elizabeth, this final resting place, a garden, the thing their father had loved so much, had shared with each of them. They'd all flourished under his patient tending, daughters and plants alike.

But now, with the hearse stopped at the foot of the steps, a funeral director blocked the door of the limousine. It was obvious he did not want the widow and daughters sitting under the tent yet. People were still walking to the grave and the casket was being carried to its final resting place.

As if on cue, each daughter directed their focus towards their mother. A jolt of reality jerked through Elizabeth as the walnut casket, flanked by pallbearers, took center stage.

Elizabeth saw Audrey grab her mom's hand, sending her the 'I've been here' encouragement. Elizabeth knew each of her sisters occupied a special duty station for their mom. Rebecca reached for the tissue box and passed it around. Each took a couple just in case. Audrey was focused on their mom. Mallory seemed to be standing watch as the funeral director stayed near the limo door. The silence was broken by their mother's sudden change in posture.

Elizabeth stiffened and hoped… wait, there it was, an old familiar attitude —fortitude— rising back into Rose's eyes. But, God forbid—not drama! Not now, Mom…. please, Elizabeth thought, trying to resist saying it out loud.

"I'm sorry I haven't been much help the past few days," Rose said, setting aside Audrey's hand. Her eyes were riveted on the casket still moving towards the green-tented scene before them. Her jaw clenched in sync with her fists. She bowed her head and took in a deep breath. As she exhaled, she lifted her head and looked at each daughter, starting with Rebecca. When she got to Elizabeth, the mood softened.

"At times, your dad and I were like oil and water," Rose said. "But, somehow it worked. He was no saint—and neither was I. When he was gone, I tried to manage what we had on a Navy salary with four girls. But, he always made sure he left me encouraged. He believed in us, all of us. Don't take this the wrong way, but even when I wavered, he never doubted making and keeping us a family." Rose's voice cracked as she finished speaking.

"Mom... you did a great job!" Mallory interjected. Rose's head was shaking from side to side.

"Just give me my moment. I need to say this before we have too many people watching. I've been rehashing for several days. What might have been, what ifs... he said, he didn't say. Could I have made things easier, why did things have to be so hard? You know?"

Rose searched the faces of her girls. "Who in their right mind falls in love with a woman with four young children?" She paused and softly laughed skeptically as a couple of tears escaped. "Who falls in love with an attractive career Navy man who has to leave and then trust he's coming back? How many times did I ask myself that while watching the ship leave the pier?"

"Again Mom, you did a great job. Y'all did a great job," Mallory said and everyone in the limo nodded.

"Thank you. But, I probably never said this enough: He made me—he made each of you— strong, confident women. I can't imagine how or what I would have been for you girls without Bob Higgins. But...." Rose started to say, noting the director was headed towards the limo. "But, watching his casket rolling away from me down that sidewalk made me realize, he's not coming home this time. His job is done and we have to stay together just like we always did. He prepared us for those times before, and we can do it now. Okay, girls?" As she smiled, what fortitude had sparked in her now wilted, and her fragility peeked back through.

It seemed like an eternity but finally the director gently opened the door and invited the women to follow him up the stairs. As they crossed the last steps, under the green tent the empty first row was obviously reserved for them. The flag draped casket rested on the rack and the male family members stood soberly across the grave with eyes blazing on each of them. Elizabeth was confident they would see the strength and resolve they had learned from their parents. These women were not going to break down and dilute the military honors presented between Daddy's final resting place and their mom.

Elizabeth locked eyes with Dan and felt him question, 'are you okay?' She nodded and returned her focus on the task at hand and noticed the Navy had sent an Honor Guard. There were flags, rifles and a trumpeter. She took a deep breath and put her arm around her mother's shoulder. Audrey held her mom's hand and her other sisters sat on each side of them.

The final scriptures were read, the rifles fired, the flag folded and presented to their mom with the low and private thanks for his service. They ended with the Taps. At the playing of taps, all five shoulders resisted shaking and Kleenex absorbed a quiet slow tear from Rebecca's eyes. Elizabeth and her sisters remained focused on the casket and resisted joining in the sobs of others behind them. They collectively felt their deep loss but they had a lifetime of celebration of the man who'd taken them under his wing. Or in his case, under his blue jacket.

Elizabeth wanted her mom distracted as they lowered the casket. Audrey and the funeral director pulled their mom off to the side. Friends and family approached her to offer condolences. Dan was joined them and she saw her daughter hanging behind with her cousins.

"Are you okay? You know I'm worried," Dan said, giving her a gentle bear hug. Elizabeth felt smothered rather than comforted. She shook her head and made an excuse to break away.

"Yes, I just need to finish saying good-bye," she said and walked towards the final entombment. She wasn't sure if she was trying to force her tears to the surface or just needed another private moment. Maybe she was a masochist. She needed to step back from putting any additional pain on her already overloaded daughter's soul. *I'm the one who goes last, shares everything or handles the crisis.* She didn't need another spotlight. *Please don't break down here.*

Mallory was already standing at the dirt mound too. Neither said anything as the cranking delivered their father to his final resting place.

"You know if you're buried at sea, they would toss a floral wreath off the fan tail," Mallory said, sharing some military trivia with Elizabeth. Each picked up two pink roses from the spray they'd ordered and threw them before the dirt was shoveled. Four pink roses he dearly loved. Elizabeth plucked a large white one, and tossed it for their mom.

Elizabeth locked arms with her sister as they turned to join the group. "I miss him so much already," Mallory said, as the dirt clunked on his casket. "I wish I'd gotten to plant the last garden with him."

I think we just did Elizabeth thought, but she held her tongue. "Everyone's invited back to the house. The church has provided food. I bought a couple boxes of wine."

Two smiles escaped at the word boxes. "See, he still makes us laugh," Mallory said smiling at Elizabeth. Mallory's eyes were welling and she captured the tears before they hit her cheeks. Elizabeth was starting to feel envious and guilty.

Four hours after the burial, their black dresses were abandoned for blue jeans. The women from Dan's church had buried the kitchen in casseroles and fried chicken. Jugs of sweet tea had lined the kitchen counter with a stack of Solo cups. The trashcan was brimming with paper plates, plastic ware and chicken bones. Audrey was consolidating food while Rebecca washed the church ladies' dishes.

"Elizabeth, are you just going to sit there and watch?" Audrey asked. There was irritation in her voice.

Elizabeth felt resentment building up but stifled her reaction. "I think I can take a break from something, don't you?" The room was thick with stress. Rebecca started humming and grabbed several dishes to move into the dining room.

Elizabeth turned as Mallory walked in, probably unaware of the tension. "Mom is off with her sisters. Think it will be good for her since she'll be alone in a day or so."

Still stinging from Audrey's comment, Elizabeth spoke again. "I'll be taking Mom around and starting all the paperwork at some point." Audrey didn't react. "I told y'all that I found two boxes in Daddy's closet when we were looking for paperwork in the safe. Since we're all here, we could see what's in them. Mom's out, kids are gone. It's still kind of early."

"I'm game," Mallory said. She reached for Elizabeth's wine glass. "More? There's still a whole box left."

Elizabeth nodded. "Audrey? Rebecca? Anything?"

"I can't stay long. John won't want to babysit too long," Rebecca said. Elizabeth cringed at the word babysit and noticed she avoided eye contact. *Was caring for your own damned children babysitting?*

"Are you kidding me?" Mallory whirled around from the refrigerator door. "I think when you lose your dad, you're allowed to be a little selfish. We're never together like this."

The room was quiet but all eyes were on Rebecca's back as she headed for the last of the dishes.

"Um, we're in the same hotel," Audrey said, trying to break the strained energy in the room. "I can call Leigh to help babysit. She's probably just watching TV. We've been through a lot today. Hang out with us before you have to head home tomorrow."

"Okay, but I can't go in his bedroom," Rebecca succumbed to their pressure. "And, someone else needs to answer if John calls."

"You're a little chicken shit," Mallory said. "When did you lose your backbone? He's such a dictator."

"At least I'm married and have children," Rebecca struck back.

The room went silent. Elizabeth watched Mallory recoil as if she'd been slapped.

"Let's chill out and someone help me get the boxes," Elizabeth said, feeling like she was stepping between boxers and sending them to their corners. "Grab a drink and head to the living room. Audrey, bring that salsa and chips."

She left the room and Mallory followed her. "Sorry she said that, Mallory. I think the weight of this day has pushed us all."

"Hell, I'd rather be alone and unmarried than married and lonely," Mallory said. They opened Dad's closet and there hanging on one side were his uniforms, standing at attention among his plaid flannel shirts. Elizabeth reached out and stroked the silver eagle insignia on the left sleeve of his dress blues jacket, flying above five gold hash marks.

"That's a lot of hash marks," Mallory said. "I've only earned two. But I don't plan on retiring any time soon. I love seeing the world."

Elizabeth slid one of the boxes towards Mallory. "As long as you come home sometimes, Lieutenant!"

As they headed out of the bedroom, Elizabeth tried not to revisit the memory of Dad on the unmade bed. She pulled the door closed as they headed to the living room. They plopped down the brown cardboard boxes, each brimming with records of their dad's thirty-two year Navy career.

"Looks like a lot of stuff," Rebecca said. Elizabeth saw Mallory glare at Rebecca from the corner of her eye. She ignored them both and began filing through the blue vinyl jackets concealing accommodations and service awards. Mallory lifted a Ziploc bag with miscellaneous items from a desk. Audrey opened a small box with Vanguard uniform trimmings, gold buttons and service ribbons. She dangled his dog tags paired together on the ball chain.

"Why are there two of them?" Audrey asked.

"If military personnel are wounded or killed, one stayed with the body and the other could be used for notification," Mallory answered. "It should have his rate, name, blood type and religious preference."

Audrey read the tag out loud, "Higgins, Robert. There is his service number and I bet he could tell you that at any time. His blood type was A-negative and he was Protestant." The energy in the room froze and it seemed each daughter had sent a prayer of thanks that a dog tag had never been used during his career.

Elizabeth reached for a small gift bag that was stuffed full of cards, photos and old letters. She plucked a black and white photograph of two sailors in crackerjacks, holding a beer and posing for the camera. It was the image she needed to replace the one from his bedroom. She turned it over and realized it was a postcard. She turned it back over and tried to figure out what was in the big glass box behind them. It was a model of a Chinese junk with riggings.

"They must have been in port in Hong Kong," she said, and passed the photo around. "Seeing the world, I'm sure. Gotta' love a man in uniform!" Elizabeth felt a lump in her throat.

As each sister passed the post card, the bonds between the four seemed to repair the fracture between them. "Holy Moly, look what he saved!"

Elizabeth said and lifted four letters. Three on plain tablet paper and one on a floral piece of stationary. As she checked the signatures, she passed each to the author of the letter.

The room grew quiet as each sister read what had compelled their dad to tuck the letters away for more than two decades.

Dear Daddy

I'm so glad you get to come home soon. I hate Aberdeen. They make fun of me a lot in Middle School. I try and fit in but I'm told I look like a boy and my clothes are out of date. I have that chip on one tooth and some white spot on the other. I'm not sure how to smile.

One of my funny memories is the lunch music. I'm eating that smelly meat loaf and one of Mommy's favorite songs, Blue Velvet, played.

I do love being in the same neighborhood with Aunt Violet. Mommy lets us go over and visit with our cousins. Sometimes we get to go the park with her. But we can't go alone. I got beat up by a black girl at the bus stop, because the boy she liked sent me a ring. I don't like to fight. Don't tell mommy.

Hope to see you soon, Daddy.

Love,
Elizabeth

Elizabeth hated when he had been sent to Vietnam. She re-read the letter and the memories felt like finding a body in the basement, forgotten or not meant to be found.

Yep, Elizabeth remembered that girl acting like her friend, but eventually sucker punching her in the spine as she left the bus to walk to the small section 8 housing cottage. Her parents had decided to move them closer to Mom's family and the housing project would accommodate the military salary. She couldn't help that the cute black kid on the corner sent a ring to her through his best friend. He'd asked her to go steady. She didn't care if he was white, black or purple... she wasn't into boys yet.

She'd just experienced an admirer before they moved from Jacksonville Beach when a classmate rang the doorbell with a huge red heart of chocolates on Valentine's Day. Afterwards, Audrey had teased her for weeks. But of course, Audrey had been quick to dip into the shiny red box. Halves of rejected candies lay barren on the pleated dark brown wrappers.

In spite of her being second born, Audrey was the one who usurped gifts and holidays. It didn't matter if it was a trending game, doll or the color of their first bike, Audrey got the best. Barbie, the white rabbit fur mittens, or The Operation Game. *Wish I could've done that to Audrey's Barbie doll stash...*Elizabeth thought. *Grow the hell up, Elizabeth!*

She went back to her letter. During the war, Elizabeth had gotten sporadic news from her real dad's letters but she'd been confused when they both left for Vietnam in the same year. She needed her dad, step-dad... it didn't matter. She wanted them back. She missed living in the South.

The letter brought back another painful hurdle, one she'd fallen squarely into while attending 7th grade. She'd struggled with disclosing the need to shave her underarms with her mom. It took over a week to ask her mother's approval. Little did she know she was paving the way that no sister would have to wrestle with their female issues. They'd never make it a family announcement but they'd make fun of her as she pioneered the teenage wasteland. It was a very painful struggle. She was always protective of them... but she was their dartboard. Elizabeth remembered feeling as if she was slipping into not only puberty but stepping up to watching out for all of them.

As Elizabeth looked up at them all staring at their letters saved and placed in the box from the closet, she wondered if she could ever tell her sisters how she had felt all those years.

"Hey, Audrey. What does yours say?" Elizabeth dismissed the ghosts of Vietnam past. She hoped they wouldn't notice her holding back hers. She just wasn't ready.

Dear Daddy

How are you? I am fine. I passed 6th grade with almost all A's. My favorite subject is math. We read a lot of books and I almost won the reading contest. My favorite was The Boxcar Children. It was about these kids that *had no parents and lived together in secret in a boxcar.*

We miss you. Mommy said we'll be moving by Mallory's birthday so we can see our next school. Elizabeth went to church camp and spends the night with a friend a lot. Rebecca plays with a little boy across the street. My hair is getting long. Sometimes Mommy lets me and Elizabeth walk to the store by my school.

See you soon. Mommy wants our letters so we can go buy a stamp and mail them. I think she is putting in our school pictures.

Love,
Audrey

Elizabeth listened to Audrey's cheery voice reading her 6th grade letter. She wondered, *How can her sister's letter be so carefree and upbeat? She hated school picture day. Holding a forced smile under the scrutiny of a camera lens and some strange man behind it? Everybody loved Audrey. Why wouldn't she sound upbeat? Or did everyone love her because she was so upbeat?*

"What was the name of that mom and pop store?" Mallory asked.

"Johnny's," Audrey responded. "I can still remember being excited to go get butter or milk for Mom. We got to leave the neighborhood and cross the highway. Sometimes I'd use some of the change to buy a Coke for me and

Elizabeth to share. I'd hide the bottle behind the steps so I could take it back and get the deposit on our next errand."

Elizabeth looked at Mallory, "Only Audrey could use change to sneak a treat, I would have paid dearly!"

"I never got to go," Rebecca said. Elizabeth and her sisters stared and in unison said, "You were the baby!"

"Mallory's turn. Read your letter," Audrey said, removing herself from the spotlight.

Dear Daddy

Mommy wants us to write you a letter before we leave. I'm trying to use my cursive. Can you tell? It was kind of fun living here near my cousins. Sometimes we get to run to the corner to buy from the ice cream truck. School is okay but I like playing baseball with the boys in the park. Mom doesn't know I go alone. Elizabeth warns me that I could get in trouble. I double dare them to bother me.

We got to run around Grandmom's alley and catch fireflies in glass jars. Rebecca was afraid of the bats. Granddaddy would show his wooden leg that he had put in the corner of the kitchen. Elizabeth won't go near it. I think it is funny.

Audrey has a boy that throws rocks at our bedroom window. Mommy is usually watching TV when he sneaks over. It's hot in the bedroom but we have a screen to keep the bugs out. Mommy got us a fan and it's pretty loud so I don't think she hears us joking with him.

Elizabeth is poking me and saying Mommy wants to mail the letters soon. Hope you come home soon.

Love,
Mallory

Mallory gripped the letter and shoved her fist in the air. "Bad to the bone, baby," she said.

"Why would you tell Daddy you snuck over? Didn't you think he'd tell Mom at some point and watch you closer?" Elizabeth asked.

"Hell, Mom knew I was the one to push the envelope. I always had," Mallory answered with a dismissive shoulder shrug.

"Yea, like the time we lived in Jacksonville and we were told not to leave the yard on our bikes. You were only allowed to ride around the house on Elizabeth's or my bike," Audrey recalled.

"I wanted to go down and play with the guys at the sandlot. How would I know that I dropped the bike in a huge fire ant nest?" Mallory smiled. "Do you see a trend here?"

"We were boring?" Elizabeth asked. "I hope riding back to the house covered in fire ants with your eyes swollen shut was worth hanging with the boys."

"I think Mom didn't have the heart to punish me as she hosed the ants off. I looked like a monster for a few days," Mallory said. "And, by the way, the guys wouldn't let me play. They said I was too little."

"Poor Mom, how did she keep up with four of us?" Audrey said. "What about your letter, Rebecca?"

Elizabeth studied Rebecca's face as she started to read aloud. There was melancholy in her eyes and revealed even more in her voice.

> *Dear Daddy*
>
> *How are you? I miss you. Mommy says we are moving at the end of the summer. She takes us to the beach with Grand mom or Aunt Cissy. It smells different than Florida and has a bunch of pebbles. Sometimes we all get in the car and drive around Robinhood Road. If we get a Coke, they stop at a spring and let us fill the bottle back up. It is really cold water.*
>
> *Mommy gave me this pretty piece of paper to write on. I've lost 2 more teeth. Freddie is doing fine. Thank you for going back and getting him before we moved.*
>
> *I love you. Hope you have presents for me.*
>
> *Love,*
> *Rebecca*

"Why were we so anxious to grow up?" Rebecca said, staring at her letter. She looked up and searched each sister's eyes. "I miss him so much."

Before anyone responded, the phone rang. All heads turned to Rebecca. They knew it was John and the deal was Rebecca would not answer.

"I can handle this," Mallory said, checking her watch. "He can back off. We need this time." Elizabeth watched her head fearlessly to the phone as Rebecca chewed on her nails. "Higgins residence," Mallory said as she decoyed the expectation it was her needy brother-in-law.

"Oh, it's you. What's up?" Mallory blandly asked, rolling her eyes. "Hmmmm, hmm," she paused as the voice on the other end could be heard whining in the room. She rolled her eyes. "Are the kids asleep?" she paused again. "Mmm, hmm. Then, what's the problem?"

The whiney voice became louder and all eyes were on Mallory. "That's what room service is for," Mallory responded. Before the voice could protest, Mallory ended the conversation. "We need our sister for a little while. We just lost our dad. Suck it up." She gently dropped the phone in the cradle.

"Okay, Rebecca? You don't need to go anywhere," Elizabeth grinned.

"Y'all don't understand. He'll make it....uncomfortable... for not doing what he wants," Rebecca responded, with a tremble in her voice. They all stared at her and shook their heads.

"You can't live like this," Audrey said. "Rebecca, you're entitled to an authentic side and your own position. You are not chattel. Has he hurt you? Or the kids?"

Elizabeth knew Audrey was prying into a touchy issue. She sensed there would be no easy fix tonight and changed the focus back to Rebecca's letter. "Well, those letters were obviously precious enough for Daddy to keep all these years. Why did you question wanting to grow up?"

Rebecca stalled and re-read the letter. "There was an innocence and I felt protected. I always felt like Mommy was watching so nothing upset me. Daddy always provided what we needed. He was the only dad I really remember. He pulled my baby teeth, taught me how to ride a two wheeler but didn't let me get away with lying about taking a shower."

The room was filled with laughter. "I was headed to the bedroom when Daddy was asking you to go take your shower and firmly suggested it be long enough to get everything clean," Audrey said. "We all knew you hated to bathe."

The family home had one very small bathroom. Between the four of them, someone was always knocking or standing outside the door. Privacy was a luxury, more often non-existent.

"Yeah, he stood outside the door with his hands folded as the shower ran. You were clueless," Elizabeth added. "I felt bad for you. The ends of your hair weren't even damp. And you did not have that fresh Ivory scent."

"After he questioned me actually showering and using soap, I figured I got away with the lie. I remember my stomach dropping when he came back from the bathroom with the dry soap bar and raised one eyebrow," Rebecca said. "I knew I was headed to the bedroom for a rare spanking. I'm sure you guys didn't have a lot of sympathy."

"Well, I wouldn't go that far," Elizabeth said. "But it was refreshing that you ratted yourself out instead of always being a tattle-tale on us."

Audrey took Rebecca's wine glass and refilled it. "Do you really think it was about the soap?"

"No, Daddy knew honesty and transparency was a must for a healthy family," Elizabeth answered for her. "It's probably one of the few things Daddy brought home from the ship."

"Well, there are those stainless steel chow line pans in the china cabinet," Mallory said. Everyone had to chuckle, picturing him in a mink coat and sunglasses smuggling them off base.

The laughter felt as if it freshened the air. If air could've been a color, it would've been blue instead of brown. Elizabeth slowly drank from her favorite wine glass, usually kept on the baker's rack in the kitchen. She watched Rebecca's eyes lose their amusement as the melancholy set back in. Her sister slumped back in the chair and dropped the letter in her lap.

"I miss our trips to Grandmom's, going on car rides on Sundays down Highway 61 and stopping at the picnic areas with a cooler. Unpacking my bedroom stuff when we moved to Daddy's next ship. Saturday morning breakfasts of red gravy or chip beef with home-made biscuits. Being woken up at 4:00 a.m. to go fishing and crabbing off the Naval Weapons Station dock."

Rebecca took a long breath and seemed to struggle with something. "They say you pick a spouse like your parent," She looked at each of them and said, "How did I miss that memo?"

Chapter 17

THE LETTER – FEBRUARY 2004

She'd ignored the stack of mail on her dining room table for a few days. The junk mail and catalogues were getting overwhelming and she knew it was time to thin the pile. She wasn't a coupon clipper and quickly pulled them out for recycling. She'd keep the Venus catalogue to look at the new spring clothing and bathing suits. She was tired of the cold and hoped the spring flowers were ready to bud and bloom.

"Power bill, cable, and water bill," she said out loud, starting a new pile. She tossed a credit card application. She reached for the next white envelope and looked at the sender's address. She felt a lump in her throat and her hands slightly trembled as she tried to muster the will to open the letter. Her emotions jumped from pain to excitement for what felt like minutes. She took a deep breath and carefully opened the envelope.

As she read, the words bounced off the page and she returned to the top, trying to comprehend the information. She stared at the subject line: The adoption of Baby Boy Doe.

That was twenty-four years ago. She'd always tried to prepare herself to revisit the memories of the love of her life, Petty Officer Larry Riley. She never got the chance to tell him of the pregnancy. He'd departed for a shakedown cruise. She waited from him to contact her for over three weeks. Eventually, she called the base to confirm the ship had returned. Then she asked for the ship's office to inquire why she hadn't heard from her sailor. A tear rolled down her cheek as she recalled the conversation.

"Lt. JG Stalls. How may I help you?" he said.

"I'm the girlfriend of Petty Officer Larry Riley. I haven't heard from him since y'all were on a shakedown cruise. Can you leave him a message to call me?" she said. There was a long silence and she heard the background noises of the ship's morning activities.

"Give me your number and I'll have someone call you back," he said. She hung up the phone and couldn't dismiss the sinking feeling in her chest. Maybe he'd just played her like sailors were known to do. Before she could reach the coffee pot, her phone rang.

"Hello?" she said cautiously, praying it was Larry.

"This is Chaplain Richards," he said. "I understand you are inquiring about Petty Officer Larry Riley?"

The Chaplain, she thought and froze. "Yes, he was supposed to call me when he got back from the shakedown."

"Ma'am, I regret to inform you that he was mortally wounded by a snapped cable. He was returned to his family in Pennsylvania." Her hand immediately covered her belly as if she was trying to keep the baby from hearing the news. "I'm so sorry for your loss."

"How long ago?" she tried to sound stoic.

"It happened on our fourth day. He was heli-ed off," the Chaplain answered. "Again, I'm so sorry for your loss... If I..."

Her ears were ringing and she hung up the phone. There was no future for her and Larry. There'd be no celebrating the birth of their child together. All she could see was a lot of grief and secrecy ahead of her.

She redirected her thoughts to the letter in her hand from the adoption agency.

....in accordance to the Consent of Adoption's terms and the agreement between you and the adoptive parents, your adult son has asked us to contact you for a possible reunification. Thank you for keeping a current address in our file and we hope this is up to date. If you are still willing to meet your son, please contact the caseworker through her contact information below...

She returned the letter to its envelope and placed it in her pocketbook. Would she introduce him to her family? How did she reveal this secret… or did she? If she did, how would they react? When or what was the right time? What does he look like? Who did he grow up to be? How would she ever tell her sisters?

Chapter 18

WESTPAC – USS L. F. MASON – 1962

"**M**ess Gear. Clear the mess decks," cued the crew to prepare executing the captain's Plan of the Day. Bobby already knew his captain's plan, he'd familiarized himself earlier. He liked a heads-up regarding drills or department meetings so he could maximize reducing the repair list in his department.

They referred to damage control and engine room sailors as snipes. It wasn't uncommon for several snipe departments to collaborate and regroup as they resolved issues to keep the engine rooms running. Long hours with his welding torch and crawling into the bowels of the engine room didn't give him much break time to walk among the deck hands. Even his watches were deprived of sunshine. Bobby was behind on the damage control repair requests since they had weathered the typhoon. He was still finding tools that had escaped drawers and hooks as the ship pitched under the storm's madness. Captain Graham was pushing day 73 at sea.

Bobby loved his captain. He was a Mustang. He'd been quickly raised from the ranks of seaman through the end of WWII and promoted to officer. His command of the CONN was not only intuitive but he'd served under great mentors during sea deployments. But, the best thing that Bobby loved about his captain was his sense of humor and genuine concern about crew morale. Their departure tune was bagpipes— honoring his Scottish heritage.

Not only had the Captain Graham hunted and taunted the enemy with a hawk's eye, he loved to fly a custom created flag: HIIYA. Bobby rarely was on deck when it was hoisted but the surface men always laughed and chatted as "Hang It In Your Ass" was flagrantly displayed. Captain Graham was relentless with anti-submarine patrols. It seemed as if he could smell a submarine. Periscopes, sonar blips or radar detections would silently change the ship's course to force the dangerous torpedoed enemy to surface or sometimes, sink.

As he slid down the ladder to the fireroom, Bobby felt the temperature changing. The heat from the engine room reminded him of working in the Hole. Jones had beaten him there and was pulling a clip board off the tool wall.

"Have you ever been above when the HIIYA flag is hoisted?" Bobby asked his fellow snipe.

"Only once. I was headed to my battle station," Jones responded. "A Russian destroyer passed so close you could see their faces. Captain Graham blasted them with the bagpipes."

"I remember that day but I was already in the Hole," Bobby said. "Where's Smitty? I've got to get to the deck and weld."

"You know him, he's a little slack," Jones said. "Did you hear that some of the guys jumped him and threw him into the shower, scrubbing him with soap and deck brushes?"

"Yeah, heard that too; he's only a few racks from me. Can't blame them though. He won't bathe and the vents are not that great down in the aft quarters," Bobby said, distinctly removing himself from the gang and changing the subject. "I hear we have a swim break coming up soon. I have an idea for making a diving board."

Jones snapped alert and addressed Bobby directly. "Out of?"

"Hey, if I can make the bbqs out of the captain's oil drums, I have some ideas for a diving board," Bobby grinned. He'd observed the captain's wisdom in maintaining balance and team spirit from a crew forced to deal with all the aspects of destroyer living. Because of long weeks of sea duty, there was a lot of testosterone and little male distraction other than drills. Not everyone fired a gun, spotted a sub's periscope or alerted the Bridge of unidentified aircraft. Some sailors were there to get conscription duty over to return home, but some were there to learn the ropes and hopefully craft a career. Bobby loved the challenge; to learn something new, or pass on the experience of those that had walked before him. And he had learned that stepping up uncompelled always helped his service record.

"Can't wait, Higgins. Sounds like a good way to get Smitty in the water again," Jones laughed, grabbing a torch. "I'm off to the engine room. Still finding leaks from the storm. They don't call her Leakin' Leonard for nothing!"

"I have a door repair on deck," Bobby said. "I'll wait for Shitty Smitty so Chief has someone in the department."

He opened the filing cabinets to pull the file for the midship passageway. Everyone knew the key to keeping the ship afloat was securing hatches and bulkheads. There was a door on the starboard bulkhead that wouldn't dog down since the typhoon.

Bobby turned and pulled out his shipfitter's little blue book. It had become his cheat sheet after welding school. He wanted to re-check the heat settings and cooling recommendations. As he opened the small shipfitter's testament, he re-read: *This information was compiled to make it more accessible to the Shipfitters who are looking for quality as well as quantity in their work.* As he looked for the melting point of aluminum, his attention was diverted by a friend who worked nearby as a machinist.

"Hey, Bobby," Stanley said, slapping him on the back. "Got a break until Oscar drill. Are you welding today?"

"Yep, midway passage door. Got messed up during storm," Bobby answered, reaching for the tip for his torch. "Still want to learn some welding?"

"That's why I popped in," Stanley answered, picking up the welding rods strewn across the work table. "Hope we get back to Yokosuka soon. Ready to see some nylons and smell perfume instead of dungarees and fuel fumes."

"Or sewer lines. A cold beer sounds good, too," Bobby said. He handed Stanley the welding hat as Smitty finally walked into the shop. "Let's go before they call us to muster stations."

As they walked towards the stern, Bobby shook his head. "I'd like to throw Smitty overboard instead of poor Oscar. Can't believe he's so lazy. Maybe treading water and waiting for us to search and rescue him would get his attention."

10:00 – DAMAGE CONTROL SHOP

"Chief, I'm going to check out the door. It should be cool by now," Bobby said, popping his head into the chief's office. "I want to make sure it can be dogged down in case we're called to general quarters."

He waited as Master Chief Connerty put the caffeine stained coffee cup on his desk. As a seaman, Bobby had learned the hard way to never touch anyone's coffee mug no matter how stained. He'd been summoned to be verbally reamed after he'd returned a spanking clean white mug to his superior in the Philippines. His punishment was crawling in the bowels of an engine room inspecting sewer pipes.

"See you back at muster," Chief Connerty grumbled. "Cleaning filters after mess."

"Yes, sir." Bobby left and walked briskly through the passageway. He saw the XO headed towards him and stood aside. The XO stopped and looked at his name stenciled on the chambray shirt. "Higgins?" he asked. Bobby saluted and said, "yes sir."

"What department are you with?"

"Damage control, sir," Bobby said. "I'm checking on a door repair before muster."

"Report to my office after you're done. Don't tell anyone—and Higgins, report *straight* to my office," the XO ordered.

Bobby knew immediately that he was being kidnapped to test his department's report during overboard drill. The Oscar dummy would figuratively be called Higgins today. He had faith in his chief to alert the bridge of his absence. A few weeks earlier, a well-meaning co-worker in the forward engine room failed to report a boilerman missing.

Luckily, it was a test but heads rolled. The petty officer took a reduced rate for thirty days.

Bobby tested the repaired door and it sealed tight. He re-opened it and proceeded to the XO's office. As he approached, the XO waved him into the room. "Close the door," he said. "You know the drill, Petty Officer Higgins?"

"Yes, sir. I'm not to muster or respond to my name being sent out over the intercom," Bobby said.

"Good. I'm headed to the bridge. Sit tight until I relieve you," the XO grabbed his hat and left Bobby.

Five minutes slowly passed and the intercom came alive. "All hands muster," the OOD announced. Bobby could hear the hundreds of shoes pounding the port and starboard decks. Snipes were headed to the fantail by port, deckhands forward starboard. He resisted mustering. He stared at the citation-covered walls of the XO's office. He hoped Chief Connerty would notice his absence and report him overboard. Especially in the event that one day, God forbid, it would not be a drill.

"Petty Officer Higgins, report to your muster station," the intercom blasted.

Another minute passed and the announcement initiated the drill. "Man overboard, man overboard!" the officer repeated several times. Bobby felt the destroyer take a sudden turn to retrace and retrieve the Oscar dummy. Hopefully, it would be quick. His stomach growled, anticipating lunch while the aroma of bread teased him through the office vents. He was pretty certain the fresh bread was heading to the Ward Room for the captain and his staff.

While he waited, he perfected tossing his sailor's cap into the XO's trash can. As it sailed to the can, the door swung open and the XO ducked and grabbed it. "Bored, Higgins?" he said dryly. Bobby felt his face turn red and apologized.

"You're relieved. Thanks for your cooperation. Search and rescue had you back on the ship pretty quick," he said and handed Bobby his cap. "Sunburn free."

Bobby saluted and headed to report to his chief, anxious for lunch.

USS Leonard F. Mason – 1963, Headed to Boston Shipyard

"All non-watch personnel report to your UNREP station," was announced over the intercom.

Bobby knew the ropes of fire watch of the forward fuel bell. He grabbed his life vest and headed to the stern's fire watch station. As he exited the passageway, the seas confirmed what he'd felt below. They were churning and he was concerned as the ship tried to pace herself beside the oiler, heading into the strong head wind. Waves erratically slammed the bow, baptizing sailors with generous sprays of salt water. The linesmen were losing no time connecting to their lifelines.

"What do you think, Higgins?" Shouted Smith from the cable line, wiping spray from his eyes. Bobby shook his head at the borderline conditions and appreciated the captain's endless breakaway drills, critical if the ships were pulled too close.

"Not the easiest one we've done," Bobby yelled. "They're signaling the holding line is about to be shot." A large wave crashed the bow and Bobby's head lurched from the impact. He felt his feet slipping and he barely retained his footing. *This is going to be a mother fucker*, he said to himself.

Within five minutes, the fueling hose had been transferred to the ship's receiving bell. The ship continued to drink deeply from the oiler. The waves pounded but the helmsman was somehow holding the distance between the two ships.

Bobby looked down the row at his water-soaked shipmates handling the lines. The fuel hose was released and returned to the oiler. New stores were hoisted to the transfer line and carried away to storage. Not a moment too soon either; the galley would be able to cook something other than hotdogs served on stale buns. Bobby strained to see if there was a mailbag. He knew that mail and the exchange of movies were lowest priority, especially under these conditions. The ship would confine the crew for several weeks as they headed to Boston for a FRAM. The Leakin' Leonard was to receive updated guns and other improvements.

He grinned as he saw canvas bags being hoisted and delivered to the ship. Mail! Otherwise, they would have had to wait until they were closer to land to receive by helicopter. Bobby hoped there may be news from home— maybe from House, too.

Before he could enjoy the moment, another rogue wave hit the port deck and a line-handler was washed over. "Man overboard," screamed from the fantail. Bobby strained, looking for a life preserver among the white caps. The suction between the two ships would more than likely seal the sailor's doom. Best case scenario would be the destroyer behind waiting to refuel would receive the alert from the bridge and pick him up. But something in Bobby's stomach said the sailor was a goner.

As the lines were released, the PA system did not blast the oiler with the signature bagpipes as they broke away. Bobby had always dreaded this drill becoming a reality. His face was stinging from the pelting of the waves and his dungarees were soaked. The ship picked up speed in spite of the aggressive seas. Reluctantly, he turned and joined the men filing back to quarters, reminding himself to stay alert on the slippery deck. He overheard his friend chatting with others about the rough fuel replenishment.

"Man, I thought I was going to be Oscar today. I fell at least three times and prayed I wouldn't be fucked up between the two hulls," a pale-faced seaman said to his friend. "I wonder who the poor bastard is?"

"I think it was Shitty Smitty," his friend interjected, shaking his head. "That guy has the worst luck. Hell of a way to clean up!" The two pals chuckled while shaking their heads.

Bobby lurched at the casual comment, *that poor guy has the worst luck?* Smitty had been a pain in the ass, he admitted. But, he'd enlisted for a lot of the same reasons as Bobby. He was a small-town boy avoiding the draft. The poor kid didn't seem to catch a break and Bobby realized that he had been just as callous as the other crew members. He should have taken him under his wing like his mentors had him. He suddenly felt ashamed that complacency had crept in and distracted him. Girlie magazines, beer, poker and locker talk had lulled him away from why he was in the Navy. His parents raised him better than that and his mamma would have been disappointed. He continued to stare off the fantail, ship lurching through the chop and he prayed the ship behind them in line for refueling had found Smitty. *God? I'll make you a deal. If we get him back, I will take him under my wing— lazy smelly bastard and all!*

He turned and directed his focus on getting out of the wet salty clothes. *Time to grow up, Bobby*, he thought to himself.

"First Mail call," was announced over the intercom.

"Higgins, you're the department mail rep today. Jones is on watch," Chief Connerty shouted from his desk.

"Yes, sir," Bobby answered, and headed up the ladder to the post office. As he joined the line, he stood behind a radioman. "Hey, Sparky. Expecting anything good from home?"

"Yeah, I'm hoping my girlfriend's letters will finally hit. Maybe the guys at FPO slid in a few girlie magazines like they did at Christmas," he said, grinning. "But, all I really need is to look up at her photo I pinned up in my office. She looks just like Ava Gardner in *On the Beach*, oo-la-la!"

They both stood aside as three bags were carried away by a seaman to the fantail bosun. "I'd say by the lumpy look of those bags, we're getting packages," Bobby observed aloud.

"Reporting for communications, sir," Radioman Wickerham said.

"Packages, Wickerham. Merry Christmas," the Petty Officer said.

"Thank you, sir," Wickerham answered and hauled the stash down the passageway towards the communications area. "See you later, Higgins. Hear we have a new movie tonight!"

"Damage control, sir," Bobby stepped forward.

"There are three bags," the post office petty officer advised. "I'll bring one. Don't waste time returning for it," he growled without looking up.

Bobby grabbed two of the larger bags. "Yes, sir."

Bobby checked the engine calibrations as he anticipated four bells, relieving him of Last Dog Watch. He wanted some time to go through his mail and packages before joining the others for the new movie. Maybe after the movie he would pop down to the mess for mid-rats. Due to his watch, he'd only grabbed a few bites at dinner. It would be interesting to see how the galley would reinvent the leftovers of the day. He didn't care, he just wanted to catch up on news from home. The dials were slightly vibrating as the ship got underway against impending weather. The red lights helped him acclimate to the dark.

"New movie, men," someone yelled from behind the boilers.

"Great! Hope it is better than Landry's choices before we left port," Bobby answered. "I was pretty tired of Oklahoma. One more time and we'll all start having periods."

"What a joke! A musical?"

"Hey, it did sound like a Western. There's no guarantee what the oiler handed off either," Bobby said, defending Landry. Four bells sounded over the PA and he looked at the ladder hoping First Watch relief was on time. As he looked over his shoulder, he saw bell bottoms jog towards him. "Steady underway, 15 knots so far." Bobby pointed at his last log entries to his relief as the ship listed heavier than normal.

Bobby scurried up the ladder.

"See you at the fucking movie, Higgins."

Bobby flopped in his rack and grabbed the stack of letters. As much as he wanted to visit with family first, there was one with an APO address. House! It was post-marked December. Bobby grinned as he pried the envelope open and removed the ship issued letterhead. He leaned back to talk with his childhood friend.

Dear Bobby,

Haven't had leave for a while. Guess you've heard about the Ruskies and Cuba. We've been on carrier guard. Between anti-submarine watch and retrieving pilots that failed to land on deck, it's pretty sleepless. I didn't get a break from the radio room for several days. Communications were intense and someone brought my food to me. It was a far cry from our port to port stops between Spain and Greece. I can't even remember being in the sunlight and drinking sangria, French wine or throwing plates as we drank Ouzo. Anyway, traffic has died down since the President got Russia to back off. Most of the activity is tracking the Russian ships hauling the missiles off Cuba. It's the underwater activity that always keeps us on our toes.

Guess you heard that dad got too sick. Your mom was really good to Ma and made sure there was a lot of help. I'm worried about her now. She's lost dad but I think she is still reeling from losing Jimmy in Korea. I left his loafers behind when we joined up. She hated when I wore them anyway. I think I may ask for leave as soon as I can. I hated missing dad's funeral.

How do you like the Leakin' Leonard? Someone told me that y'all stay at sea a lot too and there are huge storms. At least you have school and Subic under your belt, bet some of the greener guys are sick as dogs. We've had several chicken wars between Ruskie destroyers when we get reassigned.

I can't help but laugh at our captain's music choices. He's from Texas. You know how we always loved our western movies. He keeps Marty Robbins tunes on hand. I've gotten to know the lyrics of El Paso well. But, I have to confess, since I heard of Pearl Miller's engagement, I'm looking for Felina. Without the shoot out of course. Want to kiss her until I'm old and grey. No Rosa's Cantina over on this side though.

What have you invented new these days? Eight bells and I need to grab some shut eye before watch.

Write soon.
House

Bobby smiled but felt sad at some of the news. He was well aware of chicken wars with Ruskie vessels. His captain was the master of anti-submarine warfare. Depth chargers were a normal activity. Leave for home? He'd put in so he could go home during the shipyard FRAM. His dad wasn't doing well either.

Bobby sorted through the other letters. He smelled the two goodwill packages. He picked his sister's with the red postmark from Atlanta. Someone snored below him and he was relieved as he hoped there would be no sharing...not yet.

Just like Christmas' pasts, he peeled the brown paper off and opened the reused cardboard box. It was from Charlie's Grill. The logo was from a local Atlanta hamburger joint. His brother-in-law was working for the railroad nearby. As he broke the brown flaps, he saw two newspapers, cookies and cigarettes. He tasted the cookie. Stale, but they were from a loving family's hand. He stared at the headline of Atlanta's paper-- JFK diffuses the Cuban Missile Crisis. How timely. House had been there, now Bobby could get more info. As he played with his rack's bounty, he heard seven bells. Thirty minutes before the new *fucking movie*, as his comrades called it. His stomach rumbled as he stashed his packages from home and rushed to join the others in the mess. He pushed a pack of Pall Malls into his shirt pocket and prepared to adjust to the white light of non-watch ship sections.

The smoking lamp was still on, as well as the red lights engaged to help watch standers adjust to the night conditions. The ocean was churning angry in spite of so recently claiming his shipmate. Poor Smitty. Between three ship's efforts, no one ever spotted him. Bobby didn't want to think the worst but the suction between the oiler and the Leonard had been unusually dangerous. As he stood under the smoking lamp and puffed on his cigarette, he heard the vibration of the propellers as they were forced out of the water. Correction...the screws were whirling above the surf line. Props, screws...propellers. The waves pulled the bow under; the fantail see-sawed and violently shuddered. Until the seas calmed, everyone's sleep would be interrupted with the bucking. Clouds hid the moon and starlight, all indicating a perfect recipe for storm conditions as they headed to the Panama Canal.

As he finished his smoke, he thought of the stars and fireflies at home. Peaceful days that seemed like a lifetime ago. Jones approached the doorway. "Come on, Bobby. You're going to miss the fucking movie. I hear it's a real Western."

Chapter 19

APRIL, 2004

E lizabeth was buried in the trail of Statements of Personal History forms clipped in the brown U.S. Navy Enlisted Service Record file folder. She observed that her stepfather's parents' names disappeared as dependent family members between 1963 and 1964. His sister and brother-in-law, along with a brother, were penned in as the new emergency contacts. Seeing her aunt's name brought back memories of Elizabeth traveling to Atlanta with Mallory many times to visit Aunt Sarah.

As she crossed into adulthood, her aunt had told her the story of her and Bobby's parents passing while he was stuck at sea. There was no choice but to miss the funeral—

they were on patrol. *Daddy always had a big heart. I can't imagine how he put the pain away,* Elizabeth reflected. As much as today's graveside service hurt, and as much as her eyes felt permanently hot and blurred with tears that still couldn't escape, she couldn't imagine not being there for it. She realized she had at least been blessed with the ability to say good-bye and share the grief of losing her dad with her sisters.

She turned to the next page—a newspaper clipping. It was yellow and there was the list of Operations. Operation Starlite, Piranha, Dagger Thrust and Double Eagle. As her eyes skimmed the article, she learned how the collateral efforts between the Navy, Marines, Army and VC Corps haunted the concentrations of the Viet Cong. According to the reporter, thousands of shells from the five-inch guns were devastatingly accurate. For six days, shore bombardment target results were reported by troops and helicopter pilots.

Elizabeth paused and did the math. 1965 minus 1958. She would have only been seven years old. Here was a lightbulb moment. The Cold War was morphing into the Vietnam War and both of her fathers had kept the family in an all-is-well cocoon. She looked back in her mind to where her mother was at the time. She'd yet to consider her mother's mindset. Or even more, her emotional state. It would be three more years before her stepfather would really blend into their lives. Both fathers were caught up in the acceleration of a war and Mom was basically home alone. But at no time that Elizabeth could remember did she sense much stress. Her mom was only twenty-six, juggling four girls, running the household and Elizabeth hoped, finding some rare social time. She felt selfish, realizing how much she depended on Dan for a one child household. She couldn't imagine–

"What are you reading, Elizabeth?" Mallory asked, waving her napkin to get her attention.

"Newspaper clipping he tucked into his file. His destroyer was involved in some Vietnam off shore bombardments," Elizabeth said. "Can you imagine being twenty-seven years old, stuck at sea for months with your very life depending on the skills of the others?"

"Yeah, with no internet or computers," Audrey added. "News from home only when mail found the ship." She'd listened to her late husband's father share stories of the glory days. "You had to hope that the captain could manage all those young guys, and with all the lack of liberties. I remember how Daddy used to exchange his stories with Jeff's father during holiday get togethers." She looked down, hiding behind her bangs.

The mood in the room paused to allow Audrey a moment. Elizabeth caught the tear sliding down her sister's cheek. She wanted to say something about the loss of her sister's husband but knew it was still a fresh topic.

"We need to write them down," Elizabeth suggested. "The stories, I mean. All of them. For our children, and their children. Hey, what's a funny memory of Daddy?" Elizabeth pointed at Audrey.

"Remember how much he loved to cook for us?" Audrey asked. Everyone agreed and the thirty-five years of savory kitchen memories warmed the mood of the room. "How about the night Daddy and Mom decided to cook lumpia?"

"I remember peeking in the kitchen and watching them paint the egg roll wrappers on that awful avocado-green electric griddle," Mallory said. "The smell of the fried pork filling that he put on the wrappers, then sealing each lumpia roll with a dab of water."

"And after the fryer stopped bubbling, he presented at least a dozen of them at the dining room table. He held one vertical, poured Worstershire from the top until it dripped onto the plate under it," Audrey added, fully recalling their first lumpia experience.

"He showed us how to eat it and we all grabbed from the platter," Mallory jumped in. "He took the platter and left to create more. All of us stood our ground at the table, greedy little birds, waiting for another batch. I certainly wasn't letting y'all eat my share."

"He must have made dozens and still I don't think there were any leftovers," Rebecca added. "Y'all didn't care if you took *my* share. He went back to the kitchen shaking his head."

"I can still see and hear him chuckling and saying '*Lord, it's like a bunch of termites,*'" Elizabeth added. "Hey, does anyone remember how Daddy met Mom?"

"Now there's a serendipitous question, Elizabeth," Mallory said immediately. "Last weekend when I was helping him get the garden ready, we were having a cold beer on the porch and talking about childhood memories and shit." Her eyes misted and she forced a smile.

"I only remember some of it," Rebecca said. "I was too little and hardly remember the divorce. Do tell!"

Chapter 20

MAYPORT, FL – MARCH, 1968

There was a pep in Bobby's step and he left a trail of English Leather as he crossed the parking lot to catch a ride. It had been a grueling week of emergency repairs, long hours and sweltering conditions in the bowels of the ships. But he'd finally traded his dixie cup for the khaki chief's hat. The shiny vinyl brim matched the impeccable luster of his shoes. The music of the cicadas in the Spanish moss laden trees accompanied his step as he approached Tiny's '64 Ford Fairmont.

Tiny laid on the horn, "Step it up, Higgins! We don't have all night." Bobby slid into the passenger's seat.

"You know the way?"

"Been there several times. I think tonight is all you can eat crab legs." Tiny looked over his shoulder and backed out of the parking space. "You'll love this bar. Country music, on the beach, complete with cute girls. A lot of the Flagler girls from St. Augustine troll the street."

Bobby took off his hat and rolled down the window. "Nice ride. Not sure if I'm going to jump into owning a car yet, but this has to be a major babe magnet. Convertible?"

"Yeah, but when you want to test a broad then it's top down all the way. I pick her up and see if she likes the wind in her hair," Tiny lowered his lights as they approached the guard shack and were waved on. Street lights were starting to flicker on as the sunset dipped below the horizon. "If she gets all prissy, you may want to bob for another apple."

Without looking, Tiny turned on the radio and immediately the DJ announced, "From the Big Ape Hall of Fame, here's a hit from Dolly Parton singing Dumb Blonde."

"What's your type, Bobby?" Tiny offered him a cigarette. Bobby dug into his pocket for the well-used Zippo.

"Well, I was stationed in the Western Pacific. WESTPAC. I really haven't taken a relationship seriously yet. You know what they say about a girl in every port?" Bobby confessed. Smoke drafted out the window. "Just having fun, I guess. What about you?"

"Keeping my distance but I'm a sucker for long legs… tits…earthy…no pearls." Tiny looked at Bobby. Both began laughing and shaking their heads. "Shit, I like them all."

The car grew quiet and the air was filled with the last of the lyrics—*When you left you thought I'd sit, An' you thought I'd wait, An' you thought I'd cry, You called me a dumb blonde, Ah, but somehow I lived through it...*

"I saw her sing that song on the Porter Wagner Show. She's tiny but can belt out a tune," Tiny turned his Fairmont onto A1A. "Just a couple more minutes and we'll be studs with suds."

"Just don't fall for a dumb blonde! Dolly warned us on that deal," Bobby grinned, flicking the cigarette butt out the window.

It was a typical Friday night and the parking spaces were full. They circled twice and finally gave in to parking a few blocks away. Putting on their chief hats, there was a pep in their steps as the noise from the juke box invited them to a room of amusements. Pool balls were cracking and expletives bounced off the walls.

Tiny spied a friend at the ping pong table and slapped Bobby on the back. "Grab those two stools and order me a Schlitz."

Bobby took his hat off and claimed the barstool real estate. He ordered the beers, popped the top off his and poured it into the frosty mug. Most of the women were dancing with sailors. The room was as thick with flirting as it was cigarette smoke. The cold beer was going down fast, releasing the anxiety from the repair emergencies. He was still adjusting to shore duty. He often felt the yearning to be back riding the ocean on a greyhound of the sea.

He loved being on destroyers. Breakaway songs—or in his case—the sound of bagpipes, steel picnics on a Sunday while jumping into the ocean from his diving board contribution to the L.F. Mason. The anticipation that was built from being at sea for weeks on end always ramped up their liberty time. He signaled the bartender for another beer. "Can I get a shot of whiskey, too?"

Bobby looked across at Tiny feeding coins into the juke box with a couple of girls pointing to songs. Tiny was in his element. A cute brunette in clam diggers (long legs of course) leaned against him. Flanking the other side was a busty red head. Both looked like college students, probably from Flagler. After Tiny pushed the last request, the two girls giggled and ran back over to the pool tables. Tiny looked across the bar, giving Bobby a crooked grin with his *what the hell* look and headed over.

"Only cost me a quarter!" Tiny said, grabbing his beer. "Hey, you already had a shot without me?" he said, signaling the bartender to refill as he held up two fingers. "Got quarters on the pool table. Want to be my partner?"

"Nah, I'm just sitting back tonight. Maybe some table shuffleboard after a few beers. Got my eye on the cute solo blonde over there. I don't see a ring or a date."

"The big blue eyes in the pigtails?" Both men looked her way but Bobby stared until she locked eyes with him.

"Yep, her." Bobby nodded and toasted his whiskey towards her before he swigged it. She batted her eyes and looked away. "Bet I can get her over here?"

"You ain't overseas, Bobby. Sailors are a dime a dozen over here. Damn, look how I fed the juke box for those doe eyed college girls," Tiny ran his fingers through his hair, taking another look at the blonde in pigtails, as if they were two bucks vying for the same doe.

"She's mine, Tiny," Bobby growled with a smile. He leaned against the wall and stared in her direction.

Two songs passed in the juke box. She was blocking out Bobby's stare. Bobby wasn't used to being ignored. The beer and whiskey were raising his impulsivity meter.

"Hey, you...." Bobby shouted across the bar. No reaction. "Hey, you!" She looked up and pointed at herself, questioning his introduction. "Yeah, you. Come over here." Her eyebrows raised, speaking volumes about his weak attempt at sweet talk.

She lifted a glass of chianti, took a swig and looked back at him. "My name isn't Hey You."

Tiny laughed and slapped Bobby on the back. "Seriously, where do you think are? You ain't in the islands no more. Good luck! My slot to play pool. Use my stool if you get lucky."

Bobby stuffed his ego down, got off the barstool and walked over to Hey You, The Pretty Blonde. "I'm sorry for coming across rude. I'm Chief Bobby Higgins and I can't help notice you are the prettiest woman in here."

She stared at him without saying anything and he thought for the briefest second that he might drown in those eyes. She seemed older, wiser, not like one of the coeds looking for a cheap date. He needed to change his approach.

"Would you...please come sit with me? I'd be honored to buy you a drink." He noticed her eyes twinkled and she tried not to smile.

"What's up with your buddy?" she asked, nodding to him standing by the pool table.

"He's trolling and said I could offer you his seat." Bobby reached for her glass. "Forgiven?"

She stepped off her stool, took his hand and he thought, she fits just right. He observed her as she walked in front of him. She was petite and moved with confidence, leaving a trail of Musk perfume. He looked for a wedding ring. Nothing there, but she was alone tonight. He just wanted to talk. She had some spunk and it intrigued him.

"I'll have a Miller, please," she said, raising one eyebrow.

Bobby motioned for the bartender, ordering her drink. He leaned against the wall with a grin. "I have presented you the Champagne of beers. May I know your name?"

"Rose."

"Beautiful. Where do you live?" He felt the icy wall melt a little.

"Jacksonville Beach, but I'm from Maryland. You're obviously stationed here but where are you from?" She went to pick up the beer mug and he noticed her hand slightly trembled. She riveted on his eyes but not before quickly glancing at his ring finger.

"No ring or tan line," Bobby called her out, offering an up-close inspection of his left hand. She feigned indifference and offered her left hand in response. He found it hard not to challenge the cute spunky woman, feeling like a schoolboy pulling on a girl's pigtails during recess.

"The single question is off the table," she laughed. "So, where are you from?"

"Alabama and been here on shore duty," he paused and leaned forward. "I'm very pleased to meet you. I hope we can get together and maybe I could take you on a proper date."

She smiled and he knew he'd melted another layer but he resisted turning back into cocky Bobby. He made a promise to God to grow up. And there was something special about Rose. "Can I have your number?"

Chapter 21

CHARLESTON, APRIL – 2004

Audrey passed around a photo of their parents. It was an aging old Kodak, a white bordered picture of them sitting at a Formica topped table. Their mother had her hair in ponytails and wore a white blouse. Their stepdad was in plain clothes, his hair combed off to the side, looking slick with hair creme.

"They sure were an attractive couple," Rebecca said, passing the picture to Mallory. "Who do you think took it?"

"Probably the neighbors, Mr. and Mrs. Parsons. She used to babysit you," Mallory said, and passed the picture to Audrey. "You played with her son."

"They were good people," Audrey said and passed it along to Elizabeth. "Those were some of my favorite memories living in Jacksonville Beach. The cook-outs and playing hide and seek 'til midnight."

Elizabeth looked up from the picture and over at Rebecca, grinning. "Here comes Rebecca. Pretend she's poison ivy... run!"

"Y'all were mean!" Rebecca said, showing the room her middle finger.

"Whatever," Mallory threw back with her own gesture. "This is supposed to be a celebration of Daddy. Look at that picture again. Those are the parents that gave us a safe place to grow up. Think about it! Every year we followed his naval transfers, all those deployments. And Mom had to manage four of us. FOUR OF US!"

The room grew quiet. Audrey leaned back in her chair. "So how long do you think it took before Mom told Daddy there were four girls at home?"

Everyone smiled at her question.

"Wasn't it a school night? I believe she made us get our homework and baths done. Pufnstuf had her kittens—four of them. What is it about the number four in our lives? Poor Daddy, he not only met us... we baptized him by fire with kittens."

Mallory laughed. "He was sitting on the couch and we were scattered around the living room. I think part of our openness was due to the Navy uniform," Mallory added. "But, I think it was on a Friday night. They were going to a movie down at the drive-in."

"And we were so proud of Pufnstuf's kittens," Rebecca added softly. "She had them in Elizabeth's pajama drawer and we had to move them into Mom's bathroom cabinet. We each ran and grabbed our kitten to show off to Mom's *new friend*."

"When I walked towards him with my tabby, I saw 'mommy's new friend' step back," Elizabeth recalled. "So, I sat on the floor off to the side, my kitten meowing for her mom. Mallory slid beside me right next to his pant leg, nudging her kitten towards his shoelace."

Mallory interrupted, "My kitten loved to climb the curtains. Who knew he was ready to shimmy up a guy's leg!"

"So typical, Mallory. You knew." Rebecca interjected.

"I remember Mallory's black kitten shimmying up his trouser. The terror of his reaction, her kitten flying across the room from his swat and all I could think was, did we ruin Mom's special friend moment? Poor Daddy," Elizabeth said. "Why would cats scare him so bad?"

"Obviously, not enough for him to stop seeing Mom," Audrey added. "And he never told Mom no if she wanted to replace a cat when it passed."

"Good home training in my eyes," Elizabeth whispered mostly to herself and flipped through more of his files. "Oh my, look at these." She started passing around several color photos, these obviously taken from a ship's deck approaching a space capsule, the doors open and two astronauts' heads poking out. They were flanked by three para-rescuers, barefoot and sporting wide smiles. The sky was blue and the sea was calm. The capsule was surrounded by green dye. Each photo had descriptions... Major David Scott and Neil Armstrong.

"I did a term paper on Gemini 8. I interviewed Daddy so I could make more than just a NASA story," Audrey said as she relished the young astronauts grinning at the photographer from the destroyer. "A mission cut very short because of one thruster. Doesn't Major Scott look like Jeff?" She softly mumbled, "A life cut short because of one drunk driver." As she stared, she was no longer in the present.

Elizabeth crossed the room and gave Audrey a gentle hug from the edge of the armchair. Two more sets of sister arms enveloped them.

"I want to come home," Audrey said weakly, reaching for the Kleenex box.

Chapter 22

MAYPORT, FL – MAY, 1968

B obby paid the cab fare, pulled the restaurant door open, and headed towards the hostess station. Rose had insisted she'd drive herself. He looked around for her and informed the hostess he was waiting on a date. "Reservation for two under the name Higgins," he said and watched her check the notebook, nodding. She looked up and shrugged, indicating his date wasn't there yet. "I'll wait at the bar."

Dean Martin crooned. Around the restaurant, retired Chianti bottles found new work as candleholders. Multi-colored wax candles dripped down the straw baskets resting on red and white-checkered tablecloths. "Old Milwaukee please and a shot of whiskey," Bobby ordered, feeling in need of a little liquid courage.

Rose shook his world and he wasn't sure why. He'd been with attractive women, desperate women, Asian women, silly women, dumb blondes and even loose women. Dating was not on the top of his priorities. But he sensed Rose hadn't put all her cards on the table either. Earlier that week, after he had made this dinner date, he'd walked into Big John's country band night and there she was—singing on stage like Dolly Parton. She was good. The men in the bar were cheering her on and motioning her to sit at their tables. She spotted Bobby in the back, dismissed her invites and asked if she could sit with him. This time her hair was down and a checkered hair band added color to her black ensemble.

"Are you part of the band?" he'd asked.

"No. They just pull me up now and then. I only do the songs I know."

Bobby was the proudest man in the room. Now he closed down his replay of that week's earlier encounter and shot his whiskey. Suddenly, she walked through the front door and approached the hostess station. He watched, admiring his Rose as the hostess pointed her in Bobby's direction. He drank in her stroll. She had on a mini-skirt and black vinyl boots. He couldn't hide his grin and stood to give her his stool. He gently led her with his hand on her lower back and she flirtatiously shot him a mysterious grin. He felt reduced to a mouse being played by a cat. At the thought of a cat touching him, he swept the feeling aside. Maybe not a cat…

"You look gorgeous," Bobby said, trying to resist looking her over her from head to toe again. "We have a table. Do you want a cocktail first?"

"Whiskey sour please," she said, cocking her head as she brazenly looked him over.

For twenty minutes, they made small talk and eventually moved to their table. It was in the corner and Bobby loved the soft candlelight on Rose's face. He guessed she was in her twenties but they'd never asked each other their age. Their conversation was easy but felt a little like an interview. Maybe exchanging ages would've put that over the top. They were both from small towns and loved country music. She'd been married to a Naval officer but had refused to move any farther from her family after his transfer to the West Coast. Her first husband had feigned indifference and Bobby used Rose's moment of confession to put his hand over hers. She didn't resist.

"I'm still trying to figure out where I'm headed," she said, blinking to prevent the tears from escaping. "I don't have any family here."

"What do you do for a living?" he prodded. Her face flushed and she avoided his stare. There was an awkward silence. He reached for the wine bottle and refreshed her glass.

"I got married out of high school. I've only been a stay at home…. mom," Rose said and Bobby felt her lock eyes with him. They'd both reached for their wine and allowed the word *mom* to wash down like a breadstick. A dry breadstick that seemed to have gotten stuck in both their throats. As if on cue, Frank Sinatra serenaded the room with *Strangers in the Night*.

Bobby noticed the song and said to himself, '*Are you kidding me?*'

Bobby knew right at that moment that he needed to step up and put out the fire. He almost grinned at the thought of using his Navy-trained damage control skills. Fire, welding and problem solving were naturals at work. "I'll bet you're a great mother," he said. "Boy or girl?" He saw her take a deep breath.

"Girls," Rose answered, emphasis on the plural. The 's' hung in the air like the smoke of the candle. Bobby smiled and patted her hand.

"Girls are so cute. So, how old are they?" Bobby hoped his effort to be calm and collected was working.

Rose withdrew her hand, wiped her mouth with the napkin and shifted her weight in the chair. "My oldest is nine and the youngest is five."

Bobby quickly subtracted nine from.... late 20s? It didn't line up as he sat across from this petite young woman. He knew the *how old are you* to his date was a no-no. "So, you had her when you were fifteen?" Jesus, this dinner was supposed to redeem him after his botched pick up attempt at Sea Turtle Inn. But then he'd never suspected the mom card would be played.

Before she could answer, the waitress approached the table. "Has anyone saved room for dessert?"

Bobby looked at Rose.

"I'm good," Rose drank deeply of her Chianti.

Bobby looked quickly at his watch. He had an hour to get back to base. "I guess we'll take the check," he said.

The conversation drifted back to reviewing their personal life resumes. "How many siblings do you have?" Rose's walls were back up and her arms were crossed. Bobby started to wonder how complicated an area this all seemed to be heading towards.

"I'm seven of nine. And you?" The waitress set the ticket with Bobby and he signaled her to wait. He pulled out a twenty-dollar bill and focused back on Rose.

"Oldest of five," she volleyed back. "Hey, I need to get home. School starts early. I have lunches to pack."

"Hold on, let me walk you to the car," Bobby offered and left the tip. The taxi corner wasn't far away and he really wanted a kiss. Her musk was seducing him to bury his face in her hair and draw this vulnerable but spunky woman into his arms.

"I'm good. I'm just a block away," she said, reaching for her purse.

"No, I insist. I still have some time," Bobby opened the door and put his hand on her lower back. It was a sexy spot and he felt a little aroused. "Which way? What car am I looking for?" He grabbed her hand and waited for directions.

"Just down the block. It's a station wagon," Rose nudged him around the corner. They silently strolled, listening to the crashing of the waves on the beach. The moon was partially covered by the clouds and wind softly rattled the palmettos. "I'm here." She dug for her keys. They stood awkwardly at the driver's door.

"I'd like to take you to a movie tomorrow night. Can you get a sitter?" Bobby tilted her chin so she had to look at him. Before she could answer, Bobby cupped her face and drew her on tiptoes to kiss her. As he pressed her into him, he felt her start to surrender but he awkwardly stopped.

"Planet of the Apes, 7:15?"

Wow, that was romantic, he said to himself. Why hadn't he let the kiss linger? Nothing about this night had been controlled. He needed to get back to base and digest the evening. His food sat heavy and he knew it wasn't heartburn.

"Sure. I'll figure it out," Rose said as she unlocked the car. He turned her back around and kissed her tenderly again.

"I look forward to it," he said, reaching for the handle. She sat and started the car. "You okay to drive?" he asked.

She nodded and put the gear into drive. She looked up with a creased brow. "Bobby, I have four girls. You can meet them tomorrow. If you get cold feet, call me."

She pulled out and didn't look back.

Bobby stood and watched the tail lights fade.

The pier had received two ships needing immediate repair. Bobby was supervising the last-minute fixes in the shop so he could get them headed out to the Panama Canal. The ships were headed to Vietnam for picket duty and off shore support. Clipboards lined his office wall. Three hoses were ready to be tested, his welders were still searching for parts for scuttles and cable for safety lines. The days were getting humid and longer. His men were fatigued. When he met with his Senior Chief, he knew that the ten-day repair window was unrealistic. Fourteen days minimum, but he'd seen worse challenges.

To increase morale under the tight deadline, Bobby was sacrificing his own senior privileges. He had given up his dating life. His career eye was on a service record endorsement to advance as a senior chief and he was so close. His next assignment was just months away and he was looking forward to getting back on a ship. But he had to admit, if only to himself, Rose and her four girls were distracting him.

Getting the ships ready was also insurance, providing a little distance. He was in real danger of giving away his heart to Rose. He was too attracted to her spunky spirit and her four adorable daughters. He'd even gotten over the damned cats. Where he'd picked up such a fear of the little furballs he didn't know, but if four little blonde pig-tailed girls loved them, he'd have to man up. But, did he want to? He probably did. How could he resist the youngest climbing in his lap for a hug? In ten years, from port to teeming port, no one had gotten this close to his heart. It rattled the memories of his own family bonds. Learning that his parents had passed while he was at sea still haunted him. Committing to a family and getting grim news? Not being able to be there again if someone needed him? Not an option for him. As he tried to dismiss the argument between the devil and angel on his shoulders the phone rang.

"Chief Higgins." He was relieved for the diversion. He needed to get his head back to the repairs.

"Sir, it's Rose."

He took his feet off the desk and was surprised at how happy he was to hear her voice. So much for diversion. It wasn't like Rose to call him at work. Before he could speak, she said, "I haven't heard from you or seen you for over a week. We need to talk."

Bobby's heart sank and skipped a beat. "Rose, I'm really busy getting these orders completed. Can I meet you later? Big John's, Sea Turtle?" He wanted to diffuse the seriousness in her voice. The other end of the line was quiet. "Rose?"

"What time? It's the last week of school for the girls," Rose's voice sounded cool but Bobby sensed the storm in the distance.

"I can be done and ready by.... 6?"

Chapter 23

MAYPORT, FL – JULY, 1968

A petite blonde woman—and four daughters—that had never been part of his plan. And yet, for two months, he looked forward to spending all his free time with them. The sex with Rose was passionate and playful. Nothing like his usual one-night stands.

But now, it was the weekend and Bobby sat in the corner, brooding. Tiny was at the pool tables hitting on the college girls. The jukebox played above the voices of patrons. Bobby thought, *same old, same old*. Something in him hoped she'd walk through the door. It had been almost two weeks since they'd met for the talk. He'd tried to explain that a marriage proposal wasn't on the table.

The look in her eyes stabbed him in the heart. As she left the room, she made it clear that he should lose her telephone number.

Bobby took inventory of his single Navy life. Huks in the Philippines, weeks at sea running drills, liberties in ports he never knew existed and various humanitarian assignments. Girls. He knew the Navy was his destiny and career choice.

Screw it, he dug for a dime for the pay phone. He tossed back his whiskey and headed to the phone in the corner. Hopefully, he could keep her on the line—if she answered. On the other hand, he hoped his sassy woman didn't cuss him like a sailor.

Tiny looked up from his pool shot and shook his head at Bobby. Bobby knew Tiny wouldn't approve of him caving. He avoided his gaze and picked up the dirty, scratched receiver from the chrome cradle. Once the dime dropped into the coin bin, two bells signaled that there was a dial tone. One more breath and he dialed her number. He felt a little panic when the phone rang on the other end. But, instead of Rose's voice, a recording informed him the number had been disconnected and was no longer in service.

Maybe I didn't dial it right, he thought. *I am nervous.* He heard the dime drop. After his two dings and a live dial tone, he dialed slowly, doublechecking his numbers. The same recording! She couldn't hate him so much that she changed her number, could she? Anger took over and he slammed the receiver several times. He turned around and shoved his way back to his barstool. Tiny was waiting on him. Two shots of whiskey sat beside the beers.

"Don't start, Tiny," Bobby said and slugged his shot.

"Did she give you the business or just not pick up?"

Bobby could feel his jaw pulsing and his face warm from embarrassment. "The phone is disconnected. What's she doing? Playing fucking games?"

"Bobby, you broke it off with her two weeks ago. I'd guess she's more hurt than you know," Tiny reminded him. "Hell, I'd want to marry you!"

Bobby just stared. "You're going to drive me by her house before we head back to base, aren't you?"

"Sure. But, I need to get a couple numbers before we go," Tiny excused himself. "Relax Higgins. Have a beer and enjoy the scenery."

The car was quiet. Bobby was smoking a cigarette and brushed away the hair from his forehead. In spite of the humidity, the wind in his face helped calm him. "Turn left on Pennman. We're almost there." The clicking of the blinker matched Bobby's heart. "She's probably already dating someone else."

"Bobby, she has four children."

"So? My mom had nine," Bobby wrestled with the rationale of the situation. "There's more to her past than just four girls. She was married to an officer. I'm just a country boy. Over there," he pointed. "It's the last house on the left."

Tiny slowed and parked in front. The house was dark, no car in the driveway, and a For Sale sign was planted in the front yard. "Are you sure it's this one?"

The passenger door slammed and Bobby was already jogging towards the house, ignoring Tiny.

He peeked into the side light window and furiously rang the door bell. In spite of the lack of light, it was obvious the house was vacant. Defeated, he walked back to the car, turning once more to look at what might have been his future.

"She's gone," Bobby dropped into the red vinyl seat. "I left my watch, I abandoned them. I've got to find her."

Chapter 24

APRIL, 2004

"I need a bathroom break," Audrey said, extracting herself from the sister cocoon. Elizabeth was shaken by Audrey's confession. Dorothy's famous line from *The Wizard of Oz* ran through her head... there's no place like home. Elizabeth watched her sister pull from the room after her tender confession. She'd wanted Audrey back home a long time ago. Their own girls were like sisters but life had limited them to phone calls instead of sleep-overs.

"I'll be out back on the porch," Rebecca said as she picked up her purse, digging deep. "I'm grabbing a smoke." She picked up her water and headed towards the kitchen door.

Elizabeth had noticed Rebecca's hands shaking and thought she heard a telltale rattle from inside her sister's purse. "Rebecca? Are you okay?"

Without turning, Rebecca answered, "After John's phone call, it's conspicuously quiet. That's unlike him. I'll be back in a minute."

"I'm going to check my cell phone and pop some popcorn," Mallory said as she gathered empty salsa bowls. "I saw some white cheddar salt and I'll make a bowl with Old Bay seasoning too." She left the living room, scrolling her phone while carrying the stacked bowls.

Elizabeth reached for her warm wine glass. She walked over to the dining room window to check on Rebecca. Unnoticed, she saw her sister on the deck popping a pill. *What's really going on, Rebecca?*

Before she could be seen, Elizabeth turned and scoured the room. Photos focused on her parents as grandparents. Built-in bookshelves were exploding with educational hardbacks. The old World Book Encyclopedias were shelved and had been replaced by the internet. The dated gold vein mirror squares clung to the wall over the couch. The eighteen-year-old parquet tile was chipping and peeling. The china cabinet held four porcelain angels, representing each month of her sisters' births. Well-used cookbooks were stacked on the lower shelf. A pole lamp guarded the cornered upholstered chair. Every square foot held a memory of her childhood, of her parents, of her little sisters.

Audrey emerged from the bathroom foyer. "You seem sad, are you okay?"

Elizabeth looked up and smiled weakly. "Just looking at all the memories. Do you remember when Mom decided to cover the hardwood with this parque tile? I was stunned."

Audrey returned to her spot on the couch. "Poor Daddy on his knees peeling off the paper and pressing this entire part of the house. I think he was trying to get us settled in before his Med-cruise."

"Yep. We moved in April and I graduated while he was at sea in June," Elizabeth said, squeezing the words past the lump in her throat. "God, I'd put them through so much that year. In spite of immersing myself in the church youth group; I was frustrated. I just wanted a normal life." Elizabeth snorted. "Exactly what *is* a normal life?"

"You're the psychologist!" Audrey volleyed back. "I don't remember a lot of that conflict, just when I told you that Mom wasn't mailing your letter to our father."

Elizabeth tried to ignore the memory of the explosion when she confronted her mom. "Well, when you are about to graduate and have no career goals, no boyfriend. I felt so lost. All my classmates had been pursuing college and I was working at McDonalds. But, in hindsight...poor Mom. Four teens and one woman, all with periods. Geez, and I just have one PMS teen."

The porch door squeaked and the popcorn stopped popping. The voices from the kitchen grew louder as they entered the living room. Elizabeth looked at Audrey and made the locked lips signal... closing the subject between them. She picked up her step-dad's service file again and flipped to a paper that documented them to the Navy as his stepdaughters. She smiled. "Y'all remember when Daddy found us in Maryland and married Mom?"

Chapter 25

MAYPORT, FL - JUNE, 1968

E lizabeth had finally climbed on her best friend's tire swing. It hung from a huge live oak with a tug of war rope hung both vertically and horizontally. All the kids in the neighborhood looked for the signal to pull back and sweep the tire and her to the top limbs. School was over. The summer days were becoming longer and kids wandered the neighborhood. Locusts sung from the live oaks.

The teen from across the street said, "Pull..." and Elizabeth felt the rope rock her several times, gaining momentum. "Let go," he instructed. Her stomach dropped and she tightened her grip when the tire swing crested the roof line.

The kids below her heckled and laughed as she squeezed her eyes and scrawny legs as the tire swing slowed. She recognized her sisters jeering but forced herself to celebrate the adrenaline rush. *This was highly overrated,* she thought. Four kids rushed the swing and she became obsolete.

For an hour she sat cross-legged under the smaller oak. She and her best friend had spent hours climbing and reading *MAD Magazine* in this tree. She loved when they learned new words to *I'm Dreaming of a White Sheep Dog* adapted to the tune of *White Christmas.* She even knew Bing Crosby sang it every holiday season. Her mom saturated their home with music. But recently the music had become sad. Things were disappearing from the house. The kittens were allowed to be out later at night and soon they had disappeared with no explanation. So had her mom's nice boyfriend.

Elizabeth was shaken from her musings when she heard the neighbor kids yelling, "The mosquito truck is on the next street." The boys whooped and dropped the tire rope. She knew they were headed home to be ready to ride bikes behind the bug spray cloud. She resigned herself to trudging home to their sad house. Her sisters ignored her call to head home. She plucked a stalk of sour weed in the spare lot. As she chewed and sucked, she heard her mom's voice in her head, *a dog could've peed on that.*

As she chomped it aggressively she thought, *Mr. Bobby hasn't been visiting.* It reminded her of the last time her father returned and confronted their mom about something. He'd left as fast as he'd arrived.

But one of the new songs playing in the house was when she learned a new word, divorce. There was a spelling song.... D-I-V-O-R-C-E. Her mom played it a lot and cried when she thought they weren't looking. Elizabeth suspected they were too much work. How could she help Mommy? She threw down the forbidden sour weed. Walking up the driveway, the car was backed up to the open garage.

She opened the front door, ignoring the odd way her mom had parked. Rebecca was chattering in her mom's back bedroom. Rebecca hadn't slept in her bunk for the last week. "Who's back?" her mom shouted.

"Me, Mom," Elizabeth answered. She smelled chicken TV dinners in the oven and smiled. She loved mixing up her corn, mash potatoes and butter in the little aluminum tray.

"Where are your sisters?"

"They were down at Susan's on the tire swing. Probably headed home," Elizabeth reported. "I tried to get them to follow me."

"Grab a shower before dinner," she shouted. "Pajamas are on the bed."

Before Elizabeth turned towards the bathroom, her mother shuffled to the garage with a cardboard box. Puzzled, Elizabeth went to get her pajamas and clean underwear. She opened the dresser drawer. It was empty.

She checked other drawers and they, too, all stood empty. She heard Audrey and Mallory teasing each other as they banged their way in through the front door. She slammed the drawers closed and climbed the bunk ladder to grab her pajamas. At least her mom remembered to add panties too. Her dolls and comic books were lined up across the white glossy shelf. Her gold Siamese dancer dolls posed with beautiful crowns. She remembered helping her father build the bunks. The old ache resurfaced. She loved following him around when he came home from sea. *Maybe we chased Mr. Bobby away...like dad.*

The aroma of chicken dinner was calling. She scuttled down the ladder and headed off to clean up. She needed to ask her mom if she could spend the night with Susan on Friday. She felt the ache go away and smiled as she walked to the bathroom.

Chapter 26

APRIL, 2004

"I remember the lights being turned on and being told to use the bathroom before we got in the car," Mallory said, putting the popcorn bowls on the coffee table. "I asked her why and she said we were going to see Grandmom. She always drove at night so I didn't think a whole lot about it."

"The back of the car was crammed with suitcases and boxes. Our cat was under the seat yowling. I tried to soothe her and got scratched," Audrey added. "She was always a little bitchy."

"I don't remember getting in the car but did wake up with my head on Mom's lap, cuddling Freddie," Rebecca recalled. "I can still smell pine trees blowing in from her rolled down window.

"And skunk!" Mallory added.

"Anyway, I'd start to drift back to sleep and she'd punch that button on the floor changing the headlights. Every time it clicked, headlights passed us and she'd go back to using the brights."

"That was a dark two-lane highway." Elizabeth joined in. "I remember the click of her changing radio stations. The beige buttons were worn and they always reminded me of chiclets,"

"Nothing on most of that highway except a few small motels with neon lights announcing vacancies. And, our beloved South of the Border signs," Audrey added. "I always knew we were close when I smelled exhaust fumes from driving through the Baltimore tunnel." She punctuated her memory with mock vomiting.

"Don't forget the taste of those saltine and peanut butter crackers. Imagine…we were clueless that summer would change our lives," Elizabeth said with a hint of melancholy. "And Daddy's." Then she smiled and grabbed some popcorn.

MAYPORT, FL - AUGUST, 1968

"I think I'm close," Bobby said, inhaling deeply from his cigarette. He looked across the bar at the stool where he'd first seen Rose. There was a brunette looking back at him. She gave him a flirtatious wave. Not wanting to be rude or worse, encouraging, Bobby nodded politely and shifted his attention to Tiny.

"It's been over a month, Bobby! Don't you think it's obvious she doesn't want to be found? Look around. There are so many women just for the pickings. Most of them with no kids."

"Damn it, Tiny! Those little girls are not a deal breaker," Bobby said, glaring at Tiny, daring him to insult Rose. "I've spent time with Rose in her home and those four girls. They're shy, charming, spunky and cute. The little one loves to sit in my lap and read Dr. Seuss books." Bobby fought back tears. "I'm tired of being alone and trolling bars. And—bachelor quarters? Jesus, I'm not a kid anymore."

"Okay, okay! I'm not here to talk you out of finding her," Tiny said and lit a cigarette. "I just hate seeing this get under your skin. Tell me why you're close?"

"Rose is good friends with the neighbors a couple doors down. They babysat Rebecca when we went out. Sometimes on the weekend, we'd all get together and cook-out. The kids played well together. It was happy. Well, lots of laughter and the usual bickering."

Bobby grew quiet and flipped his Zippo open and closed.

"Then they probably know something. Hope they like you."

Bobby felt his whiskey hitting and the pain was dulled. Before he could answer, the jukebox blared Dolly Parton's song. He flinched and felt like she was singing to him, *When you left you thought I'd sit, An' you thought I'd wait, An' you thought I'd cry, You called me a dumb blond, Ah, but somehow I lived through it...* "Bartender, another round." Bobby pointed back and forth between him and Tiny. "Remember that song was playing the night I met Rose here?"

"You remember that?" Tiny said, looking at Bobby with a lifted brow. "I can't remember the names of some of my dates the morning after."

"I saw her sing that song on the Porter Wagner show. Just thought of it as another one of those women's libber jabs," Bobby reached for his whiskey and shot it in one swig. "Touche!"

"Pretty soon they'll be pumping their own gas." Tiny raised his glass in toast fashion. "Damn girls! Making life complicated and changing all the rules. They need to watch re-runs of Leave it to Beaver." Tiny chuckled and shook his head.

"Glad you're amusing yourself. Here's a thought for you... how would you like having sex with June Cleaver?" Bobby said and they both laughed and shook their heads no. "I'll take my spunky blonde Rose."

"Good luck with that. Hope the neighbors have something for you," Tiny said and ran his fingers through his hair.

"I'm supposed to go over in the morning and talk to Ruth. I'm sure she'll try and feed me." Bobby stared into his beer. "I think she likes me. Hell, I hope so."

AUGUST, 1968 – HAVRE DE GRACE, MD

Elizabeth and Audrey were doing breakfast dishes for their grandmother. Mallory and Rebecca were in the other room watching Saturday morning cartoons. The small house had no privacy; a living room merged into the eat-in kitchen. Since Elizabeth could remember visiting her grandparents, they always made room for them. Quilts were folded into sleeping pads and someone got the couch. Her mother and grandmother were sitting across the room, drinking coffee and smoking, engaged in a barely audible discussion. Glancing over her shoulder, she watched her mom crush the butt into the ashtray. She'd been fascinated with the same well-used plaid beanbag ashtray they'd been using for years.

"Did you have fun at Aunt Daisy's?" Audrey asked Elizabeth while she dried another plate and put it on the stack.

How did she answer that? She'd been sent to her aunt's house for over a week. She was still reeling from her mother's announcement that they weren't going back to Jacksonville Beach. Mom was looking for a new home and would enroll them in school later in the summer.

"I play with Kelly while Aunt Daisy watches soap operas," Elizabeth whispered. She didn't want the adults to hear her complain. "Kelly cut up worms and put them in dirt to make muffins in her little baking toys. She pulls off lightning bug bodies and puts them on her fingers as jewelry. Aunt Daisy thinks it's cute. I don't think she likes me. I cried a lot."

Audrey shrugged and started drying the glasses. "It might not be that bad. We'll be here when it snows and we can make snowmen, ice skate or have snowball fights. Didn't you have fun at the July 4th carnival at the park?"

"We do that every summer when we're here on vacation. I want to go home and be with my best friend, play kickball in the street and watch *Dark Shadows* eating a Pop Tart," Elizabeth said in a voice hopefully low and private to her sister. She swished her hand around the dirty water for the rubber sink stopper. It reminded her of a rubber pancake and didn't always hold the water for the whole wash job.

"Are you almost done girls? It's still cool enough to go down to the waterfront. Your uncle is already there riding his mini-bike," their mom said. It was obvious she wanted them to leave so the adults could talk. Elizabeth jumped off the stepstool and headed to the living room. "Your grandmother has some stale crackers you can share with the ducks," her mom added.

"Can I finish watching Bugs Bunny first?" Elizabeth asked.

"Fine but be finding your sneakers and be ready to go outside for a while." Elizabeth couldn't put her finger on the look on her mother's face. It kind of looked like the way she got when Mr. Bobby came over, but her cigarette trembled in her hand.

Elizabeth lifted the sofa skirt and sorted through the shoes hidden and out of the way. She pulled Mallory's plaid ones, her white ones and guessed Audrey would not get her white ones dirty. "Is Rebecca going with us?" Elizabeth realized she'd interrupted the women's chattering.

"Absolutely not. Aunt Daisy is coming over in a little bit. She can play out back with Kelly," her mom answered.

Audrey plopped the wax bag of saltines on the couch and looked under it for her shoes. Mallory and Rebecca were laughing at Marvin the Martian. Elizabeth sat behind them, tying her shoes and leaning on the doorway, listening to her mom and grandmom.

"What are you going to do, Rose?" her grandmother asked, refilling their coffee cups.

"Ruth wasn't supposed to tell him where I am," she answered. "I'm on the list for subsidized housing and the base may have a job for me. I've been putting in applications downtown. A couple of classmates have already called. Mom, I'm so confused. Damn it, I'll show all of them I can take care of myself."

"But you always sounded so happy when you called."

"Mom, we've been talking about this for weeks. I can't take care of the girls or find a decent job in Florida." Her mother paused and Elizabeth heard a match strike. She looked over her shoulder and glanced at her mother. Her hand was still shaking. "I feel like I've been a single mom for a long time—even when John and I were mar-

214

ried. Maybe this is the way it's supposed to be as a Navy wife but I don't like it."

Elizabeth slowly pretended to watch cartoons but was not going to ignore the conversation in the kitchen. *Maybe their father was coming back!*

"At least tell her to give him our number. Just talk to him, Rose." Elizabeth's grandmother said it so low that Elizabeth strained to hear.

"Mom, I sold the house, the furniture and the girls' toys and souvenirs from overseas. I'd have to go back and start over." Her mom leaned over her coffee cup. Elizabeth couldn't see her eyes but could feel her sadness. "I have a better chance here to find a house and job. It's lonely down there."

Elizabeth teared up at the thought of her Siamese twin dolls that she'd left guarding her bed in what was now somebody else's bedroom. *What was so bad that her mom would do that? What had they done to make Mom so mad? Was it putting the kitten on Mr. Bobby's leg? He never seemed mad at them for that, but he must've been.*

The living room door rattled and Aunt Daisy bounced in with Kelly. For a second, Elizabeth was distracted from the kitchen talk. Kelly ran over to Rebecca and started giggling, showing her a new pink ball.

"Hey, Rose. I'm here for you, baby. Hey Mom," Aunt Daisy hugged them both and went around the corner. The sound of the metal cabinet opened and closed. The jiggling of the coffee cup on the saucer accompanied her back to the table. "I got your call this morning while I was making Kelly pancakes. I came as soon as I could."

"Girls, it's time to go play. Be back by lunch," Elizabeth's mom's voice didn't sound debatable. "Maybe we can get subs down at Viola's."

All three jumped up, Audrey grabbed the crackers and they headed for the alley. They'd walked down the hill and over to the waterfront many a summer. The smell of hamburgers hovered on the sidewalk as they passed a line of patrons out the door of Shorty's Grill.

As they crossed Eerie Street, the smell of the brackish marina grew stronger, combined with a hint of tar from the docks, all so familiar. Mallory started running towards the swings. "Later!"

"Don't leave the park!" Elizabeth yelled, sounding too much like their mother. Audrey and Elizabeth looked for a dock with less activity. Marina patrons didn't bother them if they hung out on the less busy docks.

"There's the mama duck over there... hanging by the reeds," Audrey said and pointed.

"Look how big those babies are!" Elizabeth sighed and smiled. "Give me some crackers." Both of them walked to the end of the dock and sat with their legs dangling over the water. Audrey crackled the wax paper and pulled a single cracker out. The mother duck quacked and headed towards them. Minnows skimmed the surface as if they knew the crumbs were up for grabs.

"Seriously, give me some crackers, Audrey." Elizabeth wasn't in the mood for Audrey's selfishness, especially after hearing there wasn't anything left of her stuff in Jacksonville Beach. Audrey handed her a couple more crackers. "Want to know a secret?" Elizabeth wanted to spill but wondered if she should tell Audrey anything. Maybe she should be as stingy with her intel as Audrey was with crackers. And crayons. And her Barbies.

"You found out that Mom took us to Big Cone for ice cream when you were at Aunt Daisy's?" Audrey threw her barb Elizabeth's way.

"Audrey, why do you do that? Why do you have to say stuff to hurt?" Elizabeth refused to let her see tears. *Focus on the mother duck and babies. They love me.* Audrey quietly handed her two more crackers. Elizabeth took that as an apology.

"Okay, so what's the secret?"

"Mom is talking about someone wanting to find her here. Do you think Daddy is coming back?" Elizabeth asked.

"Daddy's in California. I heard Mom say she would never go that far away from her family," Audrey answered. Now Elizabeth was confused.

"She told Grandmom that she gave everything away. The only thing I grabbed was Daddy's Bible when I grabbed my pillow for the ride," Elizabeth's voice was flat. She avoided looking at Audrey.

Neither girl spoke. They watched the ducks instead, paddling at their feet to greedily grab up the crackers. The sound of a mini-bike motor made them both turn to the playground. Mallory was hopping on the back with their uncle and he peeled back to the trail.

"She better not come back hurt," Elizabeth moaned. "It'll be my fault.... again."

No one spoke. For Elizabeth, the morning's adult conversation was complicated, too hard to figure out. Audrey didn't seem concerned. Elizabeth didn't understand moving without the Navy van. Finding the familiar brown boxes, drawing paper insulating their treasures and the anticipation of their father returning from sea. This was different, like they'd all run away from home.

The silence was broken by the sound of the train crossing the Black Bridge. The whistle blew and the tracks made their familiar clickety-clack under the weight of the boxcars' wheels. It was the same hypnotic sound Elizabeth heard three times a day, and once more at night as they settled into their beds on the floor.

"That's all the crackers," Audrey announced and balled up the wax paper. "Hey, I have a dime that I found. When we go to Viola's, want me to buy you some penny candy?"

"Can I get a Sugar Daddy?" It cost a penny or she could get something five for a penny. But Elizabeth knew how to make it last for days. She just rewrapped and hid it. There wasn't any point to chewing it. It got stuck in her teeth and became more work than fun.

"Sure," Audrey answered nonchalantly. "Let's go to the swings and try and get Mallory. We need to get home soon."

Before they'd gotten there, Mallory came around the corner on the mini-bike grimacing. Their uncle headed towards them, then squeezed the brakes, spraying dust all over them. "What's wrong?" Audrey and Elizabeth said at the same time.

"I burned my leg on the muffler," Mallory said, revealing a fresh burn on her upper calf. "Mom's going to kill me. I can't cover this in these shorts."

"My mom is going to freak out if Dad finds out," the uncle said panicked. Everyone looked at each other as they silently brainstormed.

It was Audrey who spoke first. "Before me and Elizabeth get the subs, I'll pull out my clam diggers. They should be long enough. Where should we put them?"

"How about under the steps by the laundry room door?" Elizabeth suggested and looked at Mallory. "You'll have to figure out where to change."

"Let's head back now. Y'all wait and bring the bike to the backyard in about ten minutes," Audrey said and turned around. Elizabeth and Audrey jogged towards the alley.

"I can smell the subs already and taste my Sugar Daddy," Elizabeth said grinning, refusing to think about

Mallory's burn. The three musketeers were at their finest against childhood angst. They passed the hamburger grill, up the alley with tar bubbles starting to emerge like acne. They politely opened the gate and the laundry room door, ready to take everyone's lunch order. But the room was silent and they saw their mom cradling the phone.

Elizabeth instinctively knew not to speak and her grandmother's finger at her lips confirmed. Elizabeth only heard the final words of her mother. "You can tell him to call me before my dad gets home from work. If he doesn't, I can't talk. (pause) I have to go. No, I'm not mad at you, Ruth." She hung up the receiver and turned towards the kitchen.

"Good girls. We're ready to order lunch. Where's Mallory?" Rose asked.

"She and Scott are walking back with the mini-bike," Elizabeth said. *It really isn't a lie*, she told herself. Her mom reached under the living room table for her purse.

"Three Italian subs, cut in quarters. That's four pieces," her mom instructed and handed her a ten-dollar bill. "Don't play on the way and stay away from Big John's house. You never know if he's sober or not." Elizabeth just took that as a warning. She knew the house but she hadn't had the word *sober* in a spelling bee.

"Okay, Mommy," Audrey said and gave her a hug, hiding the pants as they skipped out the back door.

After they tucked the pants, they went out the back gate. Elizabeth stepped gingerly up the tar alley, avoiding getting tar bubbles on her sneakers. Insects were singing from the cherry trees. She felt sweat rolling down her back.

"Was Mommy talking to our neighbor, Mrs. Parsons?" Audrey asked.

"That's what it sounded like to me," Elizabeth answered, trying to hide her excitement. *Maybe we'll get back home... wherever that was.*

AUGUST, 1968

It had taken two hours for Bobby to convince Ruth to admit she knew where Rose was hiding. He'd bought extra time to plead for her help by offering to make biscuits from scratch. She made it clear that Rose was moving on but wouldn't tell him where.

By the end of breakfast, she finally agreed to try and call her friend.

"I can't promise I'll reach her," Ruth said and opened her address book.

"I'll wait on the porch," Bobby said, closing the door. He looked down the street at Rose's house. The For Sale sign was gone and a red VW was in the driveway. In less than five minutes, Ruth opened the front door. She wasted no time telling him Rose needed to think about it.

"She said she would call me by lunch," Ruth said. Bobby felt numb, like the tiny blonde had him by the balls. His emotional scale would be tipped one way or the other.

"Thanks for doing that, Ruth. Do you mind if I wait?" he asked.

"Of course! I need to clean the kitchen," Ruth said, holding the door open. She gently patted his back as he walked by.

"Let me help. I made part of the mess," Bobby said politely.

"I've got this and it will help me pass time," Ruth said and tussled her son's head as he was glued to the cartoons on TV. "Terry, why don't you go play outside some before it gets too hot."

"Only if I can play with my b.b. gun," Terry said defiantly.

Ruth rolled her eyes and Bobby silently agreed. There were bigger fish to fry right now. "Bobby, do you mind getting his gun off the top of the bookshelf?" She headed for the kitchen cabinet and removed the box of b.b.s.

Terry jumped up from the TV. "Thanks Mr. Bobby." He ran towards the patio doors, stopping long enough to grab the box from his mom.

Bobby snapped the television off and picked up the morning paper. "If you really don't need help, do you mind if I read the paper? There was another nuclear test by France on Muruora Island and conflict in the Suez Canal."

Bobby knew the base activity was at an all time high alert. He hoped at least that Rose's revolt and emotional atom bomb dropped into his personal life was moving towards a faster truce. He struggled every day to push the distractions aside to keep his job from suffering. Yeah, she'd definitely shown him that she was no dumb blonde.

"Sure, but I want the crossword puzzle," Ruth shouted from the kitchen.

He settled into the chair across from the quirky Felix the Cat clock. He felt mocked as the eyes and tail ticked away each second for forty long minutes. Finally, the phone rang and Ruth rushed to answer. Bobby's heart raced and he broke out in a sweat.

"Hello? Oh hey, honey," Ruth said, looking at Bobby and shaking her head. "Everything's good but can I call you back? I need to leave the line open." (pause) "Yes, he's still here. Rose may be calling soon and I don't want the line busy." (pause) "Okay, we'll see you in a few hours." There were no words exchanged in the room as she hung up the phone.

Bobby read his way to the Sports page. The Milwaukee Braves had moved to Atlanta. He'd been a huge fan while on his Westpacs. Now, they were in the South. Last year while visiting his sister in Atlanta, they'd gone to a game. Maybe one day he would take Rose and the girls to a game. Felix was still grinning from across the room as the hands approached noon. "Hey, Ruth. Do you think Rose would like going to a baseball game?"

Before she answered, the phone rang. Ruth crossed her fingers at Bobby. "Hello?" Hey, Rose."

Bobby stood up and pointed at the patio doors. He wanted them to talk without him—plus he needed a cigarette. He just wanted to wait and hear Rose's decision without second-guessing what was being said.

Bobby paced outside. Her son was shooting his b.b. gun at beer cans lined up on a sawhorse. He wondered what Rose's girls were doing.

"Mr. Bobby, watch this," Terry shouted. The pings from his gun hit each can and for good measure, he knocked a little green plastic soldier from the sawhorse. "See that? I'm going to be an Army man!"

"Not a sailor?" Bobby asked, snubbing out his cigarette.

"I can't swim and I want to shoot guns," Terry answered. He turned around, sat cross-legged and poured more b.b.s into his Red Ryder.

The patio door slid open and Ruth motioned for Bobby to come back inside. They went into the living room. The couch was covered with clear plastic and crackled as he sat.

He saw nothing in Ruth's facial expression. "That was fast," Bobby remarked, not knowing if it was a good thing or bad news. "Just give it to me straight."

"You can have the number but you have to call before 4:00," Ruth smiled. "She's open to talking."

As he listened, he realized he had been holding his breath. "Where is she?"

"I can give you the number but she'll tell you what she wants you to know," Ruth said, protecting the trust between her and Rose. "I need to make lunch. Want a sandwich?"

"Only if it comes with a beer. Or two," Bobby said. He needed to close the deal. "I've thought about what I want to say for weeks. Suddenly, I'm drawing a blank."

Ruth held up her wedding band finger. "I believe it's, *Will you marry me?*"

Bobby felt his face flush and nodded his head. "Can I use your phone after lunch? I'll pay you for the long-distance charges."

"Of course. I'll take Terry out for ice cream down at the beach and call Frank to meet us," Ruth said, already thinking ahead to prevent Bobby from getting cold feet.

★ ★ ★

Bobby and Tiny were sitting at a table on the beach at The Seaturtle Inn. Bobby nervously cracked crab legs and washed them down with his beer.

"Did you have any problem getting leave?" Tiny said, licking cocktail sauce from his fingers. "We're slammed with work orders."

"I have a bunch of leave saved up. I think Chief Russell is hoping I'll get refocused once I bring them all back," Bobby said, digging through his steam bucket. "Everyone has been a lot of help so I did find a house and made a plane reservation. Uniform's ready and my watches are covered."

"How long are you going to be gone?"

"A week. I'll fly out in the morning and Rose is picking me up in Baltimore. She's got the..." Bobby stopped before he said it. "God, what a scary word." Bobby laughed shakily and shook his head. He stared out on the low tide line. The sound of the waves relieved some of the anxiety gripping his gut. "Rose has the marriage license. We can get married any time after tomorrow."

"What about the girls?"

"Rose's sisters are splitting them up for a couple days. They're good girls and doubt they'll be hard to handle. You need another beer?" Bobby saw the waitress heading their way.

"Sure. We'll go in later and I'll buy you your last bachelor whiskey shot!" You're breaking a lot of hearts!" Tiny said, raising his eyebrows and cocking him a shitty grin. He leaned forward and his face changed. "But, seriously, aren't you a little scared becoming a husband and an instant father?"

Bobby paused and swirled his answer in his head like brandy in a snifter. "This may sound corny but I had the best parents that a child could ask for. They always found a way to take care of all of us. Pops would share with anyone in the town that needed something. We didn't always have enough to share. It wasn't unusual to have more than one iron in the fire while they figured out how to keep food on our table, clothes on our backs."

The waitress brought the new round of beers. Bobby waited until she left the table and continued to answer Tiny's question. "I think I'm less intimidated about being a father than I am a husband. Scenarios play of the wrong guy neglecting or abusing Rose, predators on the girls... we've seen and heard it all from port to port. Bottom line is Rose makes me smile and keeps me on my toes. I want to take care of them. They bring something soft to my rough edges."

"What about their father? Her ex? Is she still in love with him?"

Bobby cringed inside as Tiny turned up the heat on the sore subject. "She said he's hardly home. Besides, he's been sent across the country to school. She won't leave the East Coast. Her family's her anchor when she's lonely," Bobby said. "And we know Navy wages don't leave a lot of room to buy plane tickets. Damn, I had to scramble for mine. Worth every dime when I get...my girls... home. Mrs. Rose Higgins and her four little women. Oh, and a damn cat! Now, is this interrogation over? We're supposed to be drinking."

"Sounds like a Doris Day and Cary Grant movie. Okay, let's go inside and have some shots. Get this testosterone party started," Tiny said and slapped Bobby on the back. "If we keep going this way, before you know it, we'll be trading our fruit of the looms for panties."

Bobby laughed and couldn't resist adding, "I see lots of panties in my future! Are you following the Braves?"

"Yankees fan."

"Of course you are," Bobby couldn't help but notice the polarities between him and Tiny. "What do we have in common?"

"The Navy," Tiny said, turning on his heel as a cute co-ed flirted at him. "And the ladies, Bobby."

HAVRE DE GRACE, MD – 1968

The living room was cramped as cousins and siblings grabbed any real estate to watch Bowling for Dollars. The smell of spaghetti and garlic bread wafted in from the kitchen. Elizabeth was distracted from the excitement of the adults eating at the table by the TV show airing from Baltimore. The emcee called the next bowling contestant to draw from the huge bin of postcards.

"You know the rules, Mr. Carter. Our jackpot is $720 and if you get a strike, you will split it with your pen pal. Please pull a postcard from the pile." The emcee opened the cage and Mr. Carter dug deep and presented it to the host. "Okay, head to the bowling lane and you will be sharing your winnings with.... Mrs. Helen Boukbumner."

Elizabeth and the entire room erupted in laughter at the last name. Mallory started pairing the last name with her sisters. "Elizabeth Boukbumner! Audrey Boukbumner!"

Uncle Scott elbowed Audrey who had grabbed a place on the couch. "Hey, your mom could be a Boukbumner." They both laughed as Elizabeth glared from the floor, cross legged in front of the small black and white TV.

"Can you be quiet so we can see if he wins the jackpot? There's a cool trip to London if he makes two strikes in a row," Elizabeth hissed. She felt cranky and hungry. She tried to ignore the smell of her grandmother's dinner. The adults were taking a long time to finish.

But the dining room was buzzing with a hidden excitement among the adult females surrounding her mom. For several days, Pig-latin was being used a lot when the kids were around.

"You know I wrote the pen pal post card address down for Grandmom? She put the stamp on and I took it to the post office," Audrey bragged. "They do this show in Baltimore near where we get the Gordon bluecrabs."

Elizabeth ignored the bragging. It was a normal exercise in these situations to get drawn into Audrey's word duels. But the visual of a bushel of blue crabs being scattered on the picnic table in the backyard reminded her again of how hungry she was. She knew how to clean a blue crab and use the little wooden hammer on the leg and claw meat. The yellow can of Old Bay seafood spice followed her family, regardless of the military moves. They used it on crabs, shrimp and even popcorn. The crashing of the bowling pins reminded Elizabeth to ignore that memory for her grumbling tummy.

"Look, he did it. He and Mrs. Boukbumner get another chance to win the trip!" Mallory shouted. "You know they might get to fly on an airplane if he wins the next part." The bowling ball spun down the lane and hit the king pin square on. Mr. Carter and his peanut galley in the studio jumped to their feet as all the ten pins viciously fell off the wooden platform.

Contrasting the melodic tenor of falling bowling pins, the sound of plates being scraped at the sink distracted her from the victory. Elizabeth watched her grandparents head to the porch door to smoke in the backyard as moms began dishing out spaghetti for the kids.

"Okay, plates are heading to the table. Come and get it but remember, Scott and Audrey have dish duty," Aunt Daisy said. There were six servings and a pitcher of Kool-Aid in the center of the table. The pitcher's purple face smiled and sweated on the red and white checked vinyl table cloth. It was just like the one in the TV commercial. But he didn't speak, just stared at all of them, waiting to be drunk.

Scott, Audrey and Mallory ran past Elizabeth as she refocused on Mr. Carter jumping up and down with his second strike. Now, he got to try for that new car after the following commercials. The Ivory soap commercial immediately played ahead of the car battery sale. Maybe Audrey was right, Grandmom filled the bathroom with Ivory soap because of wishing to be the pen pal wanna-be. For as long as she could remember when bathing in the small bathroom at their visits it always smelled like soap. The soft, soggy soap reminded her of how many had hit the shower before her.

As Elizabeth stared at the release of the third ball for the new car, she was shaken back to reality by her mom's voice. "Elizabeth, dinner time. Turn off the TV and let's get done." The ball and pins crashed and two pins remained upright.

"Coming, Mom," Elizabeth felt sorry for the man in the blue bowling shirt but had to admire his courage to take a chance on TV. He didn't win it all but his family still jumped all over him. The emcee handed him a lottery ticket and sent the audience back to a new advertisement. No one seemed to be disappointed.

She clicked the program off and headed to her plate of spaghetti. Mr. Carter hit a sore spot. She missed the circle of her family unanchored by a man who risked winning or losing in front of his loved ones. She used to feel that way about her parents. She wanted to be that brave for someone and surrounded by smiles and hugs.

"Okay girls. We'll be outside. Don't waste time if you want to play before bedtime," Rose said, grabbing two plates off the dining room table. "Rebecca and Kelly are with us. Get done and head out. I have something to tell you." Her smile was different than it had been for the past few weeks.

"Did Grandmom get picked for Bowling for Dollars?" Audrey asked. Scott nudged her, suppressing a chuckle.

Elizabeth saw a gleam in her mom's eye and her cryptic comment intrigued her. "Well, no, but we have hit the jackpot and there is an amazing adventure in our future."

Elizabeth overheard Scott whisper to Audrey, "Your new name is going to be Boukbumner and you get to look at pictures of their honeymoon in London!"

Elizabeth kept her head down and sprinkled parmesan cheese on her spaghetti. She watched her grape Kool-Aid sweat from the small glass jelly jar. Eating quietly, she finished before the others and walked to the sink with her plate. She could look out the window at the adults laughing below. The aluminum green and white woven webbed chairs circled the smoking smut pot. Before she could get trapped by Audrey to help with dishes, she snuck out to the backyard. She craved some alone time. For weeks, she felt as if she'd lived in piles. They slept in piles, crammed in the car for drives in the country and shouldered in a small room to watch TV. She missed her best friend. Ever since they'd left Florida, Elizabeth felt her life was claustrophobic. She stayed in the shadows and quietly sat at the redwood picnic table, alone with her thoughts.

Fireflies blinked and bats dove in and out of the alley street light. Elizabeth loved the graceful dance of the fireflies. They were like fairies. She'd patiently held out her hand, waiting for one to rest. She hoped they knew she had no intent to pluck the magical green pulsing light for her own selfish vanity. *My name's not Kelly*, she whispered to her fairy friends sitting on her palm.

As they rejoined the pulsating glowing tribe, she envied the joyous and gentle spirited army. Maybe they weren't just blinking but singing an ancient melody passed along for generations. But each summer, there were fewer and they were harder to find. Maybe she should have been a firefly with a chance to live their magical nights. But, deep inside she knew the beauty of this wondrous fragile creature did not survive without a fight. Some fell to predators, pesticides or Mason jars. Elizabeth realized that each year, her childhood felt like it was reduced to that of a firefly captured in a glass jar. There was no way out until the lid was taken off.

She watched the women engaged in lighthearted banter as they passed around a bottle of wine. Her grandfather's silhouette was framed by the shed window. It was obvious Granddaddy was absorbed in his own private tinkering project. The radio was playing an Orioles game. She heard her sister giggling and turned to see Audrey and Scott blowing bubbles from the dishwater at each other.

She hated summer. No, she hated *this* summer. This was not the way summer vacation was supposed to go. The rope was tightly knotted and she was tethered to her sisters. Her family was battered from something too advanced for her little girl mind. Daddy was gone. Her home was gone. Her friends didn't know where she was.

As she quietly sat on the edge of the old redwood picnic table, Rebecca ran over to her. "Lizabeth! Guess what? Mr. Bobby is on his way here!"

Elizabeth's heart jumped. "Are you sure?"

"Yeah! I get to go to Aunt Daisy's with Audrey tomorrow night," she said. "You and Mallory are staying with Aunt Violet."

"How do you know that?" Elizabeth asked, holding up her hand as a landing pad for the fireflies. Three of them fluttered over her palm.

"Kelly threw the ball too hard and it went under Mommy's chair. When I went to get it I heard her telling Aunt Daisy and Aunt Violet how long she needed help," Rebecca said. "You know what we get to do first tomorrow?" Elizabeth signaled *what*, with her cocked chin.

"We get to go to the laundromat, wash clothes and flip through that cool Bible story book. You know the one on the chain?" Rebecca bubbled. "It has the neatest pictures."

Elizabeth smiled. She suddenly felt ashamed that she'd ignored the lessons of hope and faith from the book she'd read many summers. Maybe all this had been a test. *Sorry, God.* "That is a really neat book. And don't forget, we get a cold Coke... if the vending machine works."

"Or Mommy will let you take us down to the candy store," Rebecca said, skipping back to her cousin. Suddenly it dawned on Elizabeth that her baby sister looked up to her. Her mother trusted her with the safety of her sisters. Her shoulders felt lighter and she sat up straighter, eager to make her mother proud.

Change was in the wind. Maybe Mr. Bobby would take the lid off the firefly jar and she'd rejoin her friends. Or better yet, he'd make two strikes for the jackpot and a trip to Florida! She'd jump up and down. Maybe even give him a hug, too.

It had been four hours since Tiny dropped Bobby off at the Jacksonville Imeson Airport. Bobby tried to get a MAC flight but if he secured a seat, it could be three days before he arrived in Baltimore. That would have been a huge chunk of his leave. Eastern Airlines provided a military discount and traveling in his service dress whites saved space in his suitcase. As he placed his hat on the floor under his window seat, he had to smile. In the concourse, he'd sat beside a young boy and his mother.

"Mr.? Can I try your hat on?" he asked, tapping on Bobby's right arm. The mother's head jerked up and she lost interest in her magazine article.

"Jimmy!" she said, but Bobby jumped in.

Bobby smiled at the memory of his brother putting his on young Bobby's beaming head. "Of course!" Bobby said, offering it to Jimmy. He couldn't help grinning as it fell cock-eyed on the little red headed boy. Jimmy couldn't be much older than Rebecca. Grinning and looking at his mom, there was a gap from a missing tooth.

"Thanks, Mr. Sailor. I can't wait to tell my dad that I got to wear a real Navy hat," Jimmy said, beaming as he handed it back. Jimmy's mother smiled and returned to her magazine.

On the plane, Bobby had been careful storing it so he didn't scuff the patent leather brim. He snuffed out his cigarette and closed the little ashtray built into the armrest as he focused on the pilot's approach to the airport.

Rose had never seen him in this uniform. He liked the summer whites, double-breasted jacket's CPO's eagle insignia on his left sleeve, and the way the six gold buttons trailed down the front, offering an elegant statement. No more crackerjacks for this Chief Petty Officer. He realized that shedding the crackerjacks for a chief's uniform was a rite of passage in his career, just like marrying Rose and her four daughters would be his rite of passage as a man.

The plane touched the runway and bounced a couple times, bringing Bobby back to his present task. He reached under his seat and retrieved his hat. No turning back. It had been the longest six weeks in his life. Even extended WESPAC deployments and FRAM overhauls hadn't caused the amount of anxiety he'd felt these past few weeks trying to find Rose.

The ladder had been rolled and secured at the plane's door. "Thank you," Bobby said to the stewardess, and covered his head. His patent leather shoes trotted down the metal stairs and briskly across the tarmac. Airport personnel pointed to the sidewalk leading to the glass doors. All these years in the Navy, he'd never searched the faces of families waiting at the end of the gangway. He and his single buddies usually hit the pier looking for the Chief's Club and easy women. Now as he entered the waiting area, he eagerly scanned the sea of faces. His gait had slowed down and he stepped aside. They'd agreed if she'd been delayed, they would meet at baggage. Before he'd resigned to heading out, he locked eyes with Rose entering the room. He wasn't waiting for her to reach him as he zig zagged through the crowd. He paused and looked at her blue eyes brimming with tears. Without thinking, his hand cradled her chin and they kissed. PDA was a no-no but he couldn't wait. He pulled her into his chest and smelled the familiar musk of her perfume. As hard as he tried to control his relief, a couple of sobs gently shook them both as he kissed her again.

"I love you, Rose," Bobby confessed, reaching for his handkerchief to try and recover from his emotional slip. "Sorry. Do you still want to marry me?"

"I better get you to the altar soon, Chief," Rose said, staring hungrily at him. "Do you know how handsome you are in that uniform?"

"Yeah, I had to beat them off in Jacksonville," Bobby smiled. He omitted that it was a little red-headed boy coveting his hat.

Rose shook her head. "Let'em try. You're mine."

Bobby placed his hand at the small of her back and led them towards baggage claim. "Yes, I am Mrs. Higgins."

He walked tall and proud beside his future wife. "How are the girls?"

"Everyone is fine and excited. My parents and sisters are waiting to give us their approval," Rose said. "I told them we would stop by first before heading to the motel." She looked up at him with a frisky grin.

"You're killing me, Rose," Bobby said, raising his eyebrows lustily.

Chapter 27

CHARLESTON, APRIL, 2004

"Road trip! Geez, we had a ton of those," Rebecca chimed in. "Getting a fifteen cent hamburger and ten cent chocolate shake? Heaven." They all hummed in agreement.

Mallory piped in, "Fish sandwich was a great treat, too!"

"Can't beat the french fries," Audrey said. "Gas pumps, motels and every private zoo from Maryland back to Florida seemed to be on the unwritten agenda. I thought Daddy flying up to get us was so cool."

"Planes were for the hoidy-toidy! Remember how respectful Daddy was when he met Granddaddy? You didn't win *him* easy!" Rebecca said, surprising Elizabeth that she remembered. "And, Granddaddy always gave us a whole dollar each for the trip home."

"I'm sure flying was to save time but Mommy's family *was* impressed. None of us had ever flown before," Elizabeth said, remembering how fast they headed back to Jacksonville Beach. Pulling off in the station wagon with her new dad at the wheel was romantic in 1968. But now, Elizabeth stared at the leave request in the file in her lap. She realized he hadn't been given much time to get his new family home and back to his job. Her tears welled up as she thought of the pressure he must have been under, the pressure he never shared with any of them. In the words of Gomer Pyle, "Shazaam," instant husband and father.

"That was a long drive home. Well, to our *new* home," Audrey added.

"That had to be exhausting. Mommy always drove at night avoiding traffic and us being awake. He had to make the trip back during the day. God knows how many *are we there yets* or *I gotta gos* tested them," Rebecca said, almost in a whisper.

"Hell, I wasn't timid. Girl gotta go, a girl gotta go," Mallory said, laughing. "Hey, he'd already survived the kittens. A road trip with four girls and a new wife? I say baptized with fire."

"Mallory, is there a time where you aren't so tough?" Rebecca asked, her voice loud and clear now. "Daddy made an amazing, life altering move. Where would we be today?"

The room grew quiet.

Elizabeth broke the silence. "All I remember about the end of that drive? Pulling into a strange driveway, the engine turned off and being told to wake up. Daddy said we were home and following him to the front door as he rattled keys. It may have been summer but it was foggy and I blew smoke walking to the door with some of the bags."

"Yep, it was a very empty house but it had power... and water bugs," Audrey said, shuddering. "Walking down the hallway to the bedrooms and hearing them crunch under that gross beige carpet runner."

Mallory laughed and threw a piece of popcorn at Elizabeth to see if she'd flinch. "Elizabeth freaked out when that fat pregnant one came flying down from the wall. Guess all the weight from her egg case and the sudden intrusion of light woke her up."

"Obviously, the water bugs didn't get the memo about the new kids in town," Elizabeth said, minimizing her freak out. She remembered squealing and slapping her hair to ensure there was no critter in her space. "I don't even remember what we slept on that night. I was pooped."

"I couldn't wait to figure out where Daddy had put us near our old house," Audrey said. "I think we left Pufnstuf in the car that night because she was hunkered under the seat."

"I didn't care. I wanted to make up my sleep-over with Susan and to let all my classmates know we were back," Elizabeth smiled. But, she knew that was a twenty-six year ago girlish wish list. Elizabeth secretly wished it had been as simple as recovering sleep-overs, kick ball in the old neighborhood and wandering in the woods. But, her memories of their first year were vivid. Between learning new parental boundaries and the strains of the unfamiliar adult marital issues, there was a lot of shouting behind a closed bedroom door. A new blending family, Vietnam and other social complications would soon scramble her fragile optimism, even if the sad music had disappeared.

"Who remembers peeking outside the lanai to see what the backyard looked like?" Mallory asked.

"I couldn't wait to check out the tree fort. It reminded me of the summer reading list of mystery books. A fort in our own back yard?!" Elizabeth said, recalling the scent of the mildewed canvas concealing secret handshakes and meetings between the sisters.

"How about our redneck pool?" Mallory said, chiming in. "Daddy had bought a new black 25-gallon trash can. Before he could start using it, we got the bright idea of filling it up with water and jumping in from the fort. Like a diving board!"

Audrey and Rebecca joined in the laughter.

"I remember not getting both legs in and knocking it over. It took a long time to refill it. Poor Daddy, the water bills would tell on us!" Rebecca laughed.

"Just another reason if Mommy found out we didn't take care of you!" Audrey said. "Remember when Daddy decided we needed a dog? He brought a german shepherd home and named it Chief. He was overly friendly and probably lonely. We'd stare out the back door and run to the fort to avoid him jumping on us and scratching our legs."

"Poor puppy," Mallory said, compassion in her voice. "I hope when Chief went *to the farm*, it was a good one."

"Why are kids told their missing dogs go to the farm?" Rebecca asked.

"I think the best memory that night was the distraction of someone struggling with the front door," said Mallory, ignoring Rebecca's question. "We turned around and saw them. Mom was giggling and Daddy tried not to exaggerate the difficulty of getting her over the threshold. She was tiny but I think they were exhausted from driving all day. It reminded me of one of those old movies Mom used to watch. Doris Day or Judy Garland being swept off their feet."

A tear trickled down Audrey's cheek. Audrey had been very attentive to their mom during this whole weekend. "You okay?" Elizabeth prodded.

"You know they always say you're attracted to a mate like your father? Until I married Jeff, I never realized how deeply I wanted that, and found it. Jeff was sweet, protective and always made me feel safe," Audrey confessed, trying to stop the tears.

Mallory snapped to attention, grabbed a Kleenex and held Audrey tight.

Elizabeth rarely saw this side of Mallory. It seemed out of character. "Audrey, it hasn't been that long since Jeff..." Elizabeth felt as if she had stuck her foot in her mouth. "...I'm sure you can relate with Mom on a level we're unfamiliar with."

Without looking at Elizabeth, Mallory cut in, "We all have our losses. Grieving is an individual process."

Elizabeth felt her face flush and resented Mallory's passive aggressive dig using basic psychology 101. Or at least it felt like one. *Walk a mile in my shoes, sisters.*

Chapter 28

VIETNAM, FEBRUARY, 1969

Dear Bobby,

I took the girls iceskating at Benton's Pond. They had to take turns with hand-me-down skates. They seemed to figure it out for being southern girls. Grades are good. Mom and Dad said to tell you hello. I know we agreed to save some money with this tiny house, but it's depressing. I'm glad to be near my family while you're away but it's still hard.

I keep trying to remind myself that we're halfway through. But, the thought of moving again and you leaving again on a ship is discouraging. I felt like a single mother in my first marriage, and I'm afraid I'm headed there again. I know you know how I feel about leaving the east coast.

You only have to take care of yourself. I'll admit that I've questioned that we may have gotten together too soon. I hope you're being faithful. It makes me crazy thinking about you at the Chief's Club having a good time, and I'm here watching TV with no social life or friends. Can you hear how lonely I am? Maybe even a little jealous.

I should probably stop before I get more upset. Maybe even get you upset. Good navy wives don't worry their husbands in Vietnam. I do care but I hope we get through this. I put the girls' letters in here too.

Love,
Rose

Bobby picked up the alarm clock and threw it across the room. "Damn it, Rose! I saved your letter for last." The anticipation of sexy words and love chat switched to seeing red. His chest tightened and he struggled to resist tearing up his room. She'd pushed his button again. This time from halfway around the damned world. He paced while he talked himself down. He clenched the letter and finally, furiously, ripped it to pieces.

He usually put her letters in the bedside table, especially ones that still had perfume on them. He hastily put on his shoes and slammed the door as he headed for the

Chief's Club. He wasn't going to drink alone—Jim Beam was waiting at the bar. But, as he headed there, eight words kept triggering his anger. *You only have to take care of yourself.*

How could she say that? He was teaching 33 South Vietnamese to take over small craft repair. Vietnamization was the new buzzword. He'd secluded himself and studied for the Senior Chief's exam. That was a great move for everyone. He was beyond exhausted.

By 2230 Bobby fell into his bed and sacked out immediately, carried along by whiskey-hazed dreams. He was a young boy, chasing his brothers across a quarry. No rice fields. No brown rivers. Mom was home baking the lightest biscuits an Alabama boy could want. Next, he was with Rose and the girls making dinner. He stole kisses while the girls sat at the dining room table waiting for tacos. He'd been researching recipes for corn tortillas and even had the machinists create his special taco frying tool.

Suddenly, his bed was violently shaking. As he awoke, he tried to sort dream from reality. His navy instinct kicked him into gear. He grabbed dungarees as the base sirens came alive. He stopped briefly at the sink to splash himself awake. His blood shot eyes stared back as another blast rolled through the floor of his quarters. The concussion could have come from a rocket blast.

What was I thinking? he asked himself. This would definitely be a fire and ammo situation. He needed his wits. No diversions. None. Especially a hangover.

As he headed to Military Zone 1, he could see the warm glow on the horizon. Something had been hit. There were red flares slowly drifting towards the bridge.

"Chief Higgins. There's rocket attack from the rice paddy." The MP panned the horizon with night goggles.

"We have too many PBRs at pier. Damn sappers do anything to put another notch on their belts," Bobby said.

"There's some gunfire up there. You should see all the tracers." On cue, the ground shook, slamming the boats against the ships they were moored to. The bows and sterns cracked and groaned.

"Jesus, I can't wait to get the repair orders tomorrow if we survive the night," Bobby said.

He stood outside, unable to avoid watching the damage, knowing even as he did so he was risking attack from a rogue sapper who may have penetrated the harbor under a drifting debris pile. "Probably bangalore torpedoes masking the rocket fire." Another fire ball lit up the skyline and like thunder, the concussion rocked the base, and Bobby's head.

"Sounds like an ammo hit. Down by the bridge ramp. Doubt we'll see any action."

"Red flares. They aren't getting through. Damn, NVA. Always hitting at night," Bobby said aloud. "Anyway, don't let your guard down. We got caught with our pants down during last year's TET. Pray we don't see green flares." *Just like traffic lights, red for stop and green for got in. Gotta give them credit,* he thought.

Bobby ran towards the ammo magazine to check his watch stander, hoping to hear the all clear. He needed sleep and aspirin, but he'd be damned if he was going to lose any of his men on his watch. Rose's selfish words echoed in his aching brain. *You only have to take care of yourself. Selfish woman has no idea,* he thought to himself. Hopefully, this was all just precautionary.

The next morning, Bobby stared at the Playboy Playmate calendar hanging near the coffee cups. It was suspended by a rusty nail and the semi-nude blonde had been photographed from above. Miss February's hair was arranged in a calculated loose mess, bedroom eyes inviting him to her bare breasts. But, the only blonde on his mind and heart was his wife waiting at home. *I hope she's waiting,* he thought.

He'd been in Vietnam for six months. He'd missed all the girls' birthdays, trick-or-treat, Thanksgiving, school plays and Christmas. As much as all those missed events made his heart ache, his mind kept going back to the girl on the calendar, yearning to gather his sexy wife at home in his arms. He was tired of the only excitement in his life being the constant threat of rocket and sapper fire.

He slept very little heading his small craft repair job as division Chief Petty Officer and Supervisor. Plan of the

Day was posted but on this day he couldn't help nodding off.

"Chief Higgins?"

The polite knock snapped Bobby back to consciousness. "Come on in," Bobby said, shaking to clear his head. He grabbed his white ceramic coffee cup and took a deep gulp of the cold thick coffee. The old mug was as stained and unwashed as Chief Connerty's on the Phoebe. It seemed like a lifetime ago—an adventure to see the world. Now he was in charge of training the South Vietnamese to take over the Naval base. But beyond military maneuvers, Da Nang was just another struggling port city. He'd seen too many of them. He just wanted to go home.

"Lt. Dell needs you over at YR-71. A couple of the welders blew a hole near the gun of his PBR. They have to get back out to the Delta by Thursday."

"Were they our welders or Da Nang personnel?" Bobby asked, not sure what difference it made. Either way, he suspected he had a long day ahead of him.

Chapter 29

CHARLESTON, MARCH, 2004

Since she'd contacted the adoption attorney's office, she'd chatted with her son for three weeks. Each conversation got easier in some ways, more stressful in others. Pleasantries... or as she called it to no one but herself, "the interview"-- started putting meat on the skeleton that had been in the closet for more than two decades.

He sounded comfortable and well-adjusted over the phone. But his voice was Larry's and rekindled so many memories of her lost soulmate. Hanging out at The Flying Dutchman, drinking beer and listening to bands. Strolling on Folly Beach, making love in the dunes and sharing dreams for their future. Now, as she listened to her son, she sensed he was trying to ensure her life was good. With the reunification in process, she hoped that she'd offer him something other than *given away*.

She put the car in park, grabbed the purple ball cap they'd each agreed to wear and looked into the rear-view mirror one last time. Two things they did have in common were the love of purple and Denny's French Toast Slam. She was wearing her favorite Marvin the Martian tee shirt to compliment the hat. As a child, she and her sisters sat around in matching pajamas on Saturday mornings eating from the mini boxes of cereal on their TV trays. They never grew tired of Looney Tunes. They were classics. She wondered about his childhood, if he had watched cartoons.

She approached the retro-fitted aluminum diner door, sighed and moved toward the hostess station. "Is it possible to sit in a corner booth?"

The young college student looked at the seating chart. "I have one near the back. How many?"

"One more. He should be here shortly. He'll be wearing a purple cap," she said. The hostess grabbed two menus and led her to the booth.

Ten minutes into beating up the ice in her tea with her straw, she spotted a male wearing a purple cap approaching the hostess station. She pointed him to the booth. As he turned to walk her way, she gasped. He was tall and lanky, staring right at her with Larry's blue eyes. Then he smiled, revealing dimples. Her dimples.

She was pretty good at reading people. Her job required it. As he approached, she remained a little guarded. Would he be angry, resentful or, hopefully, understanding?

"Can't resist stealing from Dr. Seuss... are you my mother?" he said, a twinkle in his eyes. His arms were extended to embrace her.

She couldn't resist her own Dr. Seuss material, "I am, I am. Do you like green eggs and ham?"

Without hesitation, he squeezed her and spontaneously answered, "I do not, I do not like green eggs and ham. I like Denny's French Toast Slam." He released her and they set themselves across from each other. The dreaded awkward pause... where did it go from here?

The waitress approached the booth and said in her Southern drawl, "Hi, my name is Dixie and I'll be serving you." She sat a glass of water in front of him. "Do you need a few more minutes to order?"

Simultaneously they shrugged, shook their heads and ordered, "French Toast Slam with bacon," both laughing as if they'd practiced for it a lifetime. "Unsweetened iced tea for me," he added.

"I can't believe it's been two hours," he said, checking his watch. "I have to get back to the base. I have duty tonight."

She smiled, "No explanation needed, Lt. I'm a Navy brat lifer!" They both reached for the check. "No, I appreciate you meeting me today, let me."

"You made the drive. Please. Let me," he said, placing his hand over hers. She wasn't used to niceties. "Please?"

His blue eyes were fixed on hers. *God, he was so Larry*, she thought. "Sure, I appreciate it," she said, pulling her hand away. Control was usually in her corner. *It's just french toast*, she thought. As he shoved cash into the check folio, that awkward silence returned.

"Can I walk you to your car?" he asked.

"Jeep," she answered.

"The purple one? I noticed it when I was walking up. My parents bought me one in high school. They asked me to give you this..." he said, leaning in and giving her a hug.

"They did a great job," she said, fighting back tears. "Now, will you consider meeting my side of the family? You have grandparents and three aunts that I'd love to introduce to you. No time soon. Maybe on Mother's Day?"

"I'll think about it. Plus, I'd want to take some leave time. I'll be in touch. Soon," he said. "Be careful driving home."

She started the Jeep and stared as he walked across the parking lot. She must have been running on adrenaline because she began to tremble. She felt a flooding mixture of guilt, relief, appreciation and anger. The wall she'd built up for twenty-five years was crumbling. It was like she had placed him for adoption all over again. All these years, out of sight, out of mind. He could've hated her but he was kind and understanding. She'd avoided stories of adoptions gone wrong. She should be ecstatic but she felt a twinge of jealousy, too, for the family who got to watch him grow up, to see him become a man. She'd only opened Pandora's box once a year—on his birthday. She'd pull out the journal she started during her pregnancy, recording her thoughts about him and his dad.

The brake lights in front of her blurred as tears welled up and she wiped them away to focus on her ride home. Maybe she'd pull the journal out, open a bottle of wine and start a new chapter.

APRIL, 2004

Audrey excused herself to the bathroom. "She'll be okay," Mallory said, reaching for her empty wine glass.

Elizabeth noticed Rebecca biting her nails and looking towards the back door. "I'm gonna go out for a smoke."

"I'll sit with you," Elizabeth said. There was tension in the room. *It's not me. We are all tired and just missing Daddy.* She followed Rebecca to the porch swing. "I wish I had one more day with him on the swing."

"I wish I'd come home more," Rebecca mumbled, drawing off the cigarette. The ember shook in the dark.

"Why didn't you? You weren't that far away." Elizabeth asked and tried to acclimate to the darkness. Rebecca was looking away and not answering. "Are you okay?"

The only response was the singing of the cicadas and crickets. Elizabeth didn't want to push too hard. There was another drag and puff looking off into the backyard.

The phone was ringing in the house. Rebecca jumped up and looked alarmed.

"God, please don't let that be John," Rebecca's voice quivered.

"Why do you let him crack you like that?" Elizabeth asked. She reached out and stroked Rebecca's arm. "Why does he seem to have so much power over you?"

Rebecca hung her head and flicked the cigarette into the yard. "You heard what Audrey said about marrying someone like your father." Elizabeth watched the steady stream of tears on Rebecca's cheeks.

"That would be a good thing for all of us. Daddy was the best," Elizabeth replied. She tried to catch Rebecca's gaze but she stared ahead shaking her head. "Rebecca, talk to me."

Rebecca glanced at the dining room window. "Who is Mallory talking to? She's been on the phone for a while."

They both looked at Mallory leaning against the wall, calmly chatting on the orange trimline receiver. "Well, it's definitely not John. She'd be ripping into him," Elizabeth said. Collectively, they sighed.

"Elizabeth, are you happy? I know you're a counselor and all, but is there such a thing as happily ever after?"

Elizabeth resisted hopping from concerned sister to trained professional. "I charge $250 an hour, sis! But, I think it's simpler. Sometimes it is just plain old ever after with happy sprinkles," she replied, putting her arm around Rebecca. "Seriously, what's going on with you?

You're jumpy, skinny and just don't seem to be taking care of yourself."

Rebecca squirmed and lit another cigarette. "I remember as a child being excited about getting older. I traded my crayons for make-up, bicycles for driving a car and playing house for dating. When John kept flirting with me when I cashiered at Doscher's, I assumed I'd always be a princess. I was so protected by Mom. I guess I was naïve."

"True. We weren't allowed to play with you. And, you were such a tattle-tale," Elizabeth said and bumped shoulders. "Again, what's going on?"

"Growing up isn't fun. Every day I wake up to put out fires. Kids, school, homework, the business, John's neediness, grocery shopping and constantly trying to find enough money to pay for it all. I feel like I'm in a gerbil wheel," Rebecca whimpered, puffing on the cigarette. "Fuck, even sex is a job."

Elizabeth had heard this behind the counselor's door before. "Rebecca, you're a kind and caring soul. He's taking advantage of your kindness. Why aren't you insisting on him remembering y'all were a couple before life got complicated?"

Rebecca made a sarcastic snort and wiped her nose with her sleeve. "Nobody tells John what to do. Even the kids know not to buck their father. I'm always walking on egg shells. He makes me quite aware that he'll leave me if

I don't keep him happy. Like Daddy did Mom when he went to sea."

Elizabeth jerked at the comment. "What do you mean? Daddy was always keeping our family together when he was home or when he was at sea."

"Mommy used to make me sleep with her. That year in Vietnam, I'd hear her talking to her sisters. She would say Daddy wasn't coming home. I prayed to God and said I'd be so good if he'd come back. One of the reasons I told on y'all was to be sure that Daddy wouldn't leave."

Elizabeth took a breath before responding. She had to acknowledge that this was her sister's reality. She realized that her own reality wasn't based on the same perspective. "Rebecca, you were so young. None of us knew how grown-ups worked. We were kids. Naive girls insulated from the messiness of life. Our biggest job was adapting to the constant change, to the Navy relocating our family."

She tapped Rebecca's shoulder to get her attention. "I'm sure your heart meant well, but I don't believe God needs to make a deal."

"I'm so fucked up! I love my kids...but I hate my life," Rebecca said, stepping harshly on her cigarette. "How did it go so wrong?"

"We've missed you," Elizabeth said softly.

"John always had excuses tying me to the house," Rebecca said, her eyebrows tensed. "Do you remember when I brought the kids in for a Mother's Day without him?" Elizabeth nodded. "I needed a break too, but he found any excuse to call with a problem. He always wanted to know what we were doing, where were we going. He insisted I come home by the end of Mother's Day. I had planned to stay until Monday morning. I didn't even get a 'Happy Mother's Day' from him. And that is just one example of the Life with John Show."

Elizabeth suddenly felt emotionally exhausted. She was running on fumes herself, but knew her baby sister was finally cracking. "Sounds like John is a classic narcissist. Unfortunately, as we say in counselors' world, the only people that benefit from therapy are the victims."

"Great," Rebecca said, her voice monotone and defeated. "He'll never let me go."

"You didn't sign up for marriage to be a prisoner. These relationships don't happen overnight. The first red flag is isolation. We've been raised to be strong women. Look at all the obstacles we had to overcome this weekend."

"I promised myself that I'd never say divorce," Rebecca said, still sounding defeated.

"Don't get mad but you'd rather raise your children to think that you and John are an example of what they should aspire to?" Elizabeth cringed inside as she released the words. She saw Mallory hanging up the phone and walking towards the deck's back door. "Mallory's coming."

Rebecca tried to wipe off the never-ending stream of tears. "Please don't tell them what we've talked about."

The door creaked open and Mallory's head popped out. "Hey guys, can we visit a little more? Audrey thinks it may be getting too late to leave the kids downtown at the hotel."

"Come on, Rebecca. Embrace our sisterhood, our dad's legacy," Elizabeth whispered as they walked back to the house.

A package deal: the real-life Hall sisters circa 1969.

Chapter 30

CHARLESTON, SC – MAY, 1976

It was the last day of his ten-day leave before he sailed from the Charleston Navy Base. Since he returned from Vietnam, he'd promised the girls he'd find a way to keep them in one school. He juggled billets on the Yellowstone and now, the USS Sierra. He knew it created some tension between him and Rose but the girls had been uprooted too many times. His girls were trying to develop social connections. Elizabeth had to push the hardest as the oldest. She was the one who approached him as the sister spokesperson after moving to Charleston in 1971.

"Daddy?" she'd said shyly.

"Yes?" Bobby looked up from his garage project.

"Can I ask you something? I mean... we all want to ask you something." She tried to hide her nervousness.

"Of course," Bobby answered, putting down the saw so she'd sense his undivided attention. He noticed the blushing little blonde girl's blue-green eyes averting his.

"I'm in 8ᵗʰ grade now. Is there any way we can stay here and finish from one school?" she stuttered.

Bobby remembered how miserable she'd been the year before in Maryland. Her letters always seemed weighted with responsibility and loneliness. Each girl had their own tier—not unlike his staff. She'd chipped and painted and owned leadership roles for her family. She wanted some liberty and security, a step up in pay, so to speak. "Well, I can't promise that I can guarantee it, but I can certainly try. I have to work with your mom too, though."

"We just wanted to ask," she responded. "We love you Daddy," she said softly. There was almost a tentative risk woven into the revelation.

Bobby got up, knelt in front of the awkward pre-teen and hugged her. "I promise to see what I can do. But right now, I need to get back to work on this fence. I'm tired of seeing the neighbor's dog charge you girls."

She grinned, pecked him on his cheek and skipped off to do homework.

That had been over four years ago. He'd received many recognitions in his record but working through all the Navy protocol was still like drawing straws. All the years he'd invested in welding and damage control had thrust him into greater seniority and the Yellowstone kept him in port. Most of her services were local pier assignments and he rarely left the shore. It kept his job secure and his home life more peaceful. But the Yellowstone was decommissioned in 1974 and eventually sold for scrap. Now his luck had run out. His new assignment, USS Sierra, was deploying to the Med in less than two days, for three months. He and Rose had found a house to purchase just a month earlier. For the past eight days, they'd rushed to pack and get the new house ready. He wanted all his girls nesting while he sailed to Spain and all the other ports of call.

Elizabeth's high school graduation was in five weeks. His pact with her in the garage had come to fruition. It hadn't been a completely perfect journey, of course. There was a lot of feminine energy in the house. Through high school, she'd been willing to give anything a try, to fish, crab or even help move the furniture. She was, as he would joke, *strong like bull*. She played by the book and was literal to a fault. In spite of all their rocky teenage years, he'd tried to navigate his way between work and hormonal women.

But still there was a strain in the house. Elizabeth kept ties with her long distance biological father, which rattled Rose. And Elizabeth's strong will was the rock for her sisters. She'd demonstrated a willingness to man her battle station with Rose, in spite of the popularity contest within the sister circle. He was put in the middle of the tug of war between Elizabeth's parents. As the stepfather he had to walk a fine line, keeping peace in his marriage, in their home, and all while not blotting his career record. Maybe Elizabeth and Rose were too much alike.

He pulled the folded piece of notebook paper out of his desk. Elizabeth had snuck it into his truck one morning on the way to the school bus stop.

> *Dear Daddy*
>
> *I know you're leaving soon and I don't want to upset you, but I've thought long and hard about what I need to do. I haven't been the best daughter this last year but at least you encouraged mom to give me some freedom.*
>
> *I haven't been able to find a way to get into college. Mom doesn't think I need it and that I should go to work. I have no car, driver's license or job with a decent wage. Mom will be overwhelmed with the girls. Now that dad is back in the country, he has agreed to drive here for graduation. He said he would help me research colleges. I don't think he'll pay but at least I can exhaust my desire to be in the mental health field. Maybe I will specialize in family counseling. I don't know. So I've decided to go back with dad to California, just for the summer maybe. I just... I just have to do something.*
>
> *I am crying because I don't know when to tell you this. But, I wanted it to come from me. Sorry for being such a difficult child this year.*

I just want a chance to test my wings. I would only be a burden for mom while you are gone.

I love you. Get back home safe.

Elizabeth

He stared at the sentimental Happy Graduation card resting on his Navy-issued grey metal desk. Rose wasn't talking to Elizabeth and had a honey-do-list with the new house. All he could do was let her know how hard it was to miss her milestone. Since Elizabeth would be on the road with her dad, he felt some pocket money would be appropriate. He knew she'd spend most of it on postcards and souvenirs for her sisters. He reached into his wallet and removed a $100 bill. The card was placed in his briefcase so he could give it to her at dinner.

Bobby walked into the new home and felt a sense of satisfaction. He was leaving his family in their permanent residence. Elizabeth's cap and gown sat on the living room table, waiting to be ironed. He smelled the green beans and potatoes in the crockpot and cornbread in the oven. He anticipated all six of them at the table enjoying a good country meal together. He hoped there was buttermilk to crumble his cornbread in. He saw spring onions chilling in a glass of ice water beside the mason jar of gardenias he'd cut for Rose the night before. A pitcher of iced tea sat in the corner of the kitchen counter. Six glasses were on the island. Then it dawned on him, when he returned it would be to one less plate and glass. Suddenly, there was a lump in his throat. The same lump he'd felt the day he married Rose.

How am I going to get through this night? He thought. He reached into the fridge for a cold one and popped the top.

"Daddy? Are you home?" Rebecca called and trotted to the kitchen. Bobby fought back the reality that he was leaving and losing one of his girls.

"Hey, kitten," he said, taking a deep draw from his beer. "How's my baby girl? Ready for supper?"

After dinner, Bobby and Rose sat on the back porch, gently pushing the green glider. The creaking reminded Bobby of how tired he was from the house move. The glider had followed them throughout the marriage and moves. It held her secrets of family discussions and giddy girlie whispers about the new boy in school. But tonight, the ambience was as thick as the May humidity. Rose leaned away, smoking her Salem cigarette. Bobby decided to cut the tension and try to soften her stand-offish mood. He wanted to ship out with nothing left on his honey-do list, including a romantic romp in their new bedroom.

"So, how do you think tonight went?" Bobby said, then took a deep swig of his beer. Rose turned her head towards the back door. Through the glow of the window panes was the clatter of dishes being washed and dried.

She didn't answer his question. Instead, "When do you think we can get the new dishwasher that fits under the cabinets?" Her voice was stripped of affection.

Bobby felt his heart sink. "Rose, I'm only gone for three months. I was hoping to talk about you and the girls tonight."

The back door opened and Audrey peeked out. "We're done. Is it okay if we watch The Carol Burnett Show?" she asked.

"Of course. We'll be in shortly," Rose said. The door shut and the kitchen light went off. Crickets were serenading and competing with the cicadas. She took a deep breath. "Bob? Why did you get so emotional at dinner tonight giving Elizabeth our graduation card?"

Ahhhh, there it was. The elephant in the room, he thought. He sighed. "When we met and got together, you said you and the girls were a package deal. I love you more than any woman I've ever met. You know that, right?" Bobby looked pleadingly, gently pulling her chin towards him. As they locked eyes, her eyes softened and he saw a slight welling of tears.

"I know you do. But Elizabeth put us through so much this year. I'm left here to deal with all the hormones of four girls," she said. "You leaving is always so hard for me. Sometimes I think you put the girls and the Navy before me."

Bobby put down his beer and pulled her over to him. "Listen. You made it clear that you never wanted to leave the East coast. You were quite aware that most of my military assignments were in the Asian theatre. I promised you and the girls I'd try and keep us here, in Charleston. My bosses have helped me on every request to find a placement for me at the Charleston Navy Base. I really hate leaving right now. But we have a home of our own and the girls will all graduate from one school. I made you all that promise.

Elizabeth is a good girl. She is just going through some growing pains. You know being the oldest makes it tougher. She's the one we depend on the most, the one we expect the most from. And at the same time, her sisters expect her to break ground for them, to challenge us as parents."

"Maybe. But, I can't believe she is leaving the day after she graduates...with *him*," Rose said.

"She'll come back. You watch." He kissed her and felt her soften. "We've all wanted to fly from the nest, right?"

The glider's creak became more rhythmic and reminded Bobby how much he wanted to be with his wife. "After the girls go to sleep, let's make love."

Rose smiled and leaned into him, resting her head on his shoulder.

Chapter 31

CHARLESTON, APRIL, 2004

Elizabeth returned to her chair in the corner of the living room. Mallory and Rebecca sat on each side of Audrey. Audrey's mood seemed to have improved since her melt-down over Jeff. Elizabeth tried to catch Rebecca's eyes, but she was in another place, absently opening and snapping shut the Zippo lighter lid. Elizabeth had found it in the baggie of desk supplies. The profile of Daddy's last ship, the Mahan, was prominently raised on the front of the brass lighter casing. Audrey leaned toward her sister and gently restrained another round of clicks.

"Guess what I found in his box?" Audrey asked, holding up four photo jackets. The brown covers were faded and seemed worn on the edges.

"Are those our senior portraits?" Elizabeth guessed. Audrey nodded and handed one to each of them. As Elizabeth opened hers she exclaimed, "Lordie, I haven't seen this in years. I look like Marsha Brady." She flipped it around to show her sisters. "Gotta love the black portrait drapes." Elizabeth flashed back to the day she and her best friend drove downtown for their senior portraits at Condon's Department Store. Both had fought against the humidity disturbing their hair and make-up. A musty odor permeated the first floor and the small antique elevator that accompanied them to the photo center creaked as if they weighed as much as four men.

Elizabeth traced the edge of the photo mat with her finger and recalled the anxiety mine field she'd navigated to get her photo. She was first to graduate. Her parents had been inundated with all the extra costs for her, school ring, cap and gown, senior portrait. She'd tried to help with saving her tip money from the W. T. Grant diner.

"Audrey, you look like Farrah Fawcett," Mallory's comment pulled Elizabeth back from her memory. "You always took good pictures. Look how skinny I was."

"That's why they nicknamed you Stringbean," Rebecca said, entering the circle of conversation. "It's obvious I graduated closer to the '80s...the hair kept getting bigger!"

"Don't these seem to be something like trophies? Dad fulfilled his promise to let us graduate from one school. Aren't these the best evidence? But more than that, we meshed with a community," Elizabeth said. She mused over the sudden impact of his sacrifices for them. "Hey, funniest memory with him?"

"Not so funny but something personal," Rebecca volunteered first. "When they married, I was losing baby teeth. Every time one got loose, Daddy put me in his lap, tied a string to it and yanked it out."

"I remember watching that one time. You obviously dreaded the sudden tug! Glad my teeth were permanents," Audrey interjected. "You were also the only one who needed braces. Guess Daddy couldn't complain since he may have had a hand in that!"

"Literally! A hand with a string in it," Mallory said, and made a hanging gesture with her tongue hanging out the side of her mouth.

"He wasn't that aggressive," Rebecca said. "And besides he paid me when he pulled it AND I got money from the tooth fairy." The girls booed and hissed.

"One of my funniest memories? The fight between Muhammad Ali and Joe Frazier," Audrey said, taking them back to 1975. "Mom didn't want anything to do with it. I remember how excited Daddy was. He was running back and forth from the TV and kitchen saying, 'Float like a butterfly, sting like a bee,' punching the air with his fists, hopping from side to side. We stood around watching him make Jiffy-Pop popcorn on the stove."

"He was from Beaufort, you know," said Mallory.

"Who? Ali?"

"No, Joe Frazier!" Mallory rolled her eyes. "Y'all obviously paid more attention to the popcorn than the boxing."

"That was more fun to watch," said Audrey. "Shaking the aluminum pan across the burner, trying to avoid burning it while the foil top inflated like a tin balloon. We'd make a pitcher of Kool-aid to wash it down with."

"No one left during the fight because he was so funny. When it was TKO, Daddy stood up and acted like Fred Sanford having a heart attack," Audrey laughed. They all smiled because he loved using that junkman imitation up until the day he passed.

"I always liked hanging out with him in the backyard. All his sheds, tools, the garden and projects," Mallory reflected. "Helping make small furniture, knick knacks."

Rebecca perked up, "I have a couple of cool pieces hanging in my hallway. He loved carpentry and was really good at it."

"Do you remember the year the wooden Dr. Scholl sandals came out?" Mallory asked. "All the girls were all wearing them with our hip hugger bell bottoms. But they were a little out of our clothing budget. There was a knock-off down at J.M. Fields but they were flying off the shelf. I'd been saving my bottle deposit money and a little of my lunch money. The sizes were so limited and they marked them down. I found a pair a size too big. I tried them on and thought about Daddy's jig saw." The living room was full of giggles.

"I couldn't believe what you asked Daddy in front of us at the dinner table," Elizabeth added, shifting in her dad's recliner. "Cut the back of the sandals down with his jig saw?"

"You wouldn't see the back of them with the bell bottoms," Mallory shrugged. "The denim drug the ground and frayed on the concrete, remember? Plus, that way I didn't spend all my savings. I had enough for a *Tiger Beat* magazine. Daddy and I went to the carport and he joked that he needed to hurry up before a neighbor saw him. We marked the line with a carpenter's pencil and he sawed away. I wore them the next day."

"Poor Daddy, he probably just wanted to go to bed instead of pulling out power tools at 7:30," Rebecca added. "Elizabeth, what was one of your favorites with Daddy?"

Elizabeth could easily remember the fall evening at their new house. Leaves and gumballs covered the backyard. Daddy had groomed his garden for winter crops and stacked split wood for the fireplace. She'd overheard him talking to someone on the phone about little quail incubators and wanted to meet to discuss a new project. "Yeah, Daddy was talking to a guy in North Charleston about a side business raising quail. You know he was always into some side way to earn income. I still remember he grabbed Mallory and me to go meet this guy."

"Why did he want us to go along, anyway?" Mallory pondered.

"You have to remember, Mom always liked to minimize all four of us in the house at once. You and I were a pair. Anyway, we jumped into Daddy's pickup truck and went to the quail man's home. His entire backyard was set up for hatching the cute quail biddies to their independent free pen. As Daddy and his mentor discussed the process of raising quail to harvesting, you and I were in love with the little biddies, chirping and fluttering their tiny wings. We picked up a couple and went over to Daddy, beaming as we showed him their cuteness," Elizabeth winked at Mallory. "You and I were distracted, discussing what we were going to name our little cute biddies."

"Daddy shook his head and looked at the quail whisperer and said 'Never mind,'" Mallory laughed.

"Guess he knew he had no shot at getting quail to the freezer for consumption with a bunch of girls wailing over their named pets," Elizabeth reminisced. "Later, I saw an old black and white movie where the kids named their turkey. At Thanksgiving, when the kids learned it was their beloved Tom, they all left the table bawling. Daddy must've seen the handwriting on the wall."

The stepdaughters grew quiet then, each of them lost in memories of this tender heart who'd taken them all on, a package deal layered in a corrugated box with his Service

Record, accommodations and mementos of his family life in his bedroom closet, buried under the shadow of his dress blues jacket with its five gold hash marks. *Funny,* Elizabeth thought to herself. *Each shining, diagonal stripe represented a term of good behavior, but to her, each was a symbol of the five "little women" he had taken on, her mom included.*

Audrey broke the silence. "If you think about it, there are so many more daddy stories throughout our dating years, and marriages, and having babies."

"I don't know how many times Daddy called my boyfriends Chester," Mallory said. "Maybe he was trying to give me a hint that my soulmate's name was Chester."

"You weren't that special. He said the same thing to me," Elizabeth added, smirking.

The other two chimed in, "me too," and "me three."

Elizabeth had been relieved they'd finally arrived in a place of happy nostalgia, and she picked up on something Audrey said. She had hit on one more link that completed the full circle of the Navy and their parents: the blessing of them becoming grandparents.

Autumn and Leigh were born a year apart. Holiday and family traditions integrated the granddaughters, and Bobby and Rose were dubbed Pop Pop and Mamama. Friday night sleepovers morphed into a road trip to the SC/NC border to visit their beloved South of the Border. Their dad loved to cook and can Charleston produce. He'd teach them short Laurel and Hardy exchanges about a man eating a hat. Stan's thumb was a magical lighter throughout *Way Out West*.

Elizabeth blurted out, "Whoever heard of anybody eating a hat?"

Audrey looked up and recited Ollie's line, "Whoever knew a man who did that?" And on cue, she flipped her thumb up like a lighter. It remained a joke that Daddy loved to invite Autumn and Leigh to answer, pretending to light their thumbs.

Elizabeth had seen her dad's face light up with the girls' willingness to engage with him. He'd return to the kitchen checking on his biscuits and chip beef gravy...

Suddenly, the dam broke. The tears that had been blocked since Thursday came unbidden, and Elizabeth began to sob. Stunned, her sisters surrounded her.

"Elizabeth?"

She gathered her grief and tried to stuff it back inside. But the stories, the sheer wealth of her dad's legacy had finally punched a hole in her, allowing her to grieve. The box and memories had slowly removed her father's jacket that she had worn for the family for years. They all had. But, tonight as adults, recognizing how they'd each been nurtured by a humble navy man and their mom opened a new door. A door between their dad and his amazing love for their mom and *the package deal*.

"I never realized how much he loved his job with us and his grandchildren," Elizabeth said, trying to squash the flood of tears. "I think I always knew it wasn't easy for them, but I just wish I could have told him. He always made sure his family would never be burdened. Even when his heart disease was diagnosed."

The small oak ship's wheel clock hanging over the mantle struck 11:00. As if on cue, the telephone rang. Audrey went to answer.

"Yes, dear," Audrey answered, staring at the huddle near their father's recliner and mouthing, "my daughter."

"Wait honey, you and Autumn are still babysitting? Where's Uncle John?"

Audrey looked across the room to catch Rebecca's eyes. "Absolutely, we're tired too. We should be there in about twenty minutes, or less, okay?"

Audrey hung up the phone and turned to her teary-eyed sisters. "Guys, the girls are watching their cousins down at the hotel. John seems to have gone AWOL. We should probably go." Rebecca rolled her eyes, snapped to and started gathering her things.

"I want to make a traditional breakfast in honor of Mom and Dad tomorrow," Mallory said. "I know we're scattering but I'd like to share something special with you first. My leave is up on Monday and I have to check in, too. I just need a couple hours to get back to Beaufort. Bring the kids. Mom may be back, too. 9:00 a.m.?"

"Leigh and I fly out tomorrow afternoon," Audrey responded.

"Can you bring Autumn with you?" Elizabeth asked. Audrey nodded and smiled, grateful the girls would have another cousin's night together.

"John and I have to be back sometime tomorrow too," sighed Rebecca. "Not a long ride. I can probably get him here or ride with Audrey and have him meet us later." Her temporary bravado seemed to have shrunk.

Everyone hugged and left Mallory at the house. Audrey and Rebecca left in the rental car. The red tail-lights disappeared as they headed to Savannah Highway. As they pulled away, Elizabeth realized she was exhausted. She took a left for home, streetlights and headlights blurring into stars from her newfound tears.

The porch light was still on as she pulled into the driveway and waited for the garage door to groan open. Elizabeth felt as fatigued as the door sounded traveling its track. She pulled forward, glanced into her rear-view mirror and grimaced at her mascara-stained face. She turned off the car and rummaged through her console for a spare Hardee's napkin. *I've got to get my game face back on*, she thought. But no matter how long she scrubbed, the red eyes could not be erased.

After five minutes, she heard the door at the top of the stairway open. "Elizabeth? Are you okay?" Dan asked. Before she could close the car door and get to the stairs, their dog raced to greet her. She knelt and cuddled his eager smiling face.

"You're a good boy, Ziggy. Who can cry looking at your happy face?" Elizabeth kissed him, stood and patted her thigh for him to follow her. Dan was standing at the top of the stairs holding a glass of wine. She smiled weakly and plopped on the tapestry couch.

"You look drained." Dan's brow creased as he absently patted Ziggy.

"We went through a box I found in Daddy's closet while grabbing his suit for Mom. Funny how each of us had our own view of the same memories." Elizabeth stared into the fire. "I feel like my life flashed before me but there were hidden doors that I'd never seen. This may sound sappy but we each painted on the canvas of life with Daddy. I guess I was usually brush stroked the dutiful one."

"No surprise. You're a typical oldest child."

"Lucky me," Elizabeth muttered, thinking how boring an oldest child was compared to her sisters. Her sisters' versions had shed new light on so many family memories. "Audrey's lived in a bubble. Mallory isn't scared to jump into life. And Rebecca? Turns out Mom being so overprotective prevented her from growing a spine."

"You're tired," Dan said and stood, yawning. "It's late. You've had a long three days. Come to bed and I'll make you breakfast."

"My head is spinning. And thank you, but Mallory is making breakfast for all of us before everyone scatters back home," Elizabeth said, her voice flat and picked up the TV remote. "I need to sift some things before I can shut my brain off. Be to bed soon?"

"Elizabeth, you need to take a break. If your dad was here, he'd tell you that your watch is over," Dan leaned over and kissed her. "Come to bed soon. Come on, Ziggy. Get in your bed."

"I need to be out of here a little before 9:00. You're welcome to come too," Elizabeth said, her voice weary. She snuggled into the overstuffed couch and turned on the TV. She heard the bedroom door click as she started to surf channels. She stopped on TCM and mindlessly joined a black and white movie.

Audrey spun through the radio channels on their short ride to the hotel, trying to fill the car with distraction. She could see Rebecca chewing on her lip as she searched through her purse. "So, what do you think John's doing?" Audrey asked, cutting to the chase.

"I'm sure there's a reason he popped out," Rebecca replied, looking straight ahead. "I'm sure Autumn and Leigh were great babysitters. I'll make John pay them something."

"No worries. They were stuck in the hotel anyway." Audrey hoped it was just nothing. But, no one had warned her that her world would be turned upside down on the other side of a doorbell. She hated feeling jaded but how could she not? Her grief still poked its head into her peace-loving lifestyle every damn day. She'd steal *Gone with the Wind*'s famous line—*I'll think about it tomorrow.*

"Going through Daddy's box was more of a surprise than I thought. God, we're all so different."

The traffic was light and the car passed The Coburg Cow, a long-standing local landmark. "Can you believe that cow dressed up in her Easter bonnet is still circling the front of the shopping center?" Rebecca said, changing the subject.

"I was on a double date with a Citadel cadet once and we climbed up to take a photo. There was a *little* beer involved," Audrey confessed.

Rebecca turned and looked at Audrey, raising her eyebrows. "You? I could believe if Mallory did that but not you... or Elizabeth."

"Elizabeth has loosened up. I don't think she feels like she has to keep her eye on us anymore," Audrey said, turning into the hotel parking lot. "She wears a brave face but I think this hasn't really hit her yet, or maybe it's just starting to."

Rebecca recalled her conversation with Elizabeth in the backyard. Elizabeth was a true oldest child, still keeping track of each of them. "At least we know she'll make sure Mom gets through this. I feel a little guilty leaving it all with her."

They grabbed their purses and walked towards reception. Rebecca scanned the parking lot for their SUV. It was missing. She dreaded going to the room. "I'm so sorry John ducked out... to God knows where. That was unfair to the girls."

"I'm sure they were fine. That's what teens are good for," Audrey said with an encouraging smile. She grabbed Rebecca and linked arms as they passed the front desk. "Hold on, I'm going to grab a few cookies for the room."

The elevator announced its arrival and Rebecca jumped, startled by the ding. Audrey cheerfully greeted the guests coming out. "Great cookies if you have a sweet tooth!" They smiled and turned towards the bar. "Let's go check on those kids," Audrey grinned and invited Rebecca into the elevator. "7th floor?" Rebecca nodded and forced a weak smile.

"Thanks again, girls," Rebecca said and quietly clicking the hotel door closed. She looked around the room and stared at her two children. Their heads were barely peeking out from the magnolia comforter. She debated changing into her own pajamas until she knew John was back. There was only one part of the girls' story that kept popping up in her brain. They said he smelled good. Where would John be going wearing cologne? Why wasn't he supporting her through the loss of her step-father? Or maybe she was being selfish. She rummaged through her purse and pulled out her prescription bottle. Her shaky hands spilled the pills onto her bed. The same question bounced around her head—how had life gotten so complicated and confusing?

"*Brush my teeth, I need to brush my teeth*," she told herself. She headed to the bathroom and caught her own reflection in the mirror. It startled her. Who was this brutally thin shell of a girl with hollow blue eyes? *What do you see?* Secrets. Tired. Neglect. Definitely, neglect. Rebecca started to feel angry as she revisited the childhood photos and stories from tonight. Suddenly, she felt angry. Angry for allowing life choices to rob her from spending more time with her parents. She had allowed others to come and steal the fruit of her family's labors. The safety and innocence of her childhood had been violated by blindly giving her trust to John. She scrubbed her teeth as if she was exorcising a demon.

She splashed water on her face, wrapped herself in a robe, grabbed her smokes and her cell phone and slipped out to the balcony, knowing she wouldn't sleep until John returned.

Three cigarettes later, no sign of John and for the briefest moment Rebecca wondered if she should worry. Then her cell phone rang. It was John's ringtone. At 12:45 a.m. *Really?*

"John? Where are you?" Rebecca whispered. "What's going on that you'd leave the kids?" She heard muffled music. No answer. "John!"

"It doesn't matter where I am," John said, his voice harsh. Rebecca recoiled at the tone of his voice and wrapped the robe tighter around her. "I hope you had a good time this weekend."

"A good time? You mean at my dad's *funeral?*" Rebecca replied. "Where the hell are you? When are you coming back?" Her voice rose even as she tried to remain quiet. She glanced through the glass door, checking to be sure the kids were still asleep.

John cleared his throat and she heard him exhale deeply. "I think this weekend showed me who you really are," he said. "I noticed that you neglected me to sit around with your family. I'm your husband and you left me and your kids to party with your sisters."

"I think this weekend was about family—all my family," Rebecca answered. "Why are you doing this now? What are you blaming me for? This is about my dad. My mom. My sisters."

"What about me, Bec? And, when I called to check on you, Mallory blasted me," John whined.

Rebecca started to boil inside. She thought about the figure in the mirror earlier. A veil was slipping off and she realized that her own husband was one of the foxes. A fox in the henhouse stealing the eggs for his own pleasure. Letting the hen do all the work.

"John, are you serious?" she asked. "I'm grieving my dad. My sisters and I get to be together how often? When do I ask you to do anything?" She flinched at the sound of a woman's muffled voice. *He smelled really good...* came to mind. "What's really going on here? Are you coming back?"

It sounded as if his hand was over the phone and she didn't want to make out him calling someone *babe*. He cleared his throat.

"I'm not coming back to the hotel. I'm headed home to pack my stuff and get my motorcycle," John's voice was flat and unemotional. It was as if he were discussing changing his boxers. "I'm moving to Lexington."

"Who is she?" Rebecca asked, her voice flat, unrecognizable to her even as she spoke. "How long has this been going on? Does she work for one of the brokers? You hook up on a sales trip? Share a room at the Motel 6? Should I check your cell phone records? Damn it, John. Now? While I'm grieving my dad?" The other end was silent except for the muffled music.

Little practicalities began to creep in. "We have closings next week and submissions need to go to underwriting. How will we get back if you take the car?"

"Since you're so tight with your family, hitch a ride," John replied, using his best bully voice. "I'll leave the keys on the foyer table." Rebecca felt slapped in the face.

"You bastard! How can you be so cold?" she yelled, no longer caring if anyone heard. "I've put my life on hold, rescued your screwed-up business deals, taken care of the house and kids?" At her lowest emotional point, she felt somehow empowered. Her chin raised and her shoulders unslumped. "Screw you!"

She cut off the phone, tempted to toss it into the marina off her balcony.

She slipped back in the room, went to the door and secured it with the deadbolt. Even John's key couldn't get in the room. Or her heart. Not anymore.

The aroma of sautéed onions, bacon and fresh coffee wafted from the kitchen to the porch. Mallory put the bloody mary and orange juice pitchers in the refrigerator. She peeked in the oven and saw the golden crowns of the biscuits. She'd baked her dad's recipe many a Saturday morning. She rummaged the pantry and found homemade jam and raw molasses. There were even a couple cans of Spam.

"Oh, Daddy! How many times you made us fried Spam," she said aloud, as if he was standing by the stove stirring the red gravy. She opened the coffee mug cabinet, reached for the USS L. F. Mason mug, still stained from all the years of use. She poured it full of piping hot Joe, opened the door for her dog and retreated to the porch swing. The martins swooped and chattered outside the gourds Dad had put up. The young tender tomato plants glistened with dew. *Yep, so begins the year of firsts... and lasts.* Last garden and last generation of martins. She needed to chat with her dad. One more time from the porch before the house was flooded by family.

She spoke out loud. "Good morning, Daddy! I really enjoyed discovering so many treasures you stored away. How little did we know the price you paid taking on Mom and all of us. I overheard references to us being your package deal. But, I never thought about all the plates spinning in the air between your career and raising us. You may have never shared a bloodline, but I see how much you loved us. I'll admit we tested you and Mom. I guess all kids do but you ruled with a velvet hammer."

She felt her eyes well up with tears. "I guess I assumed you knew the Navy always had my heart. We never knew any other lifestyle. How much was from genetics or just learned from you is a curious question. I have my own personal conundrum on that argument."

A slight morning breeze washed her with gardenia fragrance. It was from the same tree that appeared in the background of the four sisters at different times, wearing their caps and gowns.

Her dog was focused on sniffing the wood pile. In spite of Daddy's fear of kittens, he'd ignored a few generations of feral felines. Her mom had eventually tamed and snuck one inside. She always snickered when he acted put out but threw pieces of shrimp on the floor. When the cat died during a surgery, her mom was heartbroken and couldn't fathom burying her cat in a plastic bag. She'd beckoned Elizabeth to act as mortician. Her dad came home with a Craftsman toolbox for the burial. As he'd handed it to Elizabeth, he broke down in tears. Then he'd gone to the backyard to prepare a final resting place.

The oven timer was screaming and she went inside to pull the biscuits. "Oh, Daddy! There is a lifetime of stories from the front door to the garden. I love you and hope I make you proud. As proud as you make me."

The front door opened and closed. Mallory looked over her shoulder and Elizabeth strolled in. She looked exhausted but smiled encouragingly. "Bloody Mary? Mimosa? Coffee?"

"Bloody Mary! Hope you have pickled okra," Elizabeth said, opening the refrigerator. "Geez, it smells like a Daddy-Saturday-Morning in here. Sleep okay?" Elizabeth grabbed a piece of bacon as the front door closed again. The voices and footsteps of children announced the arrival of Audrey and Rebecca.

The sisters joined them while their kids headed downstairs. Mallory began taking breakfast orders, relishing her post as short-order cook.

"Grape jelly biscuit and bacon for Molly!" Rebecca said, as she stretched to retrieve a TV tray from the heavily painted cabinet. "I used to eat watching cartoons with this same tray." She grabbed the plate, disappeared but quickly returned to the kitchen. The smell of red gravy welcomed her to the table. "Did you use Daddy's canned tomatoes?"

"Absolutely! He still had some in the pantry from last summer," Mallory answered.

"I loved canning with our parents. Green beans, tomatoes, pickled okra," Elizabeth said, thinking about the hissing of the pressure cooker and the heat in the kitchen. "Command Master Chief Higgins peeling, stuffing and sealing Mason jars on a weekend." She looked around the table and studied each sister's face.

"Can I ask how last night turned out at the hotel?" Mallory said, looking at Audrey and Rebecca. Rebecca looked like she'd been crying and Audrey was too quiet. She saw them glance at each other.

"I'll give you the one-line synopsis—John's gone," Rebecca said, her voice flat. "I should have seen it sooner. There have been red flags for a long time." She blew and sipped on her coffee.

Elizabeth broke the silence. "Wait, are you saying he didn't come back last night?"

Rebecca nodded, crunching on her bacon. "He called after midnight and started whining about me not paying him enough attention. I'm at my father's damn funeral! Screw him, I don't need a third child. I think being with y'all last night was the best thing. I didn't realize how lost I was."

"Or you didn't want to see it," Mallory mumbled. She felt the sisters' eyes like laser beams. "I'm not saying that to be mean...just hope you never let douche bags distract you again. Mom and Daddy raised us better than that."

"Mallory, just give it a rest," Audrey said, stepping in. "The bastard even took the car. We need to support her, not beat her down."

Elizabeth resisted jumping into her counselor's chair. Rebecca's journey had just started and she hoped her youngest sister would protect herself. "Well, if you need someone to talk to, I'm always available. Even if you need me to get you home."

Rebecca shook her head and said, "Thanks Elizabeth. But, I'm going to have to redefine *home*. I'm not running his company, watching him flaunt his girlfriend or try to wear me down with excuses to get in the house. Mom will need some help. I'm going to talk to her about letting me get on my feet here." She quickly wiped a tear and forced a smile. "Geez, moving in with my mom in my forties. Let's talk about something else?"

The sounds of children giggling pierced the silent breakfast room. "Anyone talked to Mom today?" Mallory asked, changing the subject.

"I called her this morning from the hotel. She and her sisters are going to brunch," Audrey said, picking up her plate and headed to the dishwasher. "Good breakfast, Mal."

"Sounds like they may be talking about the good old days, too," Elizabeth said and she headed to the kitchen with her dishes. "Guys, I have to say that last night was good for me. Reliving our childhood and seeing life from his cardboard box..." Elizabeth's voice trailed off. She stared into the backyard at the newly planted vegetable garden.

Audrey was putting up left-overs. "Mom will enjoy this tomorrow." She glanced at the oven clock. "I have a couple more hours before I need to head to the airport. I have to make a phone call. I'll use the front porch." She headed out to find the cordless phone.

Mallory walked up to Elizabeth. "Hey, come sit with me on the porch for a couple minutes." She cocked her head towards the back door. "Finish your bloody mary out there." Elizabeth nodded and grabbed her tie-dyed hoodie.

As she walked towards the glider, Elizabeth recalled the conversation with Rebecca the night before. She'd counseled many oppressed women and her wreck of a sister seemed to be on the road to reclaim her voice. John had diluted Rebecca's strengths for over a decade. Elizabeth knew there was a long row to hoe and many obstacles ahead. She sat on the swing, holding it still for Mallory.

The swing creaked as the sisters sat silent. The purple martins twittered, peaking and diving into the gourd houses. The scent of the gardenia bush hung lightly in the morning air. The sun was burning off the morning dew. Mallory's dog Sparky was prancing and sniffing through the banana trees. The yellow cinder block shed housed power tools, PVC pipes and other project hardware. Everything in the backyard bore the signature of their father's passions.

"What's up Mallory?" Elizabeth opened the conversation. She wrapped her arms around her knees, bracing herself from the morning chill.

"I really do appreciate you and all you did this weekend. I'm sorry I wasn't around more but you know, the Navy is my boss," Mallory spoke, looking directly at Elizabeth. "I'll also admit I was the maverick sister."

Elizabeth grinned and nodded in agreement. "You've done a lot with Daddy. Look at his beautiful garden!"

"Well, that's not what I really wanted to chat about. I know we were all raised to be strong in times of crisis. I heard what you said earlier about our time together last night. I agree," Mallory said, with a hint of nostalgia in her voice. The eye contact was still direct but soft.

"God, why am I waiting on the stereotype question: How does that make you feel?" Mallory stated. They both smiled. "I started wondering, with all the talk of Mom, and Daddy, and our real dad. How much of a person is nature? And how much is nurture?" Mallory raised her eyebrows, waiting for Elizabeth's response.

Elizabeth sipped on the bloody mary swirling the controversial subject in her head. She and her sisters were great candidates for a psychological study. "That's a deep and complex question. But, I think our situation was a perfect example of blends. Birth order, genetics, nurture and society influence. When I work with adoption clients, we see no solid formulas. You could write a thesis on this. Why?"

"We all loved a uniform. Both dads wore them. Birth order? We are so true to our sister pecking order. Nurture? Both fathers fulfilled a role and influence for our adult paths. Obviously, the 60s and 70s were a mix of innocence and questioning authority, so there's definitely some environmental influence." Mallory stared towards the garden. "So... Daddy was helping me to reveal something on Mother's Day." She was shaking her leg.

"Mallory? What are you trying to say? I'm super confused," Elizabeth felt like she was watching Perry Mason and there was a missing clue to solving the mystery.

"Wanna be an aunt?" Mallory asked.

Audrey placed the phone back in its cradle and noticed Elizabeth and Mallory out on the swing. From where she stood the conversation looked intense. She couldn't see Elizabeth's face. She heard Rebecca playing with the kids in the TV room. She leaned across the butcher block kitchen island. Life was changing. Or had she been in a bubble? A huge blissful bubble. A big fucking bubble that popped when a drunk driver took her soulmate. A bubble that deflated when her mom's soulmate's heart failed. It was time to start living again, for herself and for her daughter, and maybe for Jeff and Daddy, too.

Mallory's body language grew more intense as she spoke to Elizabeth. *That looks a little messy*, Audrey observed and went to the refrigerator. One mimosa and the porch situation should be sorted out. Mallory didn't display deep emotions often and it was usually reserved for fur babies. Or insects, or baby birds or tadpoles.

"What's up, Audrey?" Rebecca popped into the kitchen—startling her sister.

"Good Lord, Becca," Audrey said, turning from the porch view. "Something going on out on the swing. Waiting it out a few minutes. Cheers!" Audrey lifted her glass.

Rebecca walked towards the back door and observed the intense conversation.

"Do you remember the year we moved back to Charleston and rescued the tadpoles?" Audrey asked, changing the subject. "Or, we tried to."

Rebecca wrinkled her nose. "The smell of those poor little guys dying in the trenches. Hundreds of them because of a dry spell. Heartbreaking to watch them squirming in the mud—not quite ready to be frogs."

"Mallory and Elizabeth enlisted us with buckets to try and carry water from other puddles. I'm sure they only suffered a little while longer," Audrey said, feeling as if she was back in the woods, pouring water into a huge hole. "If Mom had found out we took you with us to the woods, we'd have wished to be a tadpole."

"Yeah, especially if I'd found fire ants or a snake," Rebecca chuckled.

"Elizabeth the leader and Mallory the animal rescuer," Audrey replied. Silently, she wondered why Mallory related so much better to animals... underdogs, perhaps? "Wonder what they're out there plotting now?"

Rebecca took a harder look at the scene on the swing. "Audrey, I think Mallory's crying. She never cries." They stood side by side and watched as Mallory laid her head on Elizabeth's shoulders. Her body lurched uncontrollably. Elizabeth was asking her a question and Mallory shook her head yes.

Elizabeth sat patiently, allowing her sister's breakdown. She saw her two sisters at the window and motioned them outside.

"I think we need to join them," Audrey said, laying her mimosa glass on the counter. She heard Rebecca take a deep breath, and grabbed a couple napkins as she followed her. "Don't be too pushy," she whispered. "Mallory has her hard-ass pride."

Audrey opened the back door and was overcome with the fragrance of the gardenia bush. "Gardenias always remind me of Daddy."

Rebecca nodded. They grabbed two of the white plastic chairs. Rebecca sat to the right of the swing, Audrey sat beside Elizabeth.

"Here, Mal," Rebecca held out the napkins.

Mallory reached out but did not make eye contact. As she exhaled, she looked up. No one spoke but the birds and cicadas. Mallory blew her nose then looked at

Rebecca, Audrey and Elizabeth. There was a sense of apology in her eyes. She drew and blew one more breath as she nudged Elizabeth's shoulder. As if on cue, Sparky hopped into Mallory's lap.

"Mallory and Daddy were working on something to share on Mother's Day," Elizabeth said, laying the foundation of Mallory's breakdown. "Obviously, he's not here but I believe he will always give us little nudges." Elizabeth stood up and headed towards the back of the yard. She could feel her sisters' eyes watching her. She stopped at the gardenia bush, carefully choosing four clusters.

She returned and sat back on the swing. "When Mallory and I came out this morning, I felt hugged by the gardenias. I still expect Daddy's gardening hat to peek out from behind the garden shed."

Elizabeth continued. "Twenty-eight years ago, we moved into this house. It had been a rental and a bit neglected. Mom took on decorating the rooms...Daddy focused on the exterior. This backyard was scruffy and that gardenia bush was a Charlie Brown Christmas tree. But Daddy saw the potential and nurtured it to the beautiful, flower-laden bush that it is. I've pressed gardenia petals in my Bible. Glued them to picture frame mats for presents throughout our lives. When I was going through my senior year, I hurt both Mom and Dad with my angst. Daddy couldn't be at my graduation so he insisted on a picture in my cap and gown in front of the bush."

Elizabeth handed each sister a flower. "Afterwards, he sat with me and privately assured me they would always welcome me home. That picture we found last night was taken after and..." She stopped and swallowed in an attempt to not cry. "I felt like that gardenia bush. Daddy saw the potential. Not the gangly twigs and dead branches. My life flourishes because of my life's journey with y'all. I don't think that it's a coincidence we are sorting out the emptiness but fullness of life with or without him—surrounded by the scent of the gardenias."

Simultaneously, they each lifted their flowers. Audrey broke into tears and kissed hers. Rebecca cupped hers and breathed deeply, followed by a sneeze. Elizabeth watched as Mallory's trembling hand offered her flower to Sparky's nose.

"So, Mallory... Daddy is here and he has left us as four strong women who can face life's storms." Elizabeth nudged Mallory as if she was passing a baton in a relay race. "You can do it."

Before Mallory spoke, the front door opened and their mother was home. "Just in time," Mallory said aloud.

"If you want her to join us, I'll get her," Audrey volunteered. Mallory nodded her head and smiled weakly.

Chapter 32

CHARLESTON, SC

JUNE, 1977

Bobby sat on the swing, his Kodak on the side table flanked by a gift box topped with a pink bow. Audrey was putting on her graduation cap and gown. She'd done well in high school. He wanted a moment with her before the house exploded with graduation activity. He missed Elizabeth's walk across the stage and he would miss Audrey's. But not because of the Navy. As each year passed, he'd yet to manage the emotional attachments to the five women in his life. All his life, watch standing was ingrained from childhood to his career. His destroyers pulled picket duty off the Asian shores with orders to keep peace in international waters. There was always danger of obscure mines, torpedoes or unmanaged navigation running ship aground. However, nothing had prepared him for the damage control needed as a father letting each of his girls leave his pier—their home—for a chance to see the world. Hopefully, he and Rose would remain their North Star. A constant to steady their course in fair or foul weather. He'd yet to build the dam for the flood of tears threatening to overwhelm his aching heart. Give him an engine room fire, a boiler explosion—damn, retrieve the Gemini 8 before the Chinese could steal it! But he knew the idea of his girls graduating, getting married or becoming mothers was a foreign land that stripped him of his male bravado.

The back door opened and Audrey floated in, wearing the white robe and hat.

"You look lovely, Audrey," Bobby complimented her. "Come sit here a minute." He wiped the sweat from his brow, unsure how much was the June heat or a little bit of nerves.

"Sure, Daddy but I don't want to mess up my hair," Audrey said, fluffing her Farrah Fawcett locks. She smoothed out her robe and sat, crossing her legs.

"We'll get your picture in just a few minutes. I wanted to give you something first," Bobby reached for the jewelry box. He struggled to speak, resisting the emotion trying to escape.

He cleared his throat and looked at his daughter's large expectant eyes. "I wanted to explain why I won't be attending your graduation ceremony. And it has nothing to do with not being able to see Elizabeth's."

"You girls know the story of how your mother and I dated and married?" He asked and she nodded.

"I do. You were a very brave man to take on a gaggle of girls," Audrey said with a softness in her eyes.

"When I found your mom, I went to my first and only wedding. It is still one of the best days of my life," Bobby said, tears welling. "You girls had my heart and I wanted to make sure y'all were safe. But..." he was overwhelmed with his feelings. "I'm very proud of each of you. But, ceremonies take me a bit out of my comfort zone. Always have. It may look weak or even a little selfish but I think it best if I not go." He choked back a sob and attempted to keep a stoic face.

"Daddy, it's okay. Mom will be there," Audrey tried to assure her dad. "You are a great dad."

Bobby took a breath. "I just wanted to give you something to wear when you get that diploma. Something that reminds you how much you mean to me." His voice cracked and he held out the square box.

"I'm so proud of each of you." Bobby tried to regain his composure as Audrey opened the box gracefully. She was trying not to rip the paper. She peeked inside.

"Oh, Daddy! It's beautiful!" She lifted the charm bracelet from the soft cotton padding. Hanging from the silver links were a graduation cap, anchor and a silver heart. She squinted, holding the heart up and read a word above the embedded ruby stone. A tear rolled down her cheek as she saw the inscription: *Daughter.*

Bobby hugged her and softly made his last confession. "No matter where we go forward, know that you are my daughter and have my heart. Now, to the gardenia bush for my photo."

"Daddy? Help me put this on first," Audrey held out her wrist, handing him the bracelet. "I love you, too."

JUNE, 1979

Mallory looked at her watch. Bugs Bunny's arms were pointing at 4 and 6. She had a few minutes to get to work. She tucked her tee shirt in the denim high waisted jeans. It was Friday. She would be cleaning reptile cages at the pet store. Daddy wouldn't care what was under her cap and gown. She brushed through her chestnut hair, quickly coated her eyelashes with Maybelline and dabbed on some lip gloss.

She could hear the rattling of dishes in the kitchen, the voices of her parents in the background. She ran into the bedroom to grab her gown. The cat was napping on it. "Sorry, Rosie," Mallory scooped her up and relocated her to her pillow. She threw on the gown and grabbed her red tasseled cap.

Jogging to the kitchen she shouted, "I have to get to work. Let's do this!"

Bobby and Rose turned to respond and gasped as the unzipped gown revealed her work clothes. It was a typical display of Mallory-ism.

Rose handed Bobby the camera and inspected her daughter. "Zip up and let's get your cap on straight. I guess we'll shoot from your knees up."

"Come on, Daddy," Mallory said, rushing to the back door. "I need to use the car but I'll bring it back by 9:00."

Rose looked at Bobby before he left the kitchen. "Make sure you don't get those jeans and be sure her cap is straight." Bobby winked and followed Mallory to the gardenia bush.

JUNE, 1980

Bobby and Rose sat together in the kitchen. Three girls had graduated and moved on to chase their dreams. All were in college and Mallory had recently taken a job in Pensacola at the Navy base in Pensacola. She'd set her sights on becoming a navy officer.

Rebecca was the last one.

"The house is getting so quiet," Rose squeaked, sipping her iced tea. Bobby looked up from the pork chops simmering in gravy. "I'm gonna miss the giggles when she's on the phone. Listening for the door to close after dates or high school games."

"I'm gonna miss meeting and messing with the boyfriends," Bobby said, grinning and flipping the chops. "Four beautiful daughters and too many Chesters!"

"Elizabeth is almost done with college and I think it is getting pretty serious between her and that guy, Dan?" Rose asked. "I hope she finishes her Masters before she gets married though."

"Elizabeth's solid and focused," Bobby said as he went to the refrigerator. "Here, let me get you a beer." He stepped over the cat in the middle of the kitchen floor. "Miller High Life?"

Rose tried to force a smile but she was obviously struggling. "I always thought I'd enjoy when the girls got older. No more school projects, backtalk, or fighting. I could go home and visit when I wanted to. I guess my only job was being a mom." She stared into the backyard.

"And what a fantastic job you did," Bobby said and poked his head into the living room. He made the gesture of taking a photo to Rebecca while she was on the phone. She nodded.

He continued. "Think about this next phase like retirement. We both are retiring with over 25 years on our records." He knew Rose was thinking about his deployment coming up in three weeks.

"I guess... but I'm going to be alone. I feel...discarded?" Rose said, refusing to look at Bobby.

Bobby cringed inside when he heard the word. "Rose! It is time for us. I'll be retiring in a few years. The girls will still be here for holidays." Bobby strained for the right words.

Rose shrugged her shoulders as if defeated. Bobby turned down the burner and covered their dinner.

"You're just gonna miss my cooking," he said, trying to lighten the direction of the conversation. He grabbed a spatula and pulled her up from her chair. He slapped her ass and raised his eyebrows, implying it wasn't just hot in the kitchen.

She smiled and blew her nose. "Sexy, huh?" She turned to see Rebecca bouncing into the room in her white cap and gown.

"Let's go Daddy. I have a shift in an hour." Rebecca failed to sense the tense room. She grabbed the camera and headed out the back door. "Meet you at the gardenia bush. Finally, my turn!"

"I have to admit that you've done a good job with the girls," Rose said with the same defeated voice.

"Rose, it is not me... it is *we* that did a good job," Bobby said. He hugged his wife and headed to the gardenia bush.

Chapter 33

2004, CHARLESTON

Mallory watched Audrey hold the door open as their mother joined them. She carried the familiar crystal glass of iced tea. "Mom, sit over by Mallory," Audrey pointed to the glider and sat cross-legged on the deck beside Rebecca.

Elizabeth broke the silence. She noticed how tired their mom looked. "Did you get any sleep last night?"

"A little. I lost time reminiscing with my sisters. But I needed them," Rose replied. "How did dinner go?"

"We basically did the same," Elizabeth said and gave her mom a nod. "Lots of memories growing up with you and Daddy."

"I feel...numb? Maybe, lost?" Rose confessed. She looked towards his garden and scanned the backyard. "I know I'm going to expect him to stand up wearing that ridiculous straw hat." They all chuckled at the visual.

"I remember him wearing it in the kitchen and took a picture of him," Rebecca added, her voice cracking. "I have it on my bookshelf by the computer at..." she couldn't say the word *home*. Audrey gently patted Rebecca's knee, rubbing the heart charm between her fingers on the bracelet.

Elizabeth nudged Mallory. "Audrey has to head out in a couple hours."

Mallory looked down at her watch, taking the hint.

"You all know I've been helping Daddy with the garden," said Mallory. "But, I was also telling him about something I needed to share with the family. Mom, I was going to tell you with everyone here on Mother's Day," she continued, straightening herself on the glider. *Keep it together*, she said to herself. She felt a tornado of memories and emotions gathering force. On the trip down memory lane during the weekend, no one had shared this stop along the road. It was like a sealed court case, collecting dust in some box buried in a warehouse. She felt all their eyes on her.

"Y'all know that I am a very independent and non-conforming woman. Mom, I know I put you through so many messy situations as a child. But, in high school I knew I wanted to join the Navy. I started taking my grades seriously and joined ROTC. I wanted to prove to you and

Daddy that I could fill your shoes. Okay, so I still pushed the envelope partying with friends, but I was determined to try and make a new impression." Mallory explained.

Mallory nervously looked at her watch. 11:30. "Before I tell you more, I have someone coming over at noon. Like I said, I had hoped to do this in a couple weeks, but I didn't expect..." Mallory's voice cracked and she took a deep breath. "I didn't expect Daddy to bring us together under these circumstances. Or maybe I didn't want to see."

"I don't think anyone wanted to see," Elizabeth added. "Daddy was good at protecting us. He didn't want Mom or us to see him off duty."

"Yep. So, after graduation I went to a Navy Recruiter and discussed my options. I'd been accepted by a couple of colleges and the Navy would pay me to sign up after graduation. I'd be a lieutenant. I didn't want to give up the beach so I chose University of West Florida. Thought I'd stay around the Navy base too and work," Mallory shifted her weight on the glider. She paused to feel out her sisters' faces. Elizabeth slipped her hand on Mallory's shoulder. It anchored her back into her story.

"That summer I decided to have a last hoorah with friends. We hung at Folly Beach, waited tables for some cash and would party over on Dorchester Road. The best part of the night life were all the cute sailors," Mallory said, and looked away, trying to discreetly wipe away a tear.

"I always loved a man in uniform. You girls got that from me," Rose interjected. Everyone smiled at their mom.

"Guilty as charged!" Audrey said. "I dated a few Citadel cadets."

Mallory took a deep breath. "Well, to make a long story short, there was this cute sailor named Larry. He had the most beautiful blue eyes, complete with a twinkle. He was persistent in asking me to dance and insisted on a date. Their ship had just returned from dry dock and was getting ready to go out for a shake down. He wanted to see me as much as he could before getting pushed back out to sea." Mallory smiled at the remembrance. "We fell hard for each other. I should have focused on the fact I was moving in a few months. We had so much in common and he was so helpful on what to expect in boot camp. One word—soulmate."

Mallory stopped and tried to regroup her thoughts. She was jumping all over the place. She never thought she'd ever have this conversation, at least not without her dad to help her through.

"I think I remember hearing Daddy talking about you dating a Navy guy," said Elizabeth. "That was my third year of college. But I never heard anything about him after you went to Florida."

Mallory shook her bowed head. "Yeah, this is the tough part. We'd been dating a couple months and I had to get to school. They were still having some trouble with some issues on the ship. He was required to participate in repair and at sea shakedowns. He usually let me know he was home within a day or so. But, we all know that can change for whatever reason their captain holds them out longer." Mallory felt her grief bubbling to the surface. If she stopped now, she wouldn't finish.

"We'd made plans for me to visit sometime in October. We only could talk on the phone here and there but I wrote letters. It had been about a week since he was supposed to be back at the dock. I started to wonder if a long-distance relationship was too much for him but I stuffed that down. So, I called the ship and asked if I could speak to him. They put me on hold and next thing I know, there's a chaplain on the phone."

"Honey, please tell me it was good news," Rose said.

"Unfortunately, no. Larry had been mortally wounded during the shake down, by a snapped cable. He was already returned to his family," she said softly. "I don't even remember hanging up the phone. I was looking forward to him coming home. I needed to tell him something... something in person."

"That you were in love?" Rebecca asked.

The silence was deafening. Mallory covered her face and her body shook from silent sobs.

Audrey wanted to go to her but it was the same scene her and Rebecca witnessed earlier. She was leaning on Elizabeth, who obviously knew what was still to come.

"I was in love, yes, and...I was pregnant. I'm sure we would have worked it out together. But, I was so riveted on getting through school and becoming an officer," Mallory continued, stopping to blow her nose. "I was a kid. The thought of being a single mother without the support of the baby's father was too much. And I couldn't live with the idea of aborting the last piece of Larry. So, I wrestled for about a month and went to the school's guidance counselor. One of my options was adoption."

"Oh, Mal! You should have told us so we could have rallied behind you," Audrey said, rubbing the anchor on her bracelet.

"It was complicated. Single mothers were not as accepted back then. Even adoption was hush-hush. I couldn't bear the idea of our child not having two parents."

"So, that's why you told us y'all broke up? Why you never came home from Pensacola that first year at college?" Rose asked. "We were so disappointed on the holidays but proud that you seemed determined in your studies."

Mallory nodded. "I made arrangements to place the baby privately. I picked the family and even got to meet them. Besides losing Larry, it was the hardest day of my life. But I wanted our son to have every advantage that I could not give him at this stage of life."

"So, you had a boy?" Rose asked, with a slight hope on her face.

Mallory smiled. "Yes, a beautiful 7 lb. boy, April. Here we are celebrating Daddy in April and he was born in April."

Rose looked hard at Mallory. "Wait, is that who is coming over today?"

"I know this is a lot to digest. I didn't expect this to happen this way but Daddy and I were going to bring him here on Mother's Day. He was going to fire up the BBQ and we were going to celebrate. I got a request to reunify a couple months ago from the attorney. We've talked on the phone and met."

"Is he okay? Was he mad at you? How did you keep this a secret? I would have been a mess!" were fired at Mallory from multiple voices.

"Please, stop!" Mallory said firmly. Her hands slapped her knees. "He's an amazing young man. We have so many things in common, from physical traits to favorite foods. His personality is so very Larry."

"How do his adoptive parents feel about this?" Elizabeth asked.

"We had ... and have ... a great understanding. They're not threatened. They support his search for his other roots," Mallory responded.

For the remainder of the time on the porch, the women bonded as sisters, women, wives and mothers, including all the rawness of Mallory's delicate revelation. And then, like the strong band of "little women" that Bobby had embraced, they began preparing themselves for a noon doorbell.

The porch noise gradually faded to an awkward silence. The voices of the children were headed towards the back door. Mallory stood, her face streaked from the tears. "I'm going in and try to get my eyes unswollen. Maybe put a little make-up on," she announced. She whistled for Sparky to follow her. "I hope I didn't complicate things, Mom."

Rose stood and cupped Mallory's face. "Nonsense. I can't wait to meet my grandson." She kissed her cheek and Mallory disappeared into the house.

Elizabeth sensed Rebecca's resolve was thinning and she knew her sis had to ask their mother a big question about sticking around for a while. "Hey, Audrey, let's go in and get the kids lunch. Rebecca, you wanna stay out here with Mom?" She raised her eyebrows, nudging Rebecca to talk about her situation.

Rebecca nodded. "Sure." But her voice was soft.

"Anyone want something to eat? Drink?" Audrey asked, pointing at her mother's sweaty tea glass. The morning sun was hanging over the porch. She didn't wait for their answer. "Why don't y'all move under the awning? I'll get you some fresh tea." She jogged to catch up with Elizabeth.

Elizabeth was already making ham sandwiches. There was plenty left from their dinner after the funeral. As she savored the sweet ham crumbles, her heart sank with another reminder of their dad's absence. *It's just ham*, she scolded herself. She heard Audrey rattling the icemaker and the clink of new ice in a glass. A few stray cubes bounced and split on the linoleum.

"Always gotta sacrifice a virgin ice cube," Audrey joked. "He hated this ice maker." She scanned the doors and observed old magnets from the grandchildren's school projects. Two red hearts with Leigh and Autumn's kindergarten pictures. A thumbprint made into a mouse. Rebecca had made butterflies out of her children's footprints. A yellowed recipe for ginger dressing cut out of the newspaper.

Elizabeth was in the pantry looking for chips and glanced over her shoulder. She observed Audrey's distraction with the refrigerator door. Elizabeth had gone into her own rabbit hole with the canned goods from last year's garden. His essence was embedded into the bones of their home. In their souls and memories. Outdated Kool-Aid packets, instant pudding used to make banana pudding, the requisite Spam. *Well, Spam would never expire*, she thought and smiled to herself.

"Mom? Can we eat yet?" A child's request brought both to the task at hand.

"I'll be right back to help with drinks," Audrey said, heading out back with iced tea.

Elizabeth grabbed chips and then went to the refrigerator for the baby gherkins. "I'll be right there." She left with the four plates and headed down to where all the kids were watching TV. Almost all, she reminded herself.

When Audrey returned to the empty kitchen, she grabbed two sodas and two juice boxes. As she passed the oven, the clock reminded her she only had a couple hours before their flight.

Elizabeth returned and started making more sandwiches for the adults. She heard Audrey behind her. "Everyone good?"

"Yeah, movie and a sandwich. Happy munchkins," Audrey said, opening the refrigerator again and rummaging through all the plastic ware. "Figured we'd eat potato salad and deviled eggs. Seems to be the gift that keeps on giving at a funeral. Believe me, I know!" she tried to joke.

Mallory joined them with a fresh face and grabbed a beer. She took on the task of gathering plates and silverware for the kitchen island. Trying to keep it light, she announced, "Nothing but the best Chinet for my son!"

"You okay?" Elizabeth asked, not turning around. She kept plating ham.

Mallory ignored her and stood looking out at Rebecca and her mom. It was obvious that Rebecca was telling her about John's leaving. "Of course." Her voice was distant and she took a swig of her Corona. "Are y'all okay? I know I laid a bomb on you today."

"I'm just sad that you lost your soulmate," Audrey said, rummaging through the kitchen cabinets, the cabinets that her mom had insisted their dad paint a different color almost annually. She always felt bad when all the doors and hardware were spread all over the floor. Daddy would sand each one, paint and reassemble. Audrey offered to help but he would insist she sit and have a beer with him. "I'm not one up-ping, but I've walked in those shoes. At least I had more time."

Elizabeth walked to the kitchen island with her plate of ham. "I admit that I may have an unfair advantage as a counselor. Please do not take this next comment as glib. I tell many clients that sometimes crisis or loss is like the pressure needed to create a diamond from a piece of coal. Mallory, I cannot tell you how much I admire the way you handled the whole situation."

Mallory shrugged her shoulders. "Then I better have made one big fucking Hope Diamond." They all laughed, relieving a little of the tension in the kitchen.

And then, as if on cue, the doorbell rang.

As Mallory went to answer the door, Audrey motioned for Rebecca and her mom to come inside. "He's here!"

Elizabeth remembered her camera was in the car. She'd wait and get it after introductions. She felt surprised by the butterflies in her stomach while her mind tried to give her professional advice. She would have prepared someone else in her situation. But she surrendered to her heart's excitement over Mallory's news. She was meeting a new nephew—another relative who wore a Navy uniform. It seemed like a softening of the loss of her father. And she was glad Mallory had shared her secret with him before his death.

Footsteps headed towards the kitchen. Elizabeth could see the silhouette of a tall, slim but fit young man. She looked over at Rebecca and smiled, raising her eyebrows. She hoped it wasn't too much for her because of John's shenanigans. At least Rebecca now knew it had been a marriage of shenanigans.

Mallory blocked the kitchen doorway. "Okay! I'd like to introduce my son... Robert Mallory Lesesne. Also known as Lt. Lesesne!" She beamed and stood aside, inviting him into the room. Then she pointed and identified each woman.

Elizabeth stepped forward and gave him a hug. She searched his face for family resemblance. His blue eyes had a boyish twinkle and his grin revealed Mallory's dimples. He was wearing the Navy khaki uniform, cradling his cap on his arm embellished with the silver initials USN and gold anchor. "We are so excited to meet you," Elizabeth said, her eyes moist with joy. "And you're just in time for lunch!"

"I hope you don't feel overwhelmed by all our questions, Robert," Rose said, her eyes misting but there were no more tears. She patted his hand and her smile said what her words didn't—welcome home.

"No ma'am... I feel very blessed to find my beautiful mother, three aunts and another grandmother," Robert responded, while patting Rose's hand back. He'd been watching his cousins peeking into the kitchen and running back to watch TV. Every once in a while, he amused himself by waving or winking at the girls. "Like I said earlier, I'm so sorry for your loss. I was looking forward to meeting your Bobby. I've heard so many good things about him."

"I think he left a little bit of his essence in each of us," Audrey inserted. Everyone nodded in agreement. She walked to the sink and looked at the thermometer hanging outside the window. It was the same old dingy plastic tool that kept them informed of the hot summer sun's work or how heavy a jacket was needed to rake leaves or gumballs. "It's probably too hot to go back outside. Why don't y'all go into the living room while we finish cleaning up."

As Robert stood and motioned the women to proceed, Rose stopped, looking deep into his bright blue eyes. He was at least a foot taller as she reached up to cup his face. "I've lost a Robert and gained a Robert, all in the same weekend," she whispered. He bent to kiss her on the forehead and offered his arm to escort her into the next room. Mallory looked at all her sisters, beaming.

All throughout lunch, Robert's new family was so open, funny and well bonded. His grandmother seemed to need protecting. Elizabeth asked good questions but was a good listener, too. Audrey organized and kept order—especially over her mom. Rebecca was quiet and seemed fragile. But, he could be wrong on his first impressions. There was one thing he was becoming more convinced of—he could see what his dad had seen in his mom. She was independent, driven, funny and brave. Obstacles were challenges and failure pushed her to find new solutions. She was a complete package. They all were.

"So, Robert, how did you wind up getting family names?" Rebecca asked, as he sat beside Mallory on the loveseat. She heard the dishes rattling as Elizabeth and Audrey loaded the dishwasher. She nervously twirled her wedding band, trying not to think about John, about anything but being in this moment with her family.

"I think Mallory could answer that better than me. I was too young to remember," Robert said. They really hadn't had this conversation in depth. He only knew why he was named Mallory. His parents had never hidden that it was his biological mother's name. They always revered her for the sacrifice she made for them to become parents. He'd always assumed Robert was used to carry on his adoptive father's namesake.

Mallory sat for a moment and appeared to turn pages in a book. A book of her life's choices. Before she responded, Elizabeth and Audrey joined them. "Take a seat hookers! Rebecca wants to know how Robert got his name."

"Before you start, please don't be upset if Leigh and I have to head out soon for the airport," Audrey said, settling on the couch beside their mom.

"Of course," Mallory continued. "There's a relatively simple explanation for his names. First, I picked his parents through a private adoption attorney. I'll give you bullet points. I wanted a couple that couldn't have a child. I wanted to meet and get to know them and for them to know me. We agreed that I would keep current addresses in the attorney's file in case there was a medical or reunification decision. And finally, and perhaps most importantly, I was drawn to my couple for a silly reason—his name was Robert. Like our stepdad."

"I think that's cool, not silly," Rose interjected.

"Serendipity!" Audrey added.

"Well, I was working on my decision to join the Navy during this time," Mallory reminded them. "I wanted my child to stay in one place—if possible of course. We all bonded in a way few adoptions do. So, they wanted to give him a piece of his father and a piece of me."

"How wonderful, Mallory! How in the world did you keep this from us?" Rose asked out of politeness, hoping Mallory understood it really wasn't a rhetorical question. More of a compliment on her hard situation.

Elizabeth jumped up. "I'm going to pop out to my car and get the camera. I have an idea!"

"Uh, oh! She's on a mission," Audrey added as the keys jingled out of the worn leather saddle-bag purse. "So, when are you leaving, Rebecca?"

"We're staying the night with Mom," she answered. Rebecca drew a breath and let it out. "Just to make sure no one is surprised, Mom has offered to let me move in while I look for work."

Before anyone could say something, it was obvious something was going on in the front yard.

"Shit!" Rebecca said. She shrunk in her chair, pupils dilating like a cat getting ready to defend her territory.

Everyone's cars peppered the front yard. They all knew how to park and not block in those who needed to leave first. Elizabeth planned to stay until everyone had to head back home. She headed to her car in the corner, blocking a direct path to the front door. Her fob popped the trunk and she went to the canvas camera bag. In it was the digital Canon that revealed what it captured faster than the old days of film. Elizabeth loved photography and found it kind of exciting waiting for Kodak film to be developed, but the new tech avoided disappointment when the perfect moment wasn't captured. *I've got a job for you little camera*, she thought. *I won't miss this moment!* She couldn't wait to show Dan her new nephew. Since Thursday, her emotions had been like waves pounding the sands of her soul. Meeting Robert renewed her faith that destiny had a way of sending gifts from the Universe.

As she slammed the trunk, something...or someone... was headed up the yard. A new car had joined the crowd; Rebecca's mini-van was on the perimeter of the driveway and its driver was charging the front door.

"Hell no, John," Elizabeth screamed and blocked his way. He was disheveled, and reeking of stale tobacco and alcohol. Worse, there was a wild look in his bloodshot eyes.

"Get out of my way, Elizabeth. I'm going to see my kids," John tried to get around her. He yelled as if the message was really for Rebecca.

"John! Stop and get off the property. You made your bed," Elizabeth bowed all 5'3" of herself to stall him. Out of the corner of her eye, she could see the rest of her family observing from the living room. Under the circumstances, her dad would've beat the living crap out of John if he touched any of his girls. Any.

"Those are my kids! Rebecca is not fit. I can raise them with or without her," John shouted, staggering a little from his night of indulgence.

"You are *not* doing this on the weekend of Daddy's funeral, you selfish son of a bitch. Go back to your girl-friend," Elizabeth spat, looking over her shoulder for reinforcement. "Mom... and Rebecca have been through enough."

"Are you kidding?" Mallory asked from inside. She leapt off the love seat and took a moment to assess John's obvious intent to confront, invade or meddle. "Rebecca, don't go out there. Let us figure out what he's doing." She looked at Audrey. "Going with me?"

Audrey nodded. "Mom, you and Rebecca stay here." She briskly retrieved the phone and handed it to Rebecca. "Call 911 if he gets past us."

Robert stood, confused, his fists slightly balled. "Who is that?"

"My jerk of a husband. I'm sorry you have to see this, Robert," Rebecca said. They heard her kids saying *Daddy's here!* She blocked them from entering the living room. "Go downstairs, do not come out."

It was obvious the sisters were blocking John but his beer balls were full blown. As they watched, something Mallory said hit a nerve and John jerked his attention towards her.

Robert was trying to restrain himself but the situation seemed to be escalating—a pot of hot water and approaching a rolling boil. Then, his mind considered the worst scenario of the hotheaded man pulling a knife, or worse, a gun.

"Rebecca, could he have a weapon?" Robert asked, not letting his eyes leave the scene. Before she could answer, he heard the man yelling at his newfound mother.

"Stick your nose in one of your other sisters' lives," John yelled, spitting the words in her face. His eyes bulged and he pointed at the front door. "That's my family in there. I'm the man of the house and you have no business putting ideas in my wife's head."

"Fucker, you've done a great job of screwing your life up without anyone's help. Back up and get your shitty breath out of my face." Mallory threw down. "God knows where your mouth has been last night." Her hand swished as she turned to go back inside. "Get off the property or I'll personally call the cops."

"You bitch!" John screamed, lunging at Mallory's back. "I'll kill all of you."

Simultaneously, Robert ordered Rebecca to call 911 as he jumped over the well-worn blue couch. He bolted off the front porch and grabbed John like a ragdoll, slamming him up against the hood of Elizabeth's car. Through clenched teeth, Robert forced all his weight against John and yelled to the others, "Get inside and lock the door!"

Elizabeth and Audrey were helping Mallory get back to her feet. The white aluminum door was partially open from Robert's rush to intervene.

"You just showed us who you are—again, fucker!" Mallory screamed, wiping her lip that left blood on the backside of her hand. "And by the way, meet my son!"

It had been ten minutes since they watched the black and white police cruiser leave with John, hand-cuffed in the back seat. The last look at the back of John's head seemed to lighten Rebecca's heart. Audrey went to warn Leigh it was time to head to the airport.

"I'm sorry that you were pushed into that situation," Rebecca said, her arms crossed, hugging herself. She looked at Robert, then at Mallory.

"Hey, at least you got your car back!" Mallory said, trying to diminish the violent outburst. She looked at the washrag icing her lip. "And, yes, thank you Robert. An odd welcome to the family, I'm afraid."

"Guess this really makes you family now," Rose said, looking around the room. As if on cue, Audrey sat back down with her mom. "These are my girls—my strong little women," she said, tapping her second daughter's knee.

"I saw that and am proud to be from such good people," he said, a little embarrassed by all the attention.

"By the way, Elizabeth, what was your idea before all that went down?" Audrey asked.

Elizabeth jumped up. "Oh my God, I nearly forgot in all the drama! Remember what we were talking about earlier on the porch? Daddy's gardenia bush?" Elizabeth said, holding up the camera. Her mother cocked her head and shook it, *no*. Her sisters slowly smiled and nodded.

"Sorry, Mom, you missed us talking about the graduation pictures in front of the gardenia bush." Elizabeth tried to cut to the quick since Audrey needed to leave. "Mallory was telling us about her and Larry... and now, Robert. The fragrance of the gardenias seemed like a blessing from Daddy. Kind of a holy water to heal us. Each of us have memories of love but also, loss. Growing up with and without each other. But we're all here now. Who knows when that will happen again…" She paused to raise her eyebrows, punctuating her comment like a question mark.

"Photo booth in front of the gardenia bush?" Rebecca asked. Her hands clasped an unlit cigarette, nervously rolling it between her slightly shaking fingers.

"Robert, will you do us the honor of posing for some family photos?" Elizabeth asked. She doubted he'd refused based on his jumping in on the earlier family scuffle. She grinned and held up her Canon, pointing to the backyard.

With no hesitation, Robert stood and grabbed his hat. "I'd be honored… and I can't wait to see the world-famous Higgins garden," he bowed as he spoke. "I never knew meeting my mother would include four more amazing women. You're kind of a package deal, you know?"

Four heads snapped in his direction, as if their dad himself had entered the room. Then Rose stood and cupped his face again, with tears that would not be denied rolling down her cheeks. "You have no idea!"

The End…and a New Beginning

Acknowledgments

Nostalgia is like a grammar lesson: you find
the present tense but the past perfect!

—Owens Lee Pomeroy

Nostalgia. This is an emotional word that conjures body language from a slow sweet smile, eye rolls or a furled brow that delights the dermatologist reaching for a Botox needle. I believe it is an underrated emotion but also one that requires balance. Mental health professionals also validate the value of coping in the present by looking at the past to find hope for a future outcome. It can remind us and regroup our sense of purpose.

So, when I began to pursue the story of what became **Gardenia Duty**, I chose to marry the relationships of the adults of the Silent Generation with the Baby

Boomer descendants. This would create the social setting of the prospering America during a relatively peaceful time. Each generation would look through the eyes of a child and the eyes of an adult.

Fortunately, it is at the root of my own childhood that I knew where to draw my research. To weave the story's perspective from the young adult sisters reliving the past through the eyes of a child allowed me to use stories of many people. To educate my own perspective about the angst of the adults that were influential in my childhood, I dove into the dominant male military world of 1950s and forward. As I progressed, it softened the edges of my own painful and happy nostalgic memories.

As in the book, I started out dissecting my late stepfather's military records and mementos, which allowed me to ask relatively informed questions to the many Vets, including my own Tin-Can sailor father. Their uniforms were retired, but often a baseball cap with a military logo alerted me to their presence. The Goose Creek Tin-Can Sailor Chapter graciously endured my prodding. I met shipmates of my dad's and even developed deep friendships with a few. I explored the decks of the USS Laffey at Patriots Point. The familiar smell of diesel mixed with grey paint sent my nostalgia into overdrive. I spent time in Jacksonville Beach, Florida to launch myself into the mind of a grade school girl navigating her way as a military dependent in the 1960s.

I treasure the many glory day chats that revived the boyish spirits over a beer at ship reunions or an American Legion hall. The vulnerable confessions of the trials and tribulations of raising families under the strain of the Cold War helped me flesh out the tender undercarriages of these masculine souls.

At the announcement of "free wine for all the blondes at the bar" at a local Olive Garden, I met and became part of the Thursday lunch gang of Jack Connerty. He became so dear to the heart of my story, I promoted him to Chief in my book. His best friend, Richard *Santa* Stanley, amused me and welcomed me with that first free glass of wine. (Lynn Stanley, you're a saint!) Thank you also to Jerry and Marla Wickerham, Dwight Cargile of American Legion Post 147; John Long, who shared the photos of the recovery of Gemini VIII from the deck of the USS Leonard F. Mason (see next page); and especially to my father, Ret. LCDR Eugene Hall; and late step-father, Command Master Chief Robert Hardegree.

But, as pointed out in the story, behind all these men were wives and children. The ones who waited and kept the family together during a husband's absence. There has to be a thank you to my mother, Jeanette Hardegree and my three sisters because without the experience of being a real 'package deal,' my story would lack a realistic flare.

My mentor and writing coach, Shari Stauch, conceived the basic idea of this story and kept me motivated to never abandon ship. Her confidence in Gatekeeper

Press has finally laid the keel of my cover and launched the pages of the journey of the Higgins family. Of course, my husband, Steve Varn, gave me much needed R&R and escape with my camera underwater when the words would freeze.

I hope this book inspires readers to look into the amazing stories of their families and ancestors. I have a new appreciation of the messiness of life, but how something as simple as birth order can be a key to untangling it.

For me, the result has been profound, and I've discovered, as I hope you will, that the definition of family isn't limited to blood but to those whose hearts are so big, they prepare us to become the watchstanders at the helms of our own lives.

Thank you to generations of those who reported for duty, and to the families that served with them. I salute you…

Reader Discussion Guide

R eading this selection in your book club, or planning to? Here are some discussion questions about **Gardenia Duty** to get you going...

1. Similar to Louisa May Alcott's novel, **Little Women**, the core family consists of a military father/step-father and mother of four daughters. As in real life, birth order tends to contribute to childhood experiences. Are there situations and/ or characters you can identify with, and if so, how?

2. **Gardenia Duty** is told from male and female voices, both child and adult. Are there situations and/or characters you can identify with, if so, how?

3.   Bobby and Rose's moral and social development occurred post-WWII and The Great Depression. What cultural influences shape their actions, especially before they marry?

4.   The sisters were born into a family whose lifestyle was governed by their father's and stepfather's US Navy careers. Eventually, the oldest daughter pleads with her stepfather to find a way to put down roots in Charleston, SC. Do you think the frequent relocations had a negative impact on the childhoods of the girls? In contrast, did it provide a positive impact in their bonding?

5.   Just like Bobby's role on his naval destroyers, Rose managed the family routine during his absence at sea. Each sister's role mirrored seniority and chain of command to their mother. Do you think it contributed or hindered the relationships?

6.   Hollywood and television series centered on what was called "The Traditional Middle Class" family life. Do you think divorce was a social hurdle for the sisters in childhood or in adult choices?

7.   The book introduces Bobby turning 18 and facing registering with Selective Services due to the military conscription still in existence. This launches him to leave his childhood home

and eventually crosses paths with Rose and her daughters. The author uses Bobby's voice to show him develop from a young boy to ultimately a family man. Do you think his ability to walking into an instant husband/father situation was influenced more by his career or by values from his parents?

8. The gardenia bush that had been nurtured in the family home creates a thread in the story. The irony of a gardenia being a locally developed flower and its resilience reflects the parenting of Bobby and Rose for the sisters. Is there a family symbolism that you can relate to like the gardenia's subtle infusion from the family garden?

9. In spite of the long-distance relationships between the sisters, do you think the military family lifestyle preserved their ability to pull back together in crisis?

10. Are there any books that you would compare this one to? Why?

Made in the USA
Middletown, DE
08 June 2023

32276917R00198